The Third Round

'SAPPER' is the pen-name of Herman Cyril McNeile, born in 1888 at the Naval Prison in Bodmin, Cornwall, where his father was Governor. Educated at Cheltenham College and the Royal Military Academy, Woolwich, he served in the Royal Engineers (popularly known as the 'sappers') from 1907 to 1919, being awarded the Military Cross during World War I and finishing as a Lieutenant-Colonel. He started writing in France, adopting a pen-name because serving officers were not allowed to write under their own names. His first stories on life in the trenches in France were published in 1915 and were an enormous success. But it was his first thriller, *Bulldog Drummond* (1920), that launched him as one of the most popular novelists of his generation. It had several immensely successful sequels, including *The Black Gang* (1922), *The Third Round* (1924) and *The Final Count* (1926), and McNeile's friend, the late Gerard Fairlie, wrote several Bulldog Drummond stories after his death. Bulldog Drummond also inspired a successful play, with Gerald du Maurier playing Drummond, and several films variously starring Ronald Colman, Ray Milland, Jack Buchanan, and Ralph Richardson. *Jim Maitland* (1923), a volume of short stories featuring a footloose English sahib in foreign lands, was another popular success. Altogether McNeile published nearly 30 books. A vast public mourned his death in 1937 at the early age of 48.

JEREMY LEWIS is a freelance journalist, columnist for *The New Statesman* and an Editorial Director at a London publishing house.

'Sapper'

THE THIRD ROUND

Introduced by Jeremy Lewis

J.M. Dent & Sons Ltd
London Melbourne

First published in Great Britain by Hodder & Stoughton Ltd, 1924
This paperback edition first published by J. M. Dent & Sons Ltd, 1984
Text © The Trustees of the Estate of the late Colonel H. C. McNeile 1924
Introduction © Jeremy Lewis 1984

This book is set in 10/11½ VIP Plantin by
Inforum Ltd, Portsmouth
Printed in Great Britain by
Richard Clay (The Chaucer Press) Plc, Bungay, for
J. M. Dent & Sons Ltd
Aldine House, 33 Welbeck Street, London W1M 8LX

British Library Cataloguing in Publication Data

Sapper
    The third round.—(Classic thrillers)
    Rn: Herman Cyril McNeile   I. Title
    II. Series
    823′.912[F]   PR6025.A317

    ISBN 0–460–02246–6

CONTENTS

INTRODUCTION

Jeremy Lewis

Re-reading the books of one's youth, like re-visiting scenes of childhood or knocking up old chums from twenty years ago, is generally a hazardous business. From the ages of five to twenty one reads with an intensity and a passionate involvement it's hard to match in later life, and the books one devoured again and again (however bad) retain a special, luminous place in one's mythology of childhood and in the bouts of literary nostalgia to which many of us are tediously addicted: unless, that is, one is rash enough to try to recover that ancient magic by elbowing one's way back into Eden, rather like one of those brisk but melancholy professional old boys who can't leave well alone but hang about their schools in blazers of a virulent hue, buttonholing the masters and making themselves the object of ridicule and amazement to the current inmates. Sometimes the formula still works, as in the case of the 'William' books or Rider Haggard; but all too often these forays into one's past prove wretched, disillusioning affairs, the net effect of which is merely to cast a gloomy retrospective shadow, and to chip unhelpfully away at those sustaining myths that most of us survive by. How could I have forced my way through the bogus-mediaeval circumlocutions of *The White Company*, a book I firmly believed to be the finest ever written? Surely *Treasure Island* was a touch more exciting than it now seems, or was I confusing it all the time with *Peter Pan*? And, anxious as I am to stand up for the industrious Enid Blyton, someone must have been tinkering with her prose since those still more distant days when *The Island of Adventure* held us in thrall, stern-faced librarians notwithstanding.

From 1920, when the first Bulldog Drummond novel was published, until the late 1950s, when Sapper's books began to drop out of print—by then James Bond was doing battle with the forces of evil, and a more censorious generation had come to regard Sapper and his kind as reactionaries of the foulest dye—the Bulldog Drummond novels were staple fare for all right-minded youths from twelve to twenty, while providing equal pleasure to assorted golfers, colonels, maiden aunts, bank managers and the kind of people who haunted Boot's libraries in places like Eastbourne and

Tunbridge Wells in search of a really good read ('but not, please, one of those difficult modern novels'). Although I always felt that, in terms of sheer urbanity—and which spotty, tongue-tied adolescent doesn't dream of playing the languid, sophisticated man-of-the-world?—Simon Templar *alias* the Saint was in a class of his own as he addressed the bumbling Inspector Teale in a patronising drawl or puffed smoke in the face of a master criminal, Bulldog Drummond I loved above all. So when, a couple of years ago, I decided to read the four Carl Peterson novels to my eldest daughter, I did so in the fear that—like Dickens coming face to face with Maria Beadnell—it could all prove a sorry mistake, and that Irma and Algy Longworth and the Revd. Theodosius Longmoor would find themselves relegated to that unhappy limbo reserved for those with whom one had had much in common, once . . .

I needn't have worried. Middle-aged readers contemplating a return trip can rest assured that Sapper holds up very well indeed, while Bulldog himself—still resident, I assume, in Half Moon Street, though somewhat hemmed in by Arabian banks and advertising agencies—is far from showing his age. The novels remain exciting, action-packed and as fast-moving as Drummond's nifty 30 h.p. two-seater, the confrontations between our hero and the Petersons as sinuous and as fraught with hazards as ever, and the world of goofy clubmen with nerves of steel reassuringly intact. Even better, there are bonuses to be had. I hadn't realised, for example, what a good writer Sapper was. He may have knocked out his novels far too fast and been prone to inconsistency and repetition, but he wrote the strong, plain prose—clear, unadorned and to the point—that one admiringly associates with military men who take to the typewriter. (H. C. McNeile—Sapper in real life—had been a professional soldier from 1907 to 1919; his first stories were written from the trenches and published by Lord Northcliffe, who bestowed his pseudonym on him.) Nor had I appreciated that he is given to comic flights of a Wodehousian variety, with Bulldog and his pals exchanging the kind of jocular badinage familiar from the lips of Gussie Fink-Nottle or Catsmeat Potter-Purbright. 'Why don't you let out your face as a grouse moor?' is the kind of crack Bertie Wooster might have reached for when confronted by a particularly repellent variety of red-bearded revolutionary.

The very mention of revolutionaries—particularly of the Bolshevik variety—introduces an aspect of the novels which modern readers find hard to stomach and which, like the good writing and the jokes, quite washed over me thirty years ago: Sapper's anti-semitism, so redolent and so representative of its period, and so particularly unpalatable in the anachronistic light of hindsight. Sapper was, it seems, a bluff, hearty figure, keen on his golf and a stiff drink to follow, unknown and uninterested in the literary or intellectual world, and reflecting—in the direct, uncomplicated way of popular middlebrow writers—the views and the prejudice of his period, and his readers. His attitude to Jews, however representative, is extremely unappealing, but in this he was no worse a sinner than many more eminent and revered contemporaries, from Belloc and Chesterton to Ezra Pound, and very similar to Buchan or Baroness Orczy. This doesn't make the notorious scene in *The Black Gang* in which Drummond and his black-masked gang horsewhip the cringing Jewish revolutionaries any more tolerable; one can only say in defence that Sapper's anti-semitism is by no means as all-pervasive as his detractors suggest (it features not at all in *The Third Round*), and that it should be judged, if not excused, in the context of its period.

But the time has come to introduce our hero to new readers, while reminding the forgetful of what they have been missing. Neatly summarised by Richard Usborne as 'the Monarch of Muscle and the Sultan of Swat', Captain Hugh Drummond DSO, MC, late of His Majesty's Royal Loamshires, is—like so many of the giant figures of world literature, from Mr Pickwick to Mr Pooter—the kind of person it's probably better to read about than to encounter in the flesh. He was, we're told by the suitably overawed narrator of *The Final Count*, 'just six feet in his socks, and turned the scale at over fourteen stone. And of that fourteen stone not one ounce was made up of superfluous fat. He was hard muscle and bone through and through, and the most powerful man I have ever met in my life. He was a magnificent boxer [so much so that 'his nose had never quite recovered from the final one year in the Public Schools Heavy Weights'], a lightning and deadly shot with a revolver, and utterly lovable.' So far so good, and still more so when we learn that although 'his best friend would not have called him good looking . . . he was the fortunate possessor of that cheerful type of ugliness which inspires immediate confidence in its owner.' Only his eyes, it seems, 'redeemed his face from being what is known in the vernacular as the Frozen Limit. Deep-set and steady, with eyelashes that many a woman had envied, they showed the man for what he was—a sportsman and a gentleman. And the combination of the two is an unbeatable production.'

And so it is. But it's hard for those of us with lurid memories of rugger scrums or towel-flicking school changing-rooms to suppress an unworthy feeling that the real-life Drummond might, at times, have been a bit hard to take: a beefy, genial hearty who when confronted by his chums—or, for that matter, complete strangers, provided they're not foreigners, revolutionaries or uppity members of the working classes—will 'burble at them genially, knock them senseless with a blow of greeting on the back, and resuscitate them with a large tankard of ale', served up, no doubt, by his long-suffering manservant, Denny, the Jeeves of Half Moon Street, though lacking the latter's powerful intellect.

Altogether more endearing—and very English—is Drummond's pose as a brainless, indolent buffoon, the man with the pea-sized brain who yet notices everything about him and, when roused from his apparent torpor, can not only out-fight but out-wit the most serpentine and intellectually well-endowed of foreigners, particularly 'Communists and other unwashed people of that type'. Drummond is the ultimate embodiment of the English, public school cult of the superiority of character over intellect, of native wit and common sense over more formal but fallible forms of ratiocination. From the same stable, in theory at least, comes his cool imperturbability and general good humour (unless some cad has gone too far, usually with a woman, in which case he will be treated to the alarming spectacle—and sensation—of Drummond going 'beserk'). Bulldog himself, in a moment of rare profundity, referred to 'that air of masterly tranquillity which is the mark of the Anglo-Saxon under stress'—a phrase which in itself suggests that the notion that reading books was quite beyond the old boy may have been a self-inflicted libel, designed to deceive friend and foe alike, and that his leisure time may well have been devoted to reading learned works before the fire.

For there is no doubt that, in between thwarting the enemies of England, Drummond must have had time enough on his hands. He had enjoyed a 'good' war on the Western Front, padding silently between the front lines and disposing of unwary Huns with the infallible technique learned from the legendary Japanese, Olaki. No doubt he had ample private means, and once the war was over he obviously found it hard—like many of his flesh-and-blood equivalents—to readjust to the boredom of civilian life, and was more than delighted at the prospect of a 'show'. Indeed, Drummond's involvement with the master-criminal Carl Peterson stems entirely from his placing a small ad in the paper offering his services: 'Demobilised officer, finding peace incredibly tedious, would welcome diversion. Legitimate if possible, but crime, if of a comparatively humorous nature, no objection . . .' Phyllis, his wife-to-be and the object of Drummond's instant adoration, answers the ad. since her foolish old father has fallen into the hands of the arch-fiend. The rest is history.

But before we move on to this particular slice of history—by way of introducing Peterson himself, and the slinky Irma, cigarette-holder permanently to hand—a word about the rest of the gang: Peter Darrell, Toby Sinclair, Jerry Seymour, Ted Jerningham and, of course, Algy Longworth. Algy is a Wooster-like silly ass who plays a key role in *The Third Round* by falling in love with the daughter of an absent-minded professor of the kind one still finds firing on all cylinders in the pages of *Dandy* and *Beano*, along with cane-swishing schoolmasters in mortar boards and gowns. This process converts the lovesick 'old bean' from being, in Drummond's view, an 'ordinary, wanting specimen' into a 'raving imbecile'. But more of that anon. Like Drummond, his friends appear to spend a reasonable amount of time exchanging facetious quips, strolling about the West End, dropping in at the Carlton and behaving for all the world like paid-up members of the Drones Club (to which, for all we know, they may well have belonged). Yet like their leader—and Drummond is every inch the man in charge—even Algy becomes a changed man at the merest whiff of foul play or the remotest prospect of action. Vacuous smiles are replaced by looks of steely concentration; lazy eyes gaze sternly into the middle distance; chinless wonders are suddenly be-chinned; spats and top hats prove perfectly compatible with the rapid laying of plans, and the impeccable execution thereof.

As for the Demon King, Carl Peterson, who knows where he comes from, what his nationality is, even what his real name is? Peterson is the cosmopolitan incarnate—a pejorative by definition, one imagines, for the stoutly patriotic Sapper, despite his long years of tax exile in Switzerland. Peterson is at home in every country yet loyal to none, the master of innumerable languages (had he Hungarian, we wonder? How would he have fared in the Gaeltacht?) and still more innumerable disguises: suave, urbane, bulging with brains, just the sort of fellow any self-respecting Englishman would view with immediate suspicion as altogether too clever by half. Peterson is, or appears to be, a prototype millionaire socialist, though his socialism is as nothing to his greed for gain and, still better, power. In his anxiety to amass a personal fortune *and* sway the destiny of nations *and* do every possible harm to the fortunes of England, he ferments Bolshevik revolution in the Home Counties (readers of the opening volume, *Bulldog Drummond*, will remember that he made his headquarters near Godalming), consorts with the most unsavoury type of revolutionary—all of them dirty, many of them bearded, like grubbier versions of Tintin's friend, Captain Haddock—and comes to these shores equipped with an entirely unsporting range of lethal gorillas, poisons, tarantulas in cardboard boxes and the like. And, of course, he brings with him his daughter Irma, a sophisticated kind of woman much given to speaking French. (I gather from the experts that Irma was, for all the official disclaimers, probably Peterson's mistress. Innocent as a schoolboy, and credulous still, I obediently continue to think of her as the child of his loins.) Irma, who speaks in a low purr, has rather a crush on the 'adorable' Hugh, though this doesn't prevent her from pursuing an unending vendetta against him after he has finally disposed of Carl in *The Final Count* (new readers should have closed their eyes at this point).

Drummond's relationship to Peterson is intimate, teasing, and—though this is not the kind of comment one can imagine Sapper relishing in the clubhouse after a strenuous day on the links—oddly voluptuous. Of course Peterson is the devil in human form and must be thwarted at every turn, and eventually destroyed; but life without the arch-fiend spells tedium indeed, causing Drummond to gaze wistfully into the distance and mutter his antagonist's name over and over again ('Carl—my Carl—it cannot be that we shall never meet again . . .'). Brought face to face, the two of them treat each other with elaborate politeness—Peterson suave, smooth, in perfect control of himself despite Drummond's maddening habit of fouling up his plans for World Dominion; Drummond affectionate, joshing and well aware (for most of the time) of the need to keep a long spoon in his hand.

Every now and then Peterson proves himself the lesser man—and confirms that, whatever else he may be, he is no Englishman—by losing control of himself. A good deal of snarling takes place on such occasions, and if by any chance Drummond happens to be lying trussed on the sitting-room floor of a rented country house, Carl will combine the snarling with a sharp kick to the rib-cage. Such lapses are quickly behind us, however, and seconds later the master criminal is lighting a fresh cigar with firm, untrembling fingers.

First published in 1924 by Hodder & Stoughton, *The Third Round* was, as its title suggests, the third of the four novels devoted to Drummond's protracted battle with Carl Peterson, following after *Bulldog Drummond* and *The Black Gang*. As expected, it sold extremely well, and continued to do so until the early 1950s at least. Hodder published initially at 7/6*d*, printing 20,000 copies and reprinting in 1925 and 1926. In 1926 they reprinted it in a 3/6*d* edition (30,000 copies) and in 1927 in a 2*s* edition (60,000 copies, almost all of which had been sold by the end of that year). The bumper volume including all four Carl Peterson novels—and a companion to similar tomes devoted to John Buchan's Richard Hannay, the Scarlet Pimpernel, Inspector Thorndyke and other firm favourites from the richly endowed Hodder stable—first appeared in 1930 in a printing of 13,000 copies, priced at 7/6*d*.

Small wonder, perhaps, that Sapper should have moved to the village of Territêt near Montreux with his wife and his son (a second child was born in Montreux), not returning to England until 1931, after Britain had been taken off the gold standard. *The Third Round* begins and ends in a villa on the edge of Lake Geneva where Carl Peterson, temporarily trading under the name of Mr Edward Blackton, is enjoying an ill-earned rest and idly wondering where his next million is to come from. It is rather different to its two predecessors—and, indeed, *The Final Count*. No doubt Carl still dreams of bringing England to her knees and fermenting Bolshevik revolution, but if so he is keeping his political aspirations in the background for once, concentrating more on the means than the ends, and spending less time than usual consorting with red-bearded Russians and the like. Irma has a modest though, as it turns out, essential part to play. Phyllis, worn out perhaps by the heavy demands made upon her in previous incarnations, appears to be putting her feet up at home (with Mrs Denny to hand, she is unlikely to be ironing Bulldog's shirts or ordering up the kegs of 'ale' with which he stops to refresh himself). Neither the peppery but slow-witted Inspector MacIver—Sapper's answer to Inspectors Lestrade and Teale—nor 'Tum-Tums' (a.k.a. Sir Bryan Johnstone, the Home Secretary, for whom the disrespectful Drummond once fagged) are called upon to do their stuff. Of course Carl plans to dominate the world and do all manner of dreadful things once he has made his pile; but from the point of view of the story line, *The Third Round* is a more conventional tale of crime and (attempted) punishment than its predecessors, and none the worse for that.

The story is simplicity itself. Suffice it to say that the absent-minded Professor Goodman, in between inventing a 'new albumen food for infants and adults' and brooding on 'atomic theory with special reference to carboniferous quartz' (no tiresome specialisations for the likes of him), has come up with a flawless method for the manufacture of artificial diamonds, involving 'no fewer than thirty-nine salts' and so perfect that not even the experts can tell them from the genuine article. Not the most worldly of figures, the Professor wanders the streets with the secret formulae, scribbled on odd scraps of paper, loose in his pocket 'along with some peppermint bullseyes and bits of string'. Even Algy, rendered imbecilic by his impending marriage to the Prof's daughter, plainly feels that the old gentleman is clearly certifiable and should be contained within the four walls of his laboratory if he is to come to no harm ('It's a perfect factory of extraordinary smells, but the old dear seems to enjoy himself . . . .'). Blissfully unaware of the disastrous effect his invention is likely to have on the international diamond market, the Prof plans to publish his findings and to read a paper on the subject to a gathering of his fellow absent-minded professors. The Metropolitan Diamond Syndicate, headed by the self-important and bad-tempered Sir Raymond Blantyre, realise that their entire livelihood is threatened, and approach Peterson about the possibility of the Professor being—perhaps—persuaded to see reason. Peterson seizes the chance of a lifetime to double-cross the diamond dealers and get his own hands on the magic formula, only to find that, once again, the unspeakable Drummond is blocking his path. For not only is Algy engaged to young Miss Goodman, but, by one of the many and pleasing coincidences with which the novel is replete, Toby Sinclair happens to work in the Syndicate as well (which proves that one, at least, of the gang was unfortunate enough to have to do a touch of work from time to time).

To say more would be the act of a cad and a spoilsport, not least to the novice reader. Ingredients in this rich and stimulating pudding include Drummond's chewing small cubes of soap in order to foam at the mouth and so convince his captors that he is indeed 100 per cent demented; a thrilling pursuit across Southampton Water (Ted Jerningham just happens to be playing around in his boat at the time); the appearance of an even scruffier professor of chemistry, a 'dirty old beast with egg all over his coat'; the lovelorn Algy discovered reading the poems of Ella Wheeler Wilcox on the morning of the Derby ('matters looked black'); a massive explosion in central London; and a dazzling display of quick-change disguises by Carl who, making cunning use of a whole changing room full of wigs, false whiskers, grease-paint, egg-stained garments and a curious putty-like substance liberally applied to the face, transforms himself in a flash from Edward Blackton to William Anderson to Professor Scheidstrun to a bufferish country squire named William Robinson, deceiving even the lynx-eyed Drummond in the process.

At the end of the day, of course, the important thing, for readers and participants alike, is that Drummond and Peterson should slog it out—hand-to-hand, ideally, with no question of involving pals or police on one side or red-bearded revolutionaries or unpleasant-sounding foreigners on the other. This knightly spirit is nowhere more apparent than in *The Third Round*, with Carl disdaining help in disposing of the pestilential clubman at a time when poor Hugh is hardly in a position to answer back ('That supreme joy must be mine and mine alone'); while Drummond, impressed as ever by Peterson's nerves of steel as he faces what must surely be the end of the road, 'saluted his adversary in spirit as a foeman worthy of his steel'. Whether or nor this elegiac note was a trifle premature, I leave you now to find out.

THE THIRD ROUND

CHAPTER 1

In Which the Metropolitan Diamond Syndicate Holds Converse with Mr Edward Blackton

With a sigh of pleasure Mr Edward Blackton opened the windows of his balcony and leaned out, staring over the lake. Opposite, the mountains of Savoy rose steeply from the water; away to the left the Dent du Midi raised its crown of snow above the morning haze.

Below him the waters of the lake glittered and scintillated with a thousand fires. A steamer, with much blowing of sirens and reversing of paddle-wheels, had come to rest at a landing-stage hard by, and was taking on board a bevy of tourists, while the gulls circled round shrieking discordantly. For a while he watched them idly, noting the quickness with which the birds swooped and caught the bread as it was thrown into the air, long before it reached the water. He noted also how nearly all the food was secured by half a dozen of the gulls, whilst the others said a lot but got nothing. And suddenly Mr Edward Blackton smiled.

'Like life, my dear,' he said, slipping his arm round the waist of a girl who had just joined him at the window. 'It's the fool who shouts in this world: the wise man says nothing and acts.'

The girl lit a cigarette thoughtfully, and sat down on the ledge of the balcony. For a while her eyes followed the steamer puffing fussily away with its load of sightseers and its attendant retinue of gulls: then she looked at the man standing beside her. Point by point she took him in: the clear blue eyes under the deep forehead, the aquiline nose, the firm mouth and chin. Calmly, dispassionately she noted the thick brown hair greying a little over the temples, the great depth of chest, and the strong, powerful hands: then she turned and looked once again at the disappearing steamer. But to the man's surprise she gave a little sigh.

'What is it, my dear?' he said solicitously. 'Bored?'

'No, not bored,' she answered. 'Whatever may be your failings, *mon ami*, boring me is not one of them. I was just wondering what it would feel like if you and I were content to go on a paddle-wheel

3

steamer with a Baedeker and a Kodak, and a paper bag full of bananas.'

'We will try tomorrow,' said the man, gravely lighting a cigar.

'It wouldn't be any good,' laughed the girl. 'Just once in a way we should probably love it. I meant I wonder what it would feel like if that was our life.'

Her companion nodded.

'I know, *carissima*,' he answered gently. 'I have sometimes wondered the same thing. I suppose there must be compensations in respectability, otherwise so many people wouldn't be respectable. But I'm afraid it is one of those things that we shall never know.'

'I think it's that,' said the girl, waving her hand towards the mountains opposite—'that has caused my mood. It's all so perfectly lovely: the sky is just so wonderfully blue. And look at that sailing boat.'

She pointed to one of the big lake barges, with its two huge lateen sails, creeping gently along in the centre of the lake. 'It's all so peaceful, and sometimes one wants peace.'

'True,' agreed the man; 'one does. It's just reaction, and we've been busy lately.' He rose and began to pace slowly up and down the balcony. 'To be quite honest, I myself have once or twice thought recently that if I could pull off some really big coup— something, I mean, that ran into the millions—I would give things up.'

The girl smiled and shook her head.

'Don't misunderstand me, my dear,' he went on. 'I do not suggest for a moment that we should settle down to a life of toping and ease. We could neither of us exist without employing our brains. But with really big money behind one, we should be in a position to employ our brains a little more legitimately, shall I say, than we are able to at present, and still get all the excitement we require.

'Take Drakshoff: that man controls three of the principal Governments of Europe. The general public don't know it; the Governments themselves won't admit it: but it's true for all that. As you know, that little job I carried out for him in Germany averted a second revolution. He didn't want one at the time, and so he called me in. And it cost him in all five million pounds. What was that to him?'

He shrugged his shoulders contemptuously.

'A mere flea-bite—a bagatelle. Why, with that man an odd million or two one way or the other wouldn't be noticed in his pass-book.'

He paused and stared over the sunlit lake, while the girl watched him in silence.

'Given money as big as that, and a man can rule the world. Moreover, he can rule it without fear of consequences. He can have all the excitement he requires; he can wield all the power he desires—and have special posses of police to guard him. I'm afraid we don't have many to guard us.'

The girl laughed and lit another cigarette.

'You are right, *mon ami*, we do not. Hullo! who can that be?'

Inside the sitting-room the telephone bell was ringing, and with a slight frown Mr Edward Blackton took off the receiver.

'What is it?'

From the other end came the voice of the manager, suitably deferential as befitted a client of such obvious wealth installed in the most palatial suite of the Palace Hotel.

'Two gentlemen are here, Mr Blackton,' said the manager, 'who wish to know when they can have the pleasure of seeing you. Their names are Sir Raymond Blantyre and Mr Jabez Leibhaus. They arrived this morning from England by the Simplon Orient express, and they say that their business is most urgent.'

A sudden gleam had come into Mr Blackton's eyes as he listened, but his voice as he answered was almost bored.

'I shall be pleased to see both gentlemen at eleven o'clock up here. Kindly have champagne and sandwiches sent to my sitting-room at that hour.'

He replaced the receiver, and stood for a moment thinking deeply.

'Who was it?' called the girl from the balcony.

'Blantyre and Leibhaus, my dear,' answered the man. 'Now, what the deuce can they want with me so urgently?'

'Aren't they both big diamond men?' said the girl, coming into the room.

'They are,' said Blackton. 'In romantic fiction they would be described as two diamond kings. Anyway, it won't do them any harm to wait for half an hour.'

'How did they find out your address? I thought you had left strict instructions that you were not to be disturbed.'

There was regret in the girl's voice, and with a faint smile the man tilted back her head and kissed her.

'In our profession, *cara mia*,' he said gently, 'there are times when the strictest instructions have to be disobeyed. Freyder would never have dreamed of worrying me over a little thing, but unless I am much mistaken this isn't going to be little. It's going to be big: those two below don't go chasing half across Europe because they've mislaid a collar stud. Why—who knows?—it might prove to be the big coup we were discussing a few minutes ago.'

He kissed her again; then he turned abruptly away and the girl gave a little sigh. For the look had come into those grey-blue eyes that she knew so well: the alert, keen look which meant business. He crossed the room, and unlocked a heavy leather dispatch-case. From it he took out a biggish book which he laid on the table. Then, having made himself comfortable on the balcony, he lit another cigar, and began to turn over the pages.

It was of the loose-leaf variety, and every page had entries on it in Blackton's small, neat hand-writing. It was what he called his 'Who's Who', but it differed from that excellent production in one marked respect. The people in Mr Edward Blackton's production had not compiled their own notices, which rendered it considerably more truthful even if less complimentary than the orthodox volume.

It was arranged alphabetically, and it contained an astounding wealth of information. In fact in his lighter moments the author was wont to say that when he retired from active life he would publish it, and die in luxury on the large sums paid him to suppress it. Mentioned in it were the names of practically every man and woman possessed of real wealth—as Blackton regarded wealth—in Europe and America.

There were, of course, many omissions, but in the course of years an extraordinary amount of strange and useful information had been collected. In many cases just the bare details of the person were given: these were the uninteresting ones, and consisted of people who passed the test as far as money was concerned but about whom the author had no personal knowledge.

In others, however, the entries were far more human. After the name would be recorded certain details, frequently of a most scurrilous description. And these details had one object and one object only—to assist at the proper time and place in parting the victim from his money.

6

Not that Mr Edward Blackton was a common blackmailer—far from it. Blackmailing pure and simple was a form of amusement which revolted his feelings as an artist. But to make use of certain privately gained information about a man when dealing with him was a different matter altogether.

It was a great assistance in estimating character when meeting a man for the first time to know that his previous wife had divorced him for carrying on with the housemaid, and that he had then failed to marry the housemaid. Nothing of blackmail in that: just a pointer as to character.

In the immense ramifications of Mr Blackton's activities it was of course impossible for him to keep all these details in his head. And so little by little the book had grown until it now comprised over three hundred pages. Information obtained first-hand or from absolutely certain sources was entered in red; items not quite so reliable in black. And under Sir Raymond Blantyre's name the entry was in red.

'Blantyre, Raymond. Born 1858. Vice-President Metropolitan Diamond Syndicate. Married daughter of John Perkins, wool merchant in London. Knighted 1904. Something shady about him in South Africa—probably I.D.B. Races a lot. Wife a snob. Living up to the limit of his income. 5.13.'

Mr Blackton laid the book on his knee and looked thoughtfully over the lake. The last three figures showed that the entry had been made in May 1913, and if he was living up to the limit of his income then, he must have had to retrench considerably now. And wives who are snobs dislike that particularly.

He picked up the book again and turned up the dossier of his other visitor, to find nothing of interest. Mr Leibhaus had only bare details after his name, with the solitary piece of information that he, too, was a Vice-President of the Metropolitan Diamond Syndicate.

He closed the book and relocked it in the dispatch-case; then he glanced at his watch.

'I think, my dear,' he said, turning to the girl, 'that our interview had better be apparently private. Could you make yourself comfortable in your bedroom, so that you will be able to hear everything and give me your opinion afterwards?' He opened the door for her and she passed through. 'I confess,' he continued, 'that I'm a little puzzled. I cannot think what they want to see me about so urgently.'

But there was no trace of it on his face as five minutes later his two visitors were ushered in by the sub-manager.

'See that the sandwiches and champagne are sent at once, please,' he remarked, and the hotel official bustled away.

'We shall be undisturbed, gentlemen,' he said, 'after the waiter brings the tray. Until then we might enjoy the view over the lake. It is rare, I am told, that one can see the Dent du Midi quite so clearly.'

The three men strolled into the balcony and leaned out. And it struck that exceptionally quick observer of human nature, Mr Blackton, that both his visitors were a little nervous. Sir Raymond Blantyre especially was not at his ease, answering the casual remarks of his host at random. He was a short, stocky little man with a white moustache and a gold-rimmed eyeglass, which he had an irritating habit of taking in and out of his eye, and he gave a sigh of relief as the door finally closed behind the waiter.

'Now perhaps we can come to business, Count—er—I beg your pardon, Mr Blackton.'

'The mistake is a natural one,' said his host suavely. 'Shall we go inside the room to avoid the risk of being overheard?'

'I had better begin at the beginning,' said Sir Raymond, waving away his host's offer of champagne. 'And when I've finished, you will see, I have no doubt, our reasons for disturbing you in this way. Nothing short of the desperate position in which we find ourselves would have induced us to seek you out after what Mr Freyder told my friend Leibhaus. But the situation is so desperate that we had no alternative.'

Mr Blackton's face remained quite expressionless, and the other, after a pause, went on:

'Doubtless you know who we are, Mr Blackton. I am the President of the Metropolitan Diamond Syndicate and Mr Leibhaus is the senior Vice-President. In the event of my absence at any time, he deputises for me. I mention these facts to emphasise the point that we are the heads of that combine, and that you are therefore dealing with the absolute principals, and not with subordinates.

'Now, I may further mention that although the Metropolitan is our particular syndicate, we are both of us considerably interested in other diamond enterprises. In fact our entire fortune is bound up irretrievably in the diamond industry—as are the fortunes of several other men, for whom, Mr Blackton, I am authorised to speak.

'So that I am in a position to say that not only am I here as representative of the Metropolitan Syndicate, but I am here as representative of the whole diamond industry and the enormous capital locked up in that industry.'

'You make yourself perfectly clear, Sir Raymond,' said Mr Blackton quietly. His face was as masklike as ever, but he wondered more and more what could be coming.

Sir Raymond took out his eyeglass and polished it; then he took a sip of the champagne which, despite his refusal, his host had poured out for him.

'That being so, Mr Blackton, and my position in the matter being fully understood, I will come to the object of our visit. One day about a fortnight ago I was dining at the house of a certain Professor Goodman. You may perhaps have heard of him by name? No!

'Well, he is, I understand, one of the foremost chemists of the day. He and I have not got much in common, but my wife and his became acquainted during the war, and we still occasionally dine with one another. There were six of us at dinner—our four selves, his daughter, and an extraordinarily inane young man with an eyeglass—who, I gathered, was engaged to the daughter.

'It was during dinner that my attention was caught by a rather peculiar ornament that the daughter was wearing. It looked to me like a piece of ordinary cut glass mounted in a claw of gold, and she was using it as a brooch. The piece of glass was about the size of a large marble, and it scintillated so brilliantly as she moved that I could not help noticing it.

'I may say that it struck me as a distinctly vulgar ornament—the sort of thing that a housemaid might be expected to wear when she was out. It surprised me, since the Goodmans are the last people one would expect to allow such a thing. And, of course, I should have said nothing about it had not the vapid youth opposite noticed me.

' "Looking at the monkey nut?" he said, or something equally foolish. "Pretty sound bit of work on the part of the old paternal parent."

'Professor Goodman looked up and smiled, and the girl took it off and handed it to me.

' "What do you think of it, Sir Raymond?" she asked. "I put it on especially for your benefit tonight."

'I glanced at it, and to my amazement I found that it was a perfectly flawless diamond, worth certainly ten to twelve thousand pounds, and possibly more. I suppose my surprise must have been obvious, because they all began to laugh.

' "Well, what is your verdict, Blantyre?" said the Professor.

' "I will be perfectly frank," I answered. "I cannot understand how you can have placed such a really wonderful stone in such an unworthy setting."

'And then the Professor laughed still more.

' "What would you say was the value of that stone?" he inquired.

' "I should be delighted to give Miss Goodman a cheque for ten thousand pounds for it here and now," I said.

'And then he really roared with laughter.

' "What about it, Brenda?" he cried. "Do you know what that stone cost me, Blantyre? Five pounds ten shillings and sixpence—and two burnt fingers." '

Blackton leaned forward in his chair and stared at the speaker.

'Well—what then?' he said quietly.

Sir Raymond mopped his forehead and took another sip of champagne.

'You've guessed it, Mr Blackton. It was false—or when I say false, it was not false in the sense that Tecla pearls are false. But it had been made by a chemical process in Professor Goodman's laboratory. Otherwise it was indistinguishable from the genuine article: in fact'—in his agitation he thumped the table with his fist—'it *was* the genuine article!'

Blackton carefully lit another cigar.

'And what did you do?' he inquired. 'I presume that you have tested the matter fully since.'

'Of course,' answered the other. 'I will tell you exactly what has happened. That evening after dinner I sat on talking with the Professor. Somewhat naturally I allowed no hint of my agitation to show on my face.

'As you probably know, Mr Blackton, artificial diamonds have been manufactured in the past—real diamonds indistinguishable from those found in nature. But they have been small, and their cost has been greater when made artificially than if they had been found. And so the process has never been economically worth while. But this was altogether different.

'If what Professor Goodman told me was the truth—if he had indeed manufactured that diamond for five pounds in his laboratory, we were confronted with the possibility of an appalling crisis. And since he was the last person to tell a stupid and gratuitous lie, you may imagine my feelings.

'I need hardly point out to you that the whole diamond market is an artificial one. The output of stones from the mines has to be limited to prevent a slump—to keep prices up. And what would happen if the market was swamped with stones worth a king's ransom each as prices go today and costing a fiver to produce was too impossible to contemplate. It meant, of course, absolute ruin to me and others in my position—to say nothing of hundreds of big jewellers and dealers.

'I pointed this out to Professor Goodman, but'—and once again Sir Raymond mopped his forehead—'would you believe it, the wretched man seemed completely uninterested. All he was concerned about was his miserable chemistry.

' "A unique discovery, my dear Blantyre," he remarked complacently. "And two years ago I bet Professor ——" I forget the fool's name, but, at any rate, he had bet this Professor a fiver that he'd do it.'

Sir Raymond rose and walked up and down the room in his agitation.

'A fiver, Mr Blackton—a fiver! I asked him what he was going to do, and he said he was going to read a paper on it, and give a demonstration at the next meeting of the Royal Society. And that takes place in a fortnight. I tried to dissuade him; I'm afraid I was foolish enough to threaten him.

'At any rate, he rose abruptly from the table, and I cursed myself for a fool. But towards the end of the evening he recovered himself sufficiently to agree to give me and the other members of my syndicate a private demonstration. His daughter also allowed me to take away her brooch, so that I could subject it to more searching tests the next day.'

He again sat down and stared at the man opposite him, who seemed more intent on how long he could get the ash of his cigar before it dropped than on anything else.

'Next day, Mr Blackton, my worst fears were confirmed. I subjected that stone to every known test—but it was useless. *It was*

11

a diamond—perfect, flawless; and it had cost five pounds to make. I called together my syndicate, and at first they were inclined to be incredulous.

'They suggested fraud—as you know, there have been in the past several attempts made to obtain money by men who pretended they had discovered the secret of making diamonds in the laboratory. And in every case, up till now, sleight-of-hand has been proved. The big uncut diamond was not produced by the chemical reaction, but was introduced at some period during the experiment.

'Of course the idea was to obtain hush-money to suppress the supposed secret. I pointed out to my friends how impossible such a supposition was in the case of a man like Professor Goodman; and finally—to cut things short—they agreed to come round with me the following afternoon to see the demonstration.

'The Professor had forgotten all about the appointment—he is that sort of man—and we waited in an agony of impatience while his secretary telephoned for him all over London. At last she got him, and the Professor arrived profuse in his apologies.

' "I have just been watching a most interesting experiment with some blue cheese-mould," he told me, "and I quite forgot the time. Now, what is it you gentlemen want to see?" '

For the first time a very faint smile flickered on Mr Blackton's lips, but he said nothing.

'I told him,' continued Sir Raymond, 'and we at once adjourned to the laboratory. We had most of us attended similar demonstrations before, and we expected to find the usual apparatus of a mould and a furnace. Nothing of the sort, however, could we see. There was an electric furnace: a sort of bowl made of some opaque material, and a variety of chemical salts in bottles.

' "You will forgive me, gentlemen," he remarked, "if I don't give you my process in detail. I don't want to run any risk of my discovery leaking out before I address the Royal Society."

'He beamed at us through his spectacles; and—serious though it was—I really could not help smiling. That he should make such a remark to us of all people!

' "You are, of course, at liberty to examine everything that I put into this retort," he went on, "and the retort itself."

'He was fumbling in his pocket as he spoke, and he finally produced two or three dirty sheets of paper, at which he peered.

' "Dear me!" he exclaimed. "I've got the wrong notes. These are the ones about my new albumen food for infants and adults. Where can I have left them?"

' "I hope," I remarked as calmly as I could, "that you haven't left them lying about where anyone could get at them, Professor."

'He shook his head vaguely, though his reply was reassuring.

' "No one could understand them even if I had," he answered. "Ah! here they are." With a little cry of triumph he produced some even dirtier scraps which he laid on the desk in front of him.

' "I have to refer to my notes," he said, "as the process—though the essence of simplicity, once the correct mixture of the ingredients is obtained—is a difficult one to remember. There are no fewer than thirty-nine salts used in the operation. Now would you gentlemen come closer, so that you can see everything I do?"

'He produced a balance which he proceeded to adjust with mathematical precision, while we crowded round as close as we could.

' "While I think of it," he said, looking up suddenly, "is there any particular colour you would like me to make?"

' "Rose-pink," grunted someone, and he nodded.

' "Certainly," he answered. "That will necessitate the addition of a somewhat rare strontium salt—making forty in all."

'He beamed at us and then he commenced. To say that we watched him closely would hardly convey our attitude: we watched him without movement, without speech, almost without breathing. He weighed his salts, and he mixed them—and that part of the process took an hour at least.

'Then he took up the bowl and we examined that. It was obviously some form of metal, but that was as far as we could get. And it was empty.

' "Without that retort, gentlemen," he remarked, "the process would be impossible. There is no secret as to its composition. It is made of a blend of tungsten and osmium, and is the only thing known to science today which could resist the immense heat to which this mixture will be subjected in the electric furnace. Now possibly one of you would like to pour this mixture into the retort, place the retort in the furnace, and shut the furnace doors. Then I will switch on the current."

'I personally did what he suggested, Mr Blackton. I poured the mixture of fine powders into the empty bowl; I placed the bowl into the furnace, having first examined the furnace; and then I closed the doors. And I knew, and every man there knew, that there had been no suspicion of fraud. Then he switched on the current, and we sat down to wait.

'Gradually the heat grew intense—but no one thought of moving. At first the Professor rambled on, but I doubt if anyone paid any attention to him. Amongst other things he told us that from the very start of his experiments he had worked on different lines from the usual ones, which consisted of dissolving carbon in molten iron and then cooling the mass suddenly with cold water.

' "That sets up gigantic pressure," he remarked, "but it is too quick. Only small stones are the result. My process was arrived at by totally different methods, as you see."

'The sweat poured off us, and still we sat there silent—each of us busy with his own thoughts. I think even then we realised that there was no hope; we knew that his claims were justified. But we had to see it through, and make sure. The Professor was absorbed in some profound calculations on his new albumen food; the furnace glowed white in the corner; and, Mr Blackton, men worth tens of millions sat and dripped with perspiration in order to make definitely certain that they were not worth as many farthings.

'I suppose it was about two hours later that the Professor, having looked at his watch, rose and switched off the current.

' "In about an hour, gentlemen," he remarked, "the retort will be cool enough to take out. I suggest that you should take it with you, and having cut out the clinker you should carry out your own tests on it. Inside that clinker will be your rose-pink diamond—uncut, of course. I make you a present of it: all I ask is that you should return me my retort."

'He blinked at us through his spectacles.

' "You will forgive me if I leave you now, but I have to deliver my address to some students on the catalytic influence of chromous chloride. I fear I am already an hour and a half late, but that is nothing new."

'And with that he bustled out of the room.'

Sir Raymond paused and lit a cigarette.

'You may perhaps think, Mr Blackton, that I have been un-necessarily verbose over details that are unimportant,' he continued after a moment. 'But my object has been to try to show you the type of man Professor Goodman is.'

'You have succeeded admirably, Sir Raymond,' said Blackton quietly.

'Good. Then now I will go quicker. We took his retort home, and we cut out the clinker. No one touched it except ourselves. We chipped off the outside scale, and we came to the diamond. Under our own eyes we had it cut—roughly, of course, because time was urgent. Here are the results.'

He handed over a small box to Blackton, who opened it. Inside, resting on some cotton-wool, were two large rose-pink diamonds and three smaller ones—worth in all, to the expert's shrewd eye, anything up to twenty-five thousand pounds. He took out a pocket lens and examined the largest, and Sir Raymond gave a short, hard laugh.

'Believe me,' he said harshly, 'they're genuine right enough. I wish to Heaven I could detect even the trace of a flaw. There isn't one, I tell you: they're perfect stones—and that's why we've come to you.'

Blackton laid the box on the table and renewed the contemplation of his cigar.

'At the moment,' he remarked, 'the connection is a little obscure. However, pray continue. I assume that you have interviewed the Professor again?'

'The very next morning,' said Sir Raymond. 'I went round, ostensibly to return his metal bowl, and then once again I put the whole matter before him. I pointed out to him that if this discovery of his was made known, it would involve thousands of people in utter ruin.

'I pointed out to him that after all no one could say that it was a discovery which could benefit the world generally, profoundly wonderful though it was. Its sole result, so far as I could see, would be to put diamond tiaras within the range of the average scullery maid. In short, I invoked every argument I could think of to try to persuade him to change his mind. Useless, utterly useless. To do him justice, I do not believe it is simply pig-headedness. He is honestly unable to understand our point of view.

'To him it is a scientific discovery concerning carbon, and according to him carbon is so vitally important, so essentially at the root of all life, that to suppress the results of an experiment such as this would be a crime against science. He sees no harm in diamonds being as plentiful as marbles; in fact, the financial side of the affair is literally meaningless to him.

15

'Meaningless, Mr Blackton, as I found when I played my last card. In the name of my syndicate I offered him two hundred and fifty thousand pounds to suppress it. He rang the bell—apologised for leaving me so abruptly—and the servant showed me out. And that is how the matter stands today. In a fortnight from now his secret will be given to the world, unless . . .'

Sir Raymond paused, and glanced at Mr Leibhaus.

'Precisely,' he agreed. 'Unless, as you say . . .'

Mr Blackton said nothing. It was not his business to help them out, though the object of their journey was now obvious.

'Unless, Mr Blackton,' Sir Raymond took the plunge, 'we can induce you to interest yourself in the matter.'

Mr Blackton raised his eyebrows slightly.

'I rather fail to see,' he remarked, 'how I can hope to succeed where you have failed. You appear to have exhausted every possible argument.'

And now Sir Raymond was beginning to look visibly agitated. Unscrupulous business man though he was, the thing he had to say stuck in his throat. It seemed so cold-blooded, so horrible—especially in that room looking on to the sparkling lake with the peaceful, snow-tipped mountains opposite.

'It was Baron Vanderton,' he stammered, 'who mentioned the Comte de Guy to me. He said that in a certain matter connected, I believe, with one of the big European banking firms, the Comte de Guy had been called in. And that as a result—er—a rather troublesome international financier had—er—disappeared.'

He paused abruptly as he saw Blackton's face. It was hard and merciless, and the grey-blue eyes seemed to be boring into his brain.

'Am I to understand, Sir Raymond,' he remarked, 'that you are trying to threaten me into helping you?'

He seemed to be carved out of stone, save for the fingers of his left hand, which played a ceaseless tattoo on his knee.

'Good heavens! no, Mr Blackton,' cried the other. 'Nothing of the sort, believe me. I merely mentioned the Baron to show you how we got on your trail. He told us that you were the only man in the world who would be able to help us, and then only if you were convinced the matter was sufficiently big.

'I trust that now you have heard what we have to say you will consider—like Mr Freyder—that the matter is sufficiently big to warrant your attention. You must, Mr Blackton; you really must.'

He leaned forward in his excitement. 'Think of it: millions and millions of money depending on the caprice of an old fool, who is really far more interested in his wretched albumen food. Why—it's intolerable.'

For a while there was silence, broken at length by Blackton.

'And so,' he remarked calmly, 'if I understand you aright, Sir Raymond, your proposal is that I should interest myself in the—shall we say—removal of Professor Goodman? Or, not to mince words, in his death.'

Sir Raymond shivered, and into Blackton's eyes there stole a faint contempt.

'Precisely, Mr Blackton,' he muttered. 'Precisely. In such a way of course that no shadow of suspicion can rest on us, or on—or on—anyone.'

Mr Blackton rose: the interview was over.

'I will let you know my decision after lunch,' he remarked. 'Shall we drink coffee together here at two o'clock? I expect my daughter will be in by then.'

He opened the door and bowed them out; then he returned to the table and picked up the bottle of champagne. It was empty, as was the plate of sandwiches. He looked at his own unused glass, and with a faint shrug of his shoulders he crossed to his dispatch-case and opened it. But when the girl came in he was making a couple of entries in his book.

The first was under the heading 'Blantyre' and consisted of a line drawn through the word 'Vice'; the second was under the heading 'Leibhaus', and consisted of the one word 'Glutton' written in red. He was thorough in his ways.

'You heard?' he said, as he replaced the book.

'Every word,' she answered, lighting a cigarette. 'What do you propose to do?'

'There is only one possible thing to do,' he remarked. 'Don't you realise, my dear, that had I heard of this discovery I should have been compelled to interfere, even if they had not asked me to. In my position I could not allow a diamond slump; as you know, we have quite a few ourselves. But there is no reason why they shouldn't pay me for it. . . .' He smiled gently. 'I shall cross to England by the Orient Express tonight.'

'But surely,' cried the girl, 'over such a simple matter you needn't go yourself.'

He smiled even more gently, and slipped his arm round her shoulders.

'Do you remember what we were talking about this morning?' he said.

'The big coup? Don't you see that even if this is not quite it, it will fill in the time?'

She looked a little puzzled.

'I'm damned if I do,' she cried tersely. 'You can't ask 'em more than half a million.'

'Funnily enough, that is the exact figure I intended to ask them,' he replied. 'But you've missed the point, my love—and I'm surprised at you. Everything that Blantyre said this morning was correct with regard to the impossibility of letting such a discovery become known to the world at large.

'I have no intention of letting it become known; but I have still less intention of letting it be lost. That would be an act of almost suicidal folly. Spread abroad, the knowledge would wreck everything; retained by one individual, it places that individual in a position of supreme power. And needless to say, I propose to be that individual.'

He was staring thoughtfully over the lake, and suddenly she seized his left hand.

'Ted—stop it.'

For a moment he looked at her in surprise; then he laughed.

'Was I doing it again?' he asked. 'It's a good thing you spotted that trick of mine, my dear. If there ever is a next time with Drummond'—his eyes blazed suddenly—'if there ever is—well, we will see. Just at the moment, however, let us concentrate on Professor Goodman.

'A telling picture that—wasn't it? Can't you see the old man, blinking behind his spectacles, absorbed in calculations on proteins for infants, with a ring of men around him not one of whom but would have murdered him then and there if he had dared!'

'But I still don't see how this is going to be anything out of the ordinary,' persisted the girl.

'My dear, I'm afraid that the balmy air of the Lake of Geneva has had a bad effect on you.' Mr Blackton looked at her in genuine surprise. 'I confess that I haven't worked out the details yet, but one point is quite obvious. Before Professor Goodman departs this life he is going to make several hundred diamonds for me, though it would never do to let the two anxious gentlemen downstairs know it. They might say that I wasn't earning my half-million.

'Those diamonds I shall unload with care and discretion during the years to come, so as not to cause a slump in prices. So it really boils down to the fact that the Metropolitan Diamond Syndicate will be paying me half a million for the express purpose of putting some five or ten million pounds' worth of stones in my pocket. My dear! it's a gift; it's one of those things which make strong men consult a doctor for fear they may be imagining things.'

The girl laughed.

'Where do I come in?'

'At the moment I'm not sure. So much will depend on circumstances. At any rate, for the present you had better stop on here, and I will send for you when things are a little more advanced.'

A waiter knocked and began to lay the table for lunch; and when at two o'clock the coffee and liqueurs arrived, closely followed by his two visitors, Mr Blackton was in a genial mood. An excellent bottle of Marcobrunner followed by a glass of his own particular old brandy had mellowed him to such an extent that he very nearly produced the bottle for them, but sanity prevailed.

It was true that they were going to pay him half a million for swindling them soundly, but there were only three bottles of that brandy left in the world.

The two men looked curiously at the girl as Blackton introduced them—Baron Vanderton had told them about the beauty of this so-called daughter who was his constant and invariable companion. Only she, so he had affirmed, knew what the man who now called himself Blackton really looked like when shorn of his innumerable disguises into which he fitted himself so marvellously.

But there were more important matters at stake than that, and Sir Raymond Blantyre's hand shook a little as he helped himself to a cigarette from the box on the table.

'Well, Mr Blackton,' he said as the door closed behind the waiter. 'Have you decided?'

'I have,' returned the other calmly. 'Professor Goodman's discovery will not be made public. He will not speak or give a demonstration at the Royal Society.'

With a vast sigh of relief Sir Raymond sank into a chair.

'And your—er—fee?'

'Half a million pounds. Two hundred and fifty thousand paid by cheque made out to Self—now; the remainder when you receive indisputable proof that I have carried out the job.'

It was significant that Sir Raymond made no attempt to haggle. Without a word he drew his cheque-book from his pocket, and going over to the writing-table he filled in the required amount.

'I would be glad if it was not presented for two or three days,' he remarked, 'as it is drawn on my private account, and I shall have to put in funds to meet it on my return to England.'

Mr Blackton bowed.

'You return tonight?' he asked.

'By the Orient Express. And you?'

Mr Blackton shrugged his shoulders.

'The view here is delightful,' he murmured.

And with that the representatives of the Metropolitan Diamond Syndicate had to rest content for the time—until, in fact, the train was approaching the Swiss frontier. They had just finished their dinner, their zest for which, though considerably greater than on the previous night in view of the success of their mission, had been greatly impaired by the manners of an elderly German sitting at the next table.

He was a bent and withered old man with a long hook nose and white hair, who, in the intervals of querulously swearing at the attendant, deposited his dinner on his waistcoat.

At length he rose, and having pressed ten centimes into the outraged hand of the head waiter, he stood for a moment by their table, swaying with the motion of the train. And suddenly he bent down and spoke to Sir Raymond.

'Two or three days, I think you said, Sir Raymond.'

With a dry chuckle he was gone, tottering and lurching down the carriage, leaving the President of the Metropolitan Diamond Syndicate gasping audibly.

CHAPTER 2

In Which Professor Goodman Realises that there are More Things in Life than Chemistry

When Brenda Goodman, in a moment of mental aberration, consented to marry Algy Longworth, she little guessed the result. From being just an ordinary, partially wanting specimen he became a raving imbecile. Presumably she must have thought it was natural as she showed no signs of terror, at any rate in public, but it was otherwise with his friends.

Men who had been wont to foregather with him to consume the matutinal cocktail now fled with shouts of alarm whenever he hove in sight. Only the baser members of that celebrated society, the main object of which is to cultivate the muscles of the left arm when consuming liquid refreshment, clung to him in his fall from grace. They found that his mental fog was so opaque that he habitually forgot the only rule and raised his glass to his lips with his right hand.

And since that immediately necessitated a further round at his expense, they gave great glory to Allah for such an eminently satisfactory state of affairs. And when it is further added that he was actually discovered by Peter Darrell reading the poems of Ella Wheeler Wilcox on the morning of the Derby, it will be readily conceded that matters looked black.

That the state of affairs was only temporary was, of course, recognised; but while it lasted it became necessary for him to leave the councils of men. A fellow who wants to trot back to the club-house from the ninth green in the middle of a four-ball foursome to blow his fiancée a kiss through the telephone is a truly hideous spectacle.

And so the sudden action of Hugh Drummond, one fine morning in June, is quite understandable. He had been standing by the window of his room staring into the street, and playing Beaver to himself, when with a wild yell he darted to the bell. He pealed it several times; then he rushed to the door and shouted:

'Denny! Where the devil are you, Denny?'

'Here, sir.'

His trusted body-servant and erstwhile batman appeared from the nether regions of the house, and regarded his master in some surprise.

'The door, Denny—the front door. Go and bolt and bar it; put the chain up; turn all the latchkeys. Don't stand there blinking, you fool. Mr Longworth is tacking up the street, and I know he's coming here. Blow at him through the letter-box, and tell him to go away. I will not have him about the house at this hour of the morning. Tell him I'm in bed with housemaid's knee. Not *the* housemaid's knee, you ass: it's a malady, not a dissecting-room in a hospital.'

With a sigh of relief he watched Denny bar the door; then he returned to his own room and sank into an arm-chair.

'Heavens!' he muttered, 'what an escape! Poor old Algy!'

He sighed again profoundly, and then, feeling in need of support, he rose and crossed to a cask of beer which adorned one corner of the room. And he was just preparing to enjoy the fruits of his labours, when the door opened and Denny came in.

'He won't go, sir—says he must see you, before you dine with his young lady tonight.'

'Great Scott! Denny—isn't that enough?' said Drummond wildly. 'Not that one minds dining with her, but it's watching him that is so painful. Have you inspected him this morning?'

'I kept the door on the chain, sir, and glanced at him. He seems to me to be a little worried.'

Drummond crossed to the window and looked out. Standing on the pavement outside was the unfortunate Algy, who waved his stick wildly as soon as he saw him.

'Your man Denny has gone mad,' he cried. 'He kept the door on the chain and gibbered like a monkey. I want to see you.'

'I know you do, Algy: I saw you coming up Brook Street. And it was I who told Denny to bar the door. Have you come to talk to me about love?'

'No, old man, I swear I haven't,' said Algy earnestly. 'I won't mention the word, I promise you. And it's really most frightfully important.'

'All right,' said Drummond cautiously. 'Denny shall let you in; but at the first word of poetry—out you go through the window.'

He nodded to his servant, and a moment or two later Algy Longworth came into the room. The newcomer was arrayed in a faultless morning coat, and Hugh Drummond eyed him non-committally. He certainly looked a little worried, though his immaculate topper and white spats seemed to show that he was bearing up with credit.

'Going to Ranelagh, old bird,' said Algy. 'Hence the bathing suit. Lunching first, don't you know, and all that—so I thought I'd drop in this morning to make sure of catching you. You and Phyllis are dining, aren't you, this evening?'

'We are,' said Hugh.

'Well, the most awful thing has happened, old boy. My prospective father-in-law to be—Brenda's dear old male parent—has gone mad. He's touched; he's wanting; he's up the pole.'

He lit a cigarette impressively, and Drummond stared at him.

'What's the matter with the old thing?' he demanded. 'I met him outside his club yesterday and he didn't seem to me to be any worse than usual.'

'My dear boy, I didn't know anything about it till last night,' cried Algy. 'He sprang it on us at dinner, and I tell you I nearly swooned. I tried to register mirth, but I failed, Hugh—I failed. I shudder to think what my face must have looked like.' He was pacing up and down the room in his agitation.

'You know, don't you, old man, that he ain't what you'd call rolling in boodle. I mean, with the best will in the world you couldn't call him a financial noise. And though, of course, it doesn't matter to me what Brenda has—if we can't manage, I shall have to do a job of work or something—yet I feel sort of responsible for the old parent.

'And when he goes and makes a prize ass of himself, it struck me that I ought to sit up and take notice. I thought it over all last night, and decided to come and tell you this morning, so that we could all have a go at him tonight.'

'What has he done?' demanded Hugh with some interest.

'You know he's got a laboratory,' continued Algy, 'where he goes and plays games. It's a perfect factory of extraordinary smells, but the old dear seems to enjoy himself. He'll probably try his new albumenised chicken food on you tonight, but that's a detail. To get to the point—have you ever noticed that big diamond Brenda wears as a brooch?'

'Yes, I have. Phyllis was speaking about it the other night.'

'You know he made it,' said Algy quietly, and Hugh stared at

23

him. 'It is still supposed to be a secret: it was to be kept dark till the next meeting of the Royal Society—but after what has happened I decided to tell you. About a fortnight ago a peculiar-looking bloke called Sir Raymond Blantyre came and dined.

'He's made his money in diamonds, and he was on to that diamond like a terrier on to a rat. And when he heard old Goodman had made it, I thought he was going to expire from a rush of blood to the head. He'd just offered Brenda a cheque for ten thousand for it, when he was told it had cost a little over a fiver to make.

'As I say, he turned a deep magenta and dropped his eyeglass in the sauce *tartare*. That was the first spasm; the next we heard last night. Apparently the old man agreed to give a demonstration to this bloke and some of his pals, and the result of the show was— great heavens! when I think of it, my brain comes out in a rash—the result, Hugh, was that they offered him a quarter of a million pounds to suppress his discovery.

'Two hundred and fifty thousand acidulated tablets—and he refused. One supreme glorious burst on fifty thousand of the best, and an income from the remaining two hundred for the rest of his life. We worked it out after dinner, my boy—Brenda and I. Two hundred thousand at five per cent. We couldn't quite make out what it would come to, but whatever it is he has cast it from him. And then you wonder at my anguish.'

With a hollow groan Algy helped himself to beer and sank into a chair.

'Look here, Algy,' said Hugh, after a pause, 'you aren't playing the fool, are you? You literally mean that Professor Goodman has discovered a method by which diamonds can be made artificially?'

'Exactly; that is what I literally mean. And I further literally mean that he has turned down an offer of a quarter of a million thick 'uns to keep dark about it. And what I want you and Phyllis to do this evening . . .'

'Dry up,' interrupted Hugh. He was staring out of the window, and his usual look of inane good temper had completely vanished. He was thinking deeply, and after a few moments he swung round on the disconsolate Algy.

'This is a pretty serious affair, Algy,' he remarked.

'You bet your life it is,' agreed his friend. 'Quarter . . .'

'Cut it out about the boodle. That's bad, I admit—but it's not that I'm thinking of.'

24

'I don't know what the deuce else there is to think about. Just because he wants to spout out his footling discovery to a bunch of old geysers at the Royal Society . . .'

Hugh regarded him dispassionately.

'I have often wondered why they ever let you leave school,' he remarked. 'Your brain is even smaller than the ten-bob helping of caviare they gave me at the Majestic last night. You don't really think it's a footling discovery, do you? You don't really think people run about the streets of London pressing two hundred and fifty thousand pounds on comparative strangers for fun?'

'Oh! I suppose the old bean has spotted a winner right enough,' conceded Algy grudgingly.

'Now, look here,' said Drummond quietly. 'I don't profess to know anything about diamonds or the diamond market. But if what you say is correct—if the Professor can manufacture a stone worth at current prices ten thousand pounds for a fiver—you don't require to know much about markets to see that diamonds will be on a par with bananas as soon as the process is known.

'Further, you don't require to know much about markets to see that such a state of affairs would be deuced unpopular with quite a lot of people. If you've got all your money in diamonds and wake up one bright morning to read in the paper that a diamond weighing half a ton has just been manufactured for three and sixpence, it's going to make the breakfast kipper look a bit jaded.'

'I know all that, old boy,' said Algy a bit wearily. 'But they're just additional reasons for the old ass taking the money. Then everyone would be happy. Only he's so confoundedly pigheaded. Why, when I sort of suggested after dinner last night during the nut-mastication period that he could do a lot with the boodle—help him no end with his albumenised chicken seed, and all that—he got quite stuffy.'

' "My dear boy," he said, "you don't understand. To offer a scientist money to suppress a discovery of possibly far-reaching importance is not only an insult to him, but it is also an insult to science. I would not suppress this for a million pounds." '

'Then he forgot to pass the port, and the meeting broke up in disorder.'

Hugh nodded thoughtfully.

'I'm afraid they will suppress it for him,' he said gravely.

Algy stared at him.

25

'How do you mean, suppress it for him?' he demanded at length.

'I haven't an idea,' answered Drummond. 'Not even the beginning of one. But people have fallen in front of tube trains before now; people have been accidentally killed by a passing car——'

'But, good heavens, man,' cried Algy dazedly, 'you don't mean to say that you think someone will murder the poor old fruit?'

Drummond shrugged his shoulders. 'Your future father-in-law has it in his power to completely ruin large numbers of extremely wealthy men. Apparently with the best will in the world he proposes to do so. He has butted into a huge vested interest, and, as far as I can make out from what you've told me, he quite fails to realise the fact.' He lit a cigarette thoughtfully.

'But what the devil are we to do, Hugh?' said Algy, now very serious himself. 'I tell you it will be impossible to make him accept that money. He's as docile as a sheep in some ways, but once he does stick his toes in over anything, a bag of gunpowder won't shift him.'

'Well, if he really is determined to go through with it, it may be necessary to get him away and keep a watchful eye on him till he gets it off his chest at the Royal Society. That's to say if he'll come. Once it's out—it's out, and the reasons for doing away with him will largely have disappeared.'

'Yes; but I say, old man—murder!' Algy harked back to his original point. 'Don't you think that's a bit over the odds?'

Hugh laughed grimly. 'You've lived the quiet life too long, Algy. There are stakes at issue now which strike me as being a deuced sight bigger than anything we played for with dear old Carl Peterson. Bigger at any rate financially.'

An almost dreamy look came into his eyes, and he sighed deeply. 'Those were the days, Algy—those were the days. I'm afraid we shall never have them again. Still—if what I'm afraid of is correct, we might have a bit of fun, looking after the old man. Dull, of course, but better than nothing.' He sighed again, and helped himself to more beer.

'Now you trot off and lunch with Brenda. Don't tell her anything about what I've said. I shall make one or two discreet inquiries this afternoon, and this evening I will bring the brain to bear over the fish and chips.'

'Right, old man,' cried Algy, rising with alacrity. 'Deuced good of you and all that. I'd hate the dear old bird to take it in the neck. His port is pretty putrid, I admit—but still——'

He waved his stick cheerfully, and a few seconds later Hugh watched him walking at speed down Brook Street. And long after Algy had disappeared he was still standing at the window staring into the street.

Hugh Drummond laid no claim to being brilliant. His brain, as he frequently remarked, was of the 'also-ran' variety. But he was undoubtedly the possessor of a very shrewd common sense, which generally enabled him to arrive at the same result as a far more brilliant man and, incidentally, by a much more direct route.

He was, it may be said, engaged in trying to arrive at what he called in military parlance, the general idea. He did it by a process of reasoning which at any rate had the merit of being easy to follow.

First, Algy, though a fool and partially demented, was not a liar. Therefore the story he had just listened to was true.

Second, the bloke who had turned a deep magenta, though possibly a liar, was certainly not a fool. If he had made his money in diamonds, he couldn't be, at any rate, as far as diamonds were concerned.

Third, since he had offered Professor Goodman no less than a quarter of a million to suppress the secret, he had evidently got a jolt in a tender spot.

Fourth, here was the great query: just how tender was that spot?

He had spoken glibly about markets to Algy, but he realised only too well that he actually knew nothing about diamonds. He recalled dimly that they were found in mines near Kimberley; beyond that his knowledge of the subject was limited to the diamond engagement ring he had bought for Phyllis. And having reached that point in his deliberations, he decided that before coming to any definite conclusion it would be well to take some expert advice on the matter.

He rose and pressed the bell: Toby Sinclair was the very man. In the intervals of backing losers, that bright particular star graced a city firm with his presence—a firm which dealt in precious stones on the wholesale side.

'Denny,' he said, as his servant came in, 'ring up Mr Sinclair in the city and ask him to come and lunch with me at the club today. Tell him it's very important.'

And five minutes later he was strolling in the same direction as that taken by Algy, but at a more leisurely rate. His face was still contorted with thought; he periodically stopped abruptly and glared into space. How big was the jolt? Was it really big enough to justify the fears he had expressed to Algy, or was he exaggerating things in his own mind? He ruminated on the point over a cocktail in the Regency; he was still ruminating as he passed into St James's Square on the way to his club.

To reach it he had to pass the doors of Professor Goodman's club, and as he walked slowly on the cause of all his profound mental activity—the worthy Professor himself—hove into sight. Drummond paused: it seemed to him that something had happened. For the Professor was muttering wildly to himself, while periodically he shook his fist in the air.

'Morning, Professor,' he remarked affably. 'Been stung by a bee, or what?'

The Professor stopped abruptly and stared at him.

'It's you, Drummond, is it?' he said. 'I've just received a most scandalous letter—perfectly scandalous. A threat, sir—an anonymous threat. Read it.'

He held out a common-looking envelope which he handed to Drummond. But that worthy only took it mechanically; his eyes—shrewd and thoughtful—were looking over the Professor's shoulder. A man had come hurriedly round King Street, only to pause with equal suddenness and stare into an area below.

'I suppose, Professor,' he remarked quietly, still holding the letter in his hand, 'that you know you're being followed.'

'I know I'm being what?' barked the Professor. 'Who is following me?'

Drummond slightly raised his voice.

'If you turn round you will see an unpleasant specimen of humanity gazing into the basement of that house. I allude to the bird with the large ears, who is beginning to go a little red about the tonsils.'

With a snarl the man swung on his heel and came towards them.

'Are you talking about me, damn you?' he said, addressing Drummond.

'I am,' remarked Drummond dispassionately. 'Mushrooms growing well down below there?' The man looked somewhat disconcerted. 'Now, who told you to follow Professor Goodman?'

'I don't know what you're talking about,' said the man surlily.

'Dear me!' remarked Drummond mildly. 'I should have thought the question was sufficiently clear even to a person of your limited intelligence. However, if it will save you any bother, the Professor is lunching with me at my club—that one over there with the warrior in uniform outside the door—and will probably be leaving about three. So you can either run away and play marbles till then, or you can stay here and watch the door.'

He put his hand through the Professor's arm, and gently propelled him towards the club, leaving the man scratching his head foolishly.

'But, my dear fellow,' mildly protested the Professor, 'this is very kind of you. I'd no idea I was lunching with you.'

'No more had I,' answered Hugh genially. 'But I think it's a jolly sort of idea, don't you? We'll get a table in the window and watch our friend earning his pay outside, while we toy with a bit of elusive Stilton.'

'But how do you know the man was following me, Drummond?' said the Professor excitedly. 'And if he was, don't you think I ought to tell the police?'

Gently but firmly Drummond piloted him up the steps of his club.

'I have an unerring instinct in such matters, Professor,' he remarked. 'And he was very bad at it—very bad. Now we will lower a Martini apiece, and I will read this threatening missive of yours.'

The Professor sank into his chair and blinked at Hugh through his spectacles. He had had a trying morning, and there was something very reassuring about this large and imperturbable young man whom he knew was his future son-in-law's greatest friend. And as he watched him reading the typewritten piece of paper, strange stories which he had heard of some of Drummond's feats in the past came back to him. They had been told him by Algy and one or two by Brenda, but he had not paid any great attention to them at the time. They were not very much in his line, but now he felt distinctly comforted as he recalled them. To have his life threatened was a new experience for the worthy Professor, and one not at all to his liking. It had interfered considerably with his work that morning, and produced a lack of mental concentration which he found most disturbing.

The letter was short and to the point.

'Unless you accept the two hundred and fifty thousand pounds recently offered to you, you will be killed.'

The Professor leaned forward as Drummond laid the sheet of paper on the table.

'I must explain, Drummond,' he began, but the other interrupted him.

'No need to, Professor. Algy came round to see me this morning, and he told me about your discovery.'

He again picked up the paper and glanced at it.

'You have no idea, I suppose, who can have sent this?'

'None,' said the Professor. 'It is utterly inconceivable that Sir Raymond Blantyre should have stooped to such a thing. He, as Algy probably told you, is the man who originally offered me this sum to suppress my discovery. But I refuse to believe for a moment that he would ever have been guilty of such a vulgar threat.'

Drummond regarded him thoughtfully.

'Look here, Professor,' he said at length, 'it seems to me that you are getting into pretty deep water. How deep I don't quite know. I tell you frankly I can't understand this letter. If, as you say, it is merely a vulgar threat, it is a very stupid and dangerous thing to put on paper. If, on the other hand, it is more than a threat—if it is an actual statement of fact—it is even more incredibly stupid and dangerous.'

'A statement of fact,' gasped the Professor. 'That I shall be killed if I don't suppress my discovery!'

He was blinking rapidly behind his spectacles, and Drummond smiled.

'A statement of fact as far as the writer of this epistle is concerned,' he remarked. 'No more than that, Professor, I hope. In fact we must take steps to ensure that it is no more than that. But this letter, on top of your being followed, shows that you're in the public eye, so to speak.'

'But I don't understand, Drummond,' said the Professor feebly.

'No more do I,' answered Hugh. 'However, that will make it all the jollier when we do. And it is possible that we may get a bit nearer the mark today at lunch. A fellow of the name of Sinclair is joining us—he's a pal of Algy's too—and he's in a big diamond merchant's office down in the city. He's a knowledgeable sort of bird, and we'll pump him. I don't want you to say a word as to your discovery—not a word. We'll just put the case to him as an academic one, and we'll get his actual opinion on it.'

'But I know their opinion about it already,' said the Professor peevishly. 'And I tell you that nothing is going to stop me announcing my discovery in ten days' time before the Royal Society.'

Drummond drained his cocktail.

'That's the spirit, Professor,' he cried cheerily. 'But for all that we may just as well see where we are. Here is Sinclair now: don't forget—not a word.'

He rose as Toby Sinclair came up.

'Morning, Toby. Do you know Professor Goodman? He is the misguided man who is allowing Algy to marry into his family.'

'Morning, sir,' said Sinclair with a grin. 'Well, old man—a cocktail, a rapid lunch, and I must buzz back. I tell you things are moving with some celerity in our line, at present. And as the bright boy of the firm, my time is fully occupied.'

He lit a cigarette, and Hugh laughed.

'With a *Lunar Guide* and the *Sportsman*. Quite so, old boy—I know.'

'No, really, Hugh,' said Toby seriously, 'the old office has not been the usual rest-cure just lately. Strong men have rushed in and out and conferred behind locked doors, and the strain has been enormous. Made one quite dizzy to see them. However, it's been better the last two or three days, ever since old Blantyre came back from Switzerland.'

Drummond adroitly kicked the Professor's leg.

'And who is old Blantyre?' he remarked carelessly, 'and why does he go to Switzerland?'

'Sir Raymond Blantyre is the head of the syndicate to which our firm belongs, though why he went to Switzerland I haven't any idea. All I can tell you is that he went out there looking like nothing on earth, and came back two days later smiling all over his face.'

'Speaks well for the Swiss air,' said Hugh dryly. 'However, let's go and inspect the menu.'

He led the way towards the dining-room, and his expression was thoughtful. If, as he had been given to understand, Sir Raymond Blantyre was now facing immediate ruin, it was a little difficult to see why he should be smiling all over his face. It showed, at any rate, a resignation to Fate which was beyond all praise. Unless, of course, something had happened in Switzerland . . . But, then, what could have happened? Had he gone over there to dispose of his stock before the crash came? He felt very vague as to whether it would be possible to do such a thing. Anyway, it mightn't be a bad idea to find out where he had been to in Switzerland. Just for future reference; in case anything happened.

'Yes—a deuced good advertisement for the Swiss air, old man,' he repeated, after they had sat down. 'Where did he go to?'

'You seem very interested in his wanderings,' said Toby with a laugh. 'As a matter of fact, I believe he went to Montreux, but since he was only there a day, the air can't have had much to do with it.'

Hugh glanced through the window; the man who had been following the Professor was still loitering about the corner of the square. And the frown on his face grew more pronounced. It beat him—the whole thing beat him completely. Especially the threatening letter. . . .

'You're marvellously merry and bright this morning, old boy.' Toby broke off his desultory conversation with the Professor and regarded Hugh with the eye of an expert. 'I don't think you can have been mother's angel-boy last night. Anyway, what is this important thing you wanted to see me about?'

With an effort his host pulled himself together.

'I was thinking, Toby,' he remarked, 'and you know what an awful effect that always has on my system. Look here, diamonds are a pretty good thing, aren't they, as a birthday present for Phyllis?'

Toby stared at him.

'I think they're a very good thing,' he remarked. 'Why?'

'No danger of them losing their value?'

'None whatever. The output is far too carefully controlled for that.'

'But supposing someone came along and manufactured them cheap?'

Toby laughed. 'You needn't worry about that, old man. It has been done in the past and the results cost more than the genuine article.'

'Yes, but supposing it did happen,' persisted Hugh. 'Supposing a process was discovered by which big stones—really big stones—could be made for a mere song—what then?'

Toby shrugged his shoulders.

'The discoverer of the process could ask practically what he liked to suppress it,' he answered.

'And if it wasn't suppressed—if it became known?'

'If it became widely known it would mean absolute ruin to

32

thousands of people. You may take it from me, old man, that in the first place such a process is never likely to be found, and, if it ever was, that it would never come out.'

Hugh flashed a warning glance at the Professor.

'There are hundreds of millions of pounds involved directly or indirectly in the diamond business,' went on Toby. 'So I think you can safely invest in a few if you want to, for Phyllis.'

He glanced at his watch and rose.

'Look here, I must be toddling. Another conference on this afternoon. If you want any advice on choosing them, old boy, I'm always in the office from eleven-thirty to twelve.'

Hugh watched him cross the room; then he turned thoughtfully to the Professor.

'So that's that,' he said. 'Now, what about a bit of Stilton and a glass of light port while we consider the matter?'

'But I knew all that before, and it has no influence on me, Drummond. None at all.' The Professor was snorting angrily. 'I will not be intimidated into the suppression of a far-reaching chemical discovery by any considerations whatever.'

'Quite so,' murmured Hugh soothingly. 'I thought you'd probably feel like that about it. But it's really Algy I'm thinking about. As you know, he's a dear old pal of mine; his wedding is fixed in about a month, and since that is the only thing that can possibly restore him to sanity, we none of us want it postponed.'

'Why should it be postponed?' cried the Professor.

'Mourning in the bride's family,' said Drummond. 'The betting is a tenner to a dried banana that you expire within a week. Have some more cheese?'

'Don't be absurd, Drummond. If you think you are going to persuade me—you're wrong. I suppose that foolish boy Algy has been trying to enlist you on his side.'

'Now look here, Professor,' said Hugh quietly. 'Will you listen to me for a moment or two? It is perfectly true that Algy did suggest to me this morning that I should try to persuade you to accept the offer Sir Raymond made you. But I am not going to do anything of the sort. I may say that even this morning it struck me that far more serious things were at stake than your acceptance or refusal of two hundred and fifty thousand pounds. I am not at all certain in my own mind that if you accepted the money you would even then be safe. You are the owner of far too dangerous a piece of knowledge.

33

However, as I say, it struck me this morning that things were serious—now I'm sure of it, after what Toby said. He evidently knows nothing about it, so the big men are keeping it dark. Moreover, the biggest man of all, according to him, seems perfectly pleased with life at the present moment. Yet it's not due to anything that you have done; you haven't told them that you will accept their offer. Then why is he pleased? Most people wouldn't be full of happiness when they were facing immediate ruin. Professor, you may take it from me—and I am not an alarmist by any means—that the jolly old situation has just about as many unpleasant snags sticking out of it as any that I have ever contemplated. And I've contemplated quite a few in my life.'

He sat back in his chair and drained his port, and the Professor, impressed in spite of himself, looked at him in perplexity.

'Then what do you suggest that I should do, Drummond?' he said. 'These sort of things are not at all in my line.'

Hugh smiled. 'No, I suppose they're not. Well, I'll tell you what I would suggest your doing. If you are determined to go through with this, I would first of all take that threatening letter to Scotland Yard. Ask for Sir Bryan Johnstone, tell him you're a pal of mine, call him Tum-tum, and he'll eat out of your hand. If you can't see him, round up Inspector McIver, and tell him—well, as much or as little as you like. Of course, it's a little difficult. You can hardly accuse Sir Raymond Blantyre of having sent it. But still it seems the only thing to do. Then I propose that you and your wife and your daughter should all come away, and Algy too, and stop with my wife and me, for a little house-warming party at a new place I've just bought down in Sussex. I'll rope in a few of Algy's pals and mine to stop there too and we'll keep an eye on you, until the meeting of the Royal Society.'

'It's very good of you, Drummond,' said the Professor uncertainly. 'I hardly know what to say. This letter, for instance.'

He fumbled in his pocket and drew out a bunch of papers, which he turned over in his hands.

'To think that there's all this trouble over that,' he continued, holding out two or three sheets of notepaper. 'Whereas nobody worries over these notes on albumenised proteins.'

Hugh stared at him in amazement.

'You don't mean to say that those are the notes of your diamond process,' he gasped. 'Carried loose in your pocket?'

34

'Yes—why not?' said the Professor mildly. 'I always carry everything loose like that, otherwise I lose them. And I should be helpless without these.'

'Good heavens! man, you must be mad,' cried Hugh. 'Do you mean to say that you couldn't carry on without those notes? And yet you carry them like that!'

'I should have to do it all over again, and it would take me months to arrive at the right proportions once more.' He was peering through the scattered sheets. 'Even now I believe I've lost one—oh! no, here it is. You see, it doesn't make much odds, because no one could understand them except me.'

Hugh looked at him speechlessly for a while: then he passed his hand dazedly across his forehead.

'My dear Professor,' he murmured, 'you astound me. You positively stagger my brain. The only remaining thing which I feel certain you have not omitted to do is to ensure that Sir Raymond and his friends know that you carry your notes about in your pocket like that. You haven't forgotten to tell them that, have you?'

'Well, as a matter of fact, Drummond,' said the Professor apologetically, 'I'm afraid they must guess that I do. You see, when I did my demonstration before them I pulled my notes out of my pockets just as I did a moment or two ago. I suppose it is foolish of me, but until now I haven't thought any more about the matter. It all comes as such a complete shock, that I really don't know where I am. What do you think I'd better do with them?'

'Deposit them at your bank the very instant you leave here,' said Hugh. 'I will come round with you, and—well, what's the matter now, Professor?'

The Professor had risen to his feet, blinking rapidly in his agitation.

'Good heavens! Drummond, I had completely forgotten. All this bother put it quite out of my head. Professor Scheidstrun—a celebrated German geologist—made an appointment with me at my house for this afternoon. He has brought several specimens of carboniferous quartz which he claims will completely refute a paper I have just written on the subject of crystalline deposits. I must get home at once, or I shall be late.'

'Not quite so fast, Professor,' said Hugh with a smile. 'I don't know anything about carboniferous quartz, but there's one thing I do know. Not for one minute longer do you walk about the streets of London with those notes in your pocket. Come into the smoking-room and we'll seal them up in an envelope. Then I'll take charge of them, at any rate until tonight when I'm coming to dine at your house. And after dinner we can discuss matters further.'

He led the agitated savant into the smoking-room, and stood over him while he placed various well-thumbed pieces of paper into an envelope. Then he sealed the envelope and placed it in his pocket, and with a sigh of relief the Professor rose. But Drummond had not finished yet.

'What about that letter and the police?' he said, holding out a detaining hand.

'My dear boy, I really haven't got the time now,' cried the old man. 'You've no idea of the importance of this interview this afternoon. Why'—he laid his hand impressively on Drummond's arm—'if what Scheidstrun claims is correct, it may cause a complete revolution in our present ideas on the atomic theory. Think of that, my friend, think of that.'

Drummond suppressed a strong desire to laugh.

'I'm thinking, Professor,' he murmured gravely. 'And even though he does all that you say and more, I still think that you ought to go to the police with that letter.'

'Tomorrow, Drummond—I will.' Like a rabbit between a line of beaters he was dodging towards the door, with Drummond after him.

'You shall come with me yourself tomorrow, I promise you. And we'll discuss matters again tonight. But the atomic theory— think of it.'

With a gasp of relief he dashed into a waiting taxi, leaving Hugh partially stupefied on the pavement.

'Tell him where to go, there's a good fellow,' cried the Professor. 'And if you could possibly lend me half-a-crown, I'd be very grateful. I've left all my money at home, as usual.'

Drummond smiled and produced the necessary coin. Then a sudden thought struck him.

'I suppose you know this German bloke, don't you?'

'Yes, yes,' cried the Professor testily. 'Of course I know him. I met him ten years ago in Geneva. For goodness' sake, my boy, tell the man to drive on.'

Drummond watched the taxi swing round into King Street; then somewhat thoughtfully he went back into his club. Discussing the

36

atomic theory with a German professor he knew, seemed a comparatively safe form of amusement, calculated, in fact, to keep him out of mischief, but he still felt vaguely uneasy. The man who had followed him seemed to have disappeared; St James's Square was warm and peaceful. From one point of view, it was hard to believe that any real danger could threaten the old man: he felt he could understand his surprised incredulity. As he had said, such things were out of his line. But as Drummond might have answered, they were not out of his, and no man living knew better that strange things took place daily in London, things which would tax the credulity of the most hardened reader of sensational fiction. And the one great dominant point which stuck out, and refused to be argued away, was this. What was the life of one old man compared to the total loss of hundreds of millions of pounds, when viewed from the standpoint of the losers? He glanced at the envelope he still held in his hand, and slipped it into his pocket. Then he went into the telephone box and rang up his chauffeur to bring round his car.

He felt he wanted some fresh air to clear his brain, and all the way down to Ranelagh the same question kept clouding it. Why had that threatening letter been sent? If the intention was indeed to kill Professor Goodman, why, in the name of all that was marvellous, be so incredibly foolish as not only to warn him, but also to put that warning on paper? And if it was merely a bluff, again why put it on paper when the writer must have known that in all probability it would be taken straight to the police? Or was the whole thing just a silly jest, and was he, personally, making an appalling fool of himself by taking it seriously?

But the last alternative was untenable. The offer of a quarter of a million pounds was no jest; not even the most spritely humorist could possibly consider it one. And so he found himself back at the beginning again, and he was still there when he saw Algy and his girl having tea.

He deposited himself in a vacant chair beside Brenda and, having assured her of his continued devotion, he consumed the last sugar-cake.

'The male parent has just lunched with me,' he remarked genially. 'And as a result I am in the throes of brain-fever. He borrowed half-a-crown, and went off in Admiral Ferguson's hat, as I subsequently discovered. I left the worthy seaman running round in small circles snorting like a bull. You should discourage your father, Brenda, from keeping pieces of paper written on with copying ink in the lining of his head-piece. Old Ferguson, who put the hat on by mistake, has a chemistry lecture written all over his forehead.'

'Did you persuade Dad not to be such an unmitigated idiot, Hugh?' asked the girl eagerly.

'I regret to state that I did not,' answered Hugh. 'In fact, honesty compels me to admit, Brenda, that I no longer wonder at his allowing you to marry Algy. He may be the outside size in chemistry, but beyond that he wants lessons. Will you believe it, that at lunch today he suddenly removed from his pocket the notes of this bally discovery of his? He has been carrying them loose, along with some peppermint bull's-eyes and bits of string!'

'Oh! but he always carries everything like that,' laughed the girl. 'What is the old dear doing now?'

'He rushed away to commune with a German professor on carboniferous quartz and the atomic theory. Seemed immensely excited about it, so I suppose it means something. But to come to rather more important matters, I have invited him and Mrs Goodman and you to come down and spend a few days with us in Sussex. We might even include Algy.'

'What's the notion, old man?' murmured Algy. 'Think he's more likely to see reason if we take him bird-nesting?'

'It's no good, Hugh,' said Brenda decisively. 'Besides, he wouldn't go.'

She turned to speak to a passing acquaintance, and Hugh bent over to Algy.

'He's damn well got to go,' he said in a low voice. 'He was being followed this morning when I met him outside the club, and he's had a letter threatening his life.'

'The devil he has!' muttered Algy.

'If you can make him see reason and suppress his discovery, so much the better,' went on Hugh. 'Personally, I think he's a pig-headed old ass, and that it undoubtedly ought to be suppressed, but there's no good telling him that at present. But if he won't, it's up to us anyway to look after him, because he's utterly incapable of doing it himself. Not a word to Brenda, mind, about the letter or his being followed. He's all right for this afternoon, and we'll fix things up this evening definitely.'

And since the afternoon was all that an afternoon should be, and no one may ask for more than that and Ranelàgh combined, it was just as well for the peace of mind of all concerned that no power of second sight enabled them to see what was happening in Professor Goodman's laboratory, where he was discussing carboniferous quartz and the atomic theory with a celebrated German geologist.

CHAPTER 3

In Which Strange Things Happen in Professor Goodman's Laboratory

At just about the same time that Algy Longworth was dancing on the pavement in Brook Street and demanding admission to Drummond's house, Sir Raymond Blantyre was holding a conference with the other members of the Metropolitan Diamond Syndicate. The proceedings were taking place behind locked doors, and had an onlooker been present he would have noticed that there was a general air of tension in the room. For good or ill the die was cast, and try as they would the seven eminently respectable city magnates assembled round the table could not rid themselves of the thought that they had deliberately hired a man to commit murder for them. Not that they admitted it even to themselves—at any rate, not as crudely as that. Mr Blackton's services had been secured to arrange matters for them with Professor Goodman—to negotiate for the suppression of his discovery. How he did it was, of course, his concern, and nothing whatever to do with them. Even Sir Raymond himself tried to lull his conscience by reflecting that perhaps the drastic measures alluded to in his interview at the Palace Hotel would not be necessary. And if they were—well, only a weak man wavered and hesitated once he was definitely committed to a particular line of action. After all, the responsibility was not his alone; he had merely been the spokesman for the combined opinions of the Syndicate reached after mature reflection. And if Professor Goodman was so pig-headed and obstinate, he must take the consequences. There were others to be considered—all those who would be ruined.

Just at first after his return from Switzerland such specious arguments had served their purpose; but during the last two days they seemed to have lost some of their soothing power. He had found himself feverishly snatching at every fresh edition of the evening paper to see if anything had happened. He had even found himself wondering whether it was too late to stop things even now, but he didn't know where the man who called himself Blackton could be found. From the moment when he had realised in the restaurant wagon that the old German professor and Mr Edward Blackton were one and the same person, he had not set eyes on him again. There had been no trace of him in Paris, and no trace on the boat. He had no idea where he was; he did not even know if he was in London.

His cheque had been presented in Paris, so he had discovered from his bank only that morning. And that was the last trace of the man he had interviewed at Montreux.

'I suppose there's no chance of this man double-crossing us.' A dark sallow man was speaking and Sir Raymond glanced up quickly. 'When all is said and done he has had a quarter of a million, and we're hardly in a position to claim it back.'

'That was one of the risks we discussed before we approached him,' said Sir Raymond. 'Of course there's a chance; that is obvious on the face of it. My impression is, however, that he will not, apart from the fact that another quarter of a million is at stake. He struck me, in a very marked degree, as being a man of his word.'

There was a silence for a while, a silence which was broken suddenly by a mild-looking middle-aged man.

'It's driving me mad, this—absolutely mad,' he cried, mopping the sweat from his forehead. 'I fell asleep last night after dinner, and I tell you, I woke up shouting. Dreams—the most awful dreams, with that poor old devil stabbed in the back and looking at me with great staring eyes. He was calling me a murderer, and I couldn't stand it any more. I know I agreed to it originally, but I can't go on with it—I can't.'

There was a moment's tense silence, and then Sir Raymond spoke.

'I don't understand you, Mr Lewisham,' he said coldly. 'It is quite impossible for you to back out of it now, without betraying us all. And anyway, I would be greatly obliged if you would lower your voice.'

With a great effort Mr Lewisham controlled himself.

'Can't we think of some other method, gentlemen?' he said. 'This seems so horribly cold-blooded.'

'What other possible method is there?' snarled Leibhaus. 'We've tried everything.'

The telephone in front of Sir Raymond rang suddenly and everyone started. It showed the condition of their nerves, and for an appreciable time the President tried to steady his hand before he picked up the receiver. And when after a few seconds he laid it down again he moistened his lips with his tongue, before he trusted himself to speak.

'Mr Blackton will be with us in a quarter of an hour, gentlemen,' he remarked, and his voice was shaking a little. 'I have no idea what he wants, and I am somewhat surprised at his coming here, since I laid especial stress on the fact that we were not to be implicated in any way with his—er—visit to England.'

He gave a brief order through a speaking-tube; then he rose and walked wearily up and down the room. The prospect of meeting Blackton again was not at all to his taste, though his dislike was not in any way due to a belated access of better feeling and remorse. It was due to the fact that Blackton as a man thoroughly frightened him, and as he paced up and down glancing at his watch every half-minute or so he felt exactly as he had felt in years long gone by when he had been told that the headmaster was awaiting him in his study. It was useless to try to bolster up his courage by reflecting that Blackton was, after all, merely the paid servant of his syndicate. He knew perfectly well that Blackton was nothing of the sort, any more than a doctor can be regarded as the paid servant of his patient. The situation in brief was that Mr Blackton for a suitable fee had agreed to assist them professionally, and any other interpretation of the position would be exceedingly unwise.

He started nervously as he heard the sound of voices on the stairs, but it was with a very creditable imitation of being at ease that he went forward as the door opened and Mr Blackton was shown in. He had discarded the disguise he had worn in the train, and appeared as he had done at their first meeting in Switzerland. He nodded briefly to Sir Raymond; then coming a few steps into the room, he favoured each man present with a penetrating stare. Then he laid his gloves on the table and sat down.

'On receiving your message, I was not quite sure in which guise we were to expect you,' said Sir Raymond, breaking the silence.

'The absurd passport regulations,' said Mr Blackton suavely, 'necessitate one's altering one's appearance at times. However, to get to business. You are doubtless wondering at my action in coming round to see you. I may say that I had no intention of so doing until this morning. I have been in London for two days, and my plans were complete—when a sudden and most unexpected hitch occurred.'

He paused and fixed his eyes on Sir Raymond.

'How many people are there who know of this discovery of Professor Goodman's?'

'His family and our syndicate,' answered the President.

'No one else in the diamond world except the gentlemen in this room knows anything about it?'

'No one,' cried Sir Raymond. 'We have most sedulously kept it dark. I feel sure I may speak for my friends.'

He glanced round the room and there was a murmur of assent.

'Then I am forced to the conclusion,' continued Mr Blackton, 'that the writer of an anonymous letter received by the Professor this morning is amongst us at the moment.'

His eyes travelled slowly round the faces of his audience, to stop and fasten on Mr Lewisham, whose tell-tale start had given him away.

'I am informed,' went on Mr Blackton—'and my informant, who was cleaning the windows amongst other things at the Professor's house, is a very reliable man—I am informed, I say, that this morning the Professor received a letter stating that unless he accepted the money you had offered him, he would be killed. Now, who can have been so incredibly foolish as to send that letter?'

Mr Lewisham fidgeted in his chair, until at length everyone in the room, noting the direction of Blackton's glance, was staring at him.

'Was it you, Lewisham?' snapped Leibhaus

Mr Lewisham swallowed once or twice; then he stood up, clutching the edge of the table.

'Yes—it was,' he said defiantly. 'It seemed to me that we ought to neglect no possible chance of getting him to agree to our terms. I typed it, and posted it myself last night.'

Smothered curses came from all sides; only Mr Blackton seemed unmoved.

'You have realised, of course, what will happen should Professor Goodman take that letter to the police,' he remarked quietly. 'The fact that it was your syndicate that offered him the money will make it a little unpleasant for you all.'

But behind the impassive mask of his face Mr Blackton's brain was busy. The thing—the only thing—with which even the most perfectly laid schemes were unable to cope had happened here. And that thing was having a chicken-hearted confederate, or, worse still, one who became suddenly smitten with conscience. Against such a person nothing could be done. He introduced an incalculable factor into any situation with which even a master-craftsman was unable to deal.

Not that he had the remotest intention of giving up the scheme—that was not Mr Blackton's way at all. A further priceless idea had come to him since the interview at Montreux, which would render this coup even more wonderful than he had at first thought. Not only would he amass a large store of diamonds himself, but after that had been done and any further necessity for the continued existence of Professor Goodman had ceased, he would still have the secret of the process in his possession. And this secret he proposed to sell for a price considerably in excess of the two hundred and fifty thousand pounds offered to its original discoverer. After which he would decide what to do with the copy he had kept.

In fact Mr Blackton fully realised that, in the hands of a master-expert like himself, the affair presented promises of such boundless wealth that at times it almost staggered even him. And now, at the last moment, this new factor had been introduced into the situation which might possibly jeopardise his whole carefully thought-out scheme. And the problem was to turn it to the best advantage.

'I don't care,' Mr Lewisham was saying obstinately to the little group of men who were standing round him. 'I don't care if that letter of mine does stop it all. I'd sooner be ruined than go through the rest of my life feeling that I was a murderer.'

'Mr Lewisham seems a little excited,' said Blackton suavely. 'Who, may I ask, has said anything about murder?'

They fell silent, and stared at him.

'When Sir Raymond Blantyre came to me in Montreux, his request to me was to prevent the publication of this secret process of Professor Goodman's. I stated that I would. I stated that the Professor would not give his lecture before the Royal Society. I believe that the word "murder" occurred in the conversation'—he gave a somewhat pained smile—'but do you really imagine, gentlemen, that my methods are as crude as that?'

He carefully lit a cigar, while his audience waited breathlessly for him to continue.

'Since I find, however, that this gentleman has been so incredibly foolish and has lost his head so pitiably, I regret to state that in all probability I shall have to wash my hands of the entire business.'

Cries of anger and dismay greeted this announcement, though the anger was entirely directed against the author of the letter.

'But, really——' stammered Mr Lewisham, plucking nervously at his collar.

'You have behaved like an hysterical schoolgirl, sir,' snapped Blackton. 'You have jeopardised the success of my entire plan, and apart altogether from the sending of this letter you have shown yourself to be totally unfitted to be mixed up in an affair of this description. Even if the police did treat it as a stupid hoax—even, in fact, if we were able to prevent the letter being shown to the police at all—you are still totally unfit to be trusted. You would probably proclaim your sin through a megaphone in Trafalgar Square, taking special care to incriminate all these other gentlemen. And so I think, since you have decided to act on your own initiative in this way, you had better undertake the affair yourself.'

He rose as if to leave, only to be, at once, surrounded by the other members of the syndicate, imploring him to reconsider his decision. And at length Mr Blackton allowed himself to be persuaded to resume his chair. His indifference was sublime; to all outward intents and purposes he was utterly bored with the whole proceedings.

'Really, Mr Blackton—I implore of you, we all implore of you, not to desert us like this.' Sir Raymond's eyeglass was dreadfully agitated. 'Can nothing be done to counteract Mr Lewisham's inconceivable stupidity?'

Mr Blackton affected to consider the point. Not for him to say that he had already decided exactly what was going to be done; not for him to say that the sole object of his recent remarks had been to produce the exact atmosphere that now existed—an atmosphere of combined antagonism to Lewisham, and an uncomfortable feeling on the part of that unfortunate man that he really had made a fool of himself. And certainly not for him to say what he had decided was a meet and fit punishment for Mr Lewisham.

He shrugged his shoulders indifferently.

'Since Mr Lewisham has caused all this trouble,' he said carelessly, 'it is up to Mr Lewisham to endeavour to rectify it.'

A chorus of approval greeted the remark, and Lewisham leaned forward a little in his chair.

'I suggest therefore that this afternoon he should pay a visit to Professor Goodman, and find out what has happened to his letter. Should it have been handed over to the police, he must endeavour to convince the Professor that it was a stupid practical joke on his part, and persuade the Professor to ring up Scotland Yard and explain things. There will be no need for Mr Lewisham's name to be mentioned, if he handles the Professor tactfully. On the other hand, if the note has not been handed over to the police, Mr Lewisham must endeavour to regain possession of it. And according to Mr Lewisham's report, I will decide whether I can continue in this matter or not.'

'That is tantamount to an avowal that the letter was sent by a member of our syndicate,' said Sir Raymond doubtfully. 'You don't think that perhaps it might be advisable to say that he had just discovered that some clerk had played a foolish practical joke?'

'The point seems really immaterial,' returned Mr Blackton indifferently. 'But if Mr Lewisham prefers to say that, by all means let him do so.'

'You will go, of course, Lewisham,' said Sir Raymond, and the other nodded.

'I will go and see what I can do,' he answered. 'And I can take it from you, Mr Blackton, that there will be no question of—of—killing Professor Goodman?'

For a brief moment there came into Mr Blackton's grey-blue eyes a faint gleam as if some delicate inward jest was tickling his sense of humour.

'You may take it from me,' he answered gravely, 'that nothing so unpleasant is likely to happen to Professor Goodman.'

Mr Lewisham gave a sigh of relief.

'What time shall I go?' he asked.

Mr Blackton paused in the act of drawing on his gloves.

'The Professor, I am told,' he remarked, 'has an appointment at three o'clock this afternoon. I would suggest therefore that you should call about two-thirty.'

'And where shall I communicate with you?'

'You can leave that entirely to me, Mr Lewisham,' murmured the other, with an almost benevolent smile. 'I will take all the necessary steps to get in touch with you. Well, gentlemen'—he turned to the others—'that is all, I think, for the present. I will report further in due course. By the way, Mr Lewisham, I wouldn't give your name to the servant, if I were you.'

With a slight bow he opened the door and passed down the stairs. He paused as he reached the crowded pavement and spoke two words to a man who was staring into a shop-window; then he deliberated whether he should call a taxi, and decided to walk. And as he strolled along—slowly, so as not to destroy the aroma of his cigar, his reflections were eminently satisfactory. If the police had not received the note, he was in clover; if they had, a little care would be necessary. But in either case the one detail which had previously been, if not lacking, at any rate not entirely satisfactory was now supplied. It gratified his intellect; it pleased his artistic sense. Just as the sudden and unexpected acquisition of a tube of some rare pigment completes a painter's joy, so this one detail completed Mr Blackton's. That it consisted of a singularly cold-blooded murder is beside the point: all artists are a little peculiar. And if fool men write fool letters, they must expect to suffer small annoyances of that sort. After all, reflected Mr Blackton with commendable thoughtfulness, the world would endure Mr Lewisham's departure with almost callous fortitude.

He realised suddenly that he had reached his destination, and throwing away his cigar he produced his latchkey and entered the house. It was situated in one of those quiet squares which lie, like placid backwaters, off the seething rivers of London. And its chief point of interest lay in the fact that it formed the invariable *pied-à-terre* of Mr Blackton when visiting England in whatever character he might at the moment be assuming. It appeared in the telephone-book as belonging to William Anderson, a gentleman who spent much of his time abroad. And it was to William Anderson that the Inland Revenue were wont yearly to address their friendly reminders as to the duties of British citizens. Ever mindful of those duties, Mr Anderson had declared his income at nineteen hundred and fifty pounds per annum, and had opened a special account at a branch bank to cope with the situation. He drew the line at admitting his liability to super-tax; but after mature reflection he decided that his method of life rendered it advisable to state that his income was unearned.

He placed his gloves and stick on the table in the hall, and slowly ascended the stairs. A few little details still required polishing up in connection with his afternoon's work, and he was still deep in thought as he entered a room on the first landing.

A man was seated at a desk, who rose as he entered—a man whose face was well-nigh as inscrutable as his chief's. He was Mr Blackton's confidential secretary, Freyder, a man with a salary of ten thousand a year plus commission. He was as completely unscrupulous as his employer, but he lacked the wonderful organising brain of the other. Given a certain specific job to do, he could carry it out to perfection; and for making arrangements in detail he was unrivalled. Which made him an ideal staff officer—a fact which the other had very soon recognised. And because Edward Blackton, like all big men, was not such a fool as to underpay an almost invaluable subordinate, he took care that Freyder's salary would be such that he would have no temptation to go. For it he demanded implicit obedience, no mistakes, and at times twenty-four hours' work out of twenty-four.

'What did you find out, Chief?' he asked curiously.

'It was sent by one of them, as I suspected,' answered Blackton, seating himself at his desk. 'A stupid little man called Lewisham, who appears to have lost his head completely. However, on my assuring him that I had no intention of killing the excellent Goodman, he agreed to go round this afternoon and talk to the Professor about the matter.'

'Go round this afternoon?' echoed Freyder, surprised. 'What do you want him there for, this afternoon?'

Blackton smiled gently.

'He happens to be about the same size as our worthy Professor,' he murmured, 'so it struck me he would come in very handy. By the way, make a note, will you, to obtain a specimen of his writing and signature. Find out if he's married, and, if so, draft a letter to his wife from him saying that he's gone to Valparaiso for the good of his health. Have it sent out to Number 13, and posted there.'

He stared thoughtfully out of the window, and Freyder waited for any further instructions.

'Anything more to be settled about the house?'

'Everything fixed, Chief; it's ready to move straight into this afternoon.'

The telephone bell rang on Freyder's table.

'Good,' he remarked a few moments later, replacing the receiver. 'Number 10 reports that he followed Goodman to St James's Square; that he is now having lunch at the Junior Sports Club, and that he has not communicated verbally with the police.'

'And since the letter was in his pocket when he left his house, presumably he has not communicated in writing. He must be a frivolous old man, Freyder, to lunch at such a club. Anyway, I trust he will have a substantial meal, as I'm afraid his constitution may be tried a little during the next few hours.'

He glanced at his watch. 'The box and the men are ready?'

'Loaded up on the car at the garage.'

'Excellent. Then I think a pint of champagne and a little caviare —and after that I must get to work. And we will drink a silent toast to the worthy Mr Lewisham for his kindly forethought in being much the same size as the Professor, and wish him *bon voyage* to—what did I say?—oh! yes, Valparaiso.'

'I don't quite get Mr Lewisham's part in this show, Chief,' remarked Freyder.

Mr Blackton positively chuckled.

'No more does he, my good Freyder—no more does he. But I can positively assure you of one thing—he is not going to Valparaiso.'

And he was still chuckling ten minutes later when he rose and passed into an inner room at the back. It was a strange place—this inner sanctum of Mr Edward Blackton. The window was extra large, and was made of frosted glass which effectually prevented any inquisitive neighbour from seeing in. Around the walls full-length mirrors set at different angles enabled him to see himself from every position—an indispensable adjunct to making up on the scale he found necessary. A huge cupboard filled one wall of the room, a cupboard crammed with clothes and boots of all sorts and descriptions; whilst on a shelf at the top, each in its separate pigeon-hole, were half a dozen wigs. But the real interest of the room lay in the small dressing-table which he proceeded to unlock. A score of little bottles containing strange liquids, brushes, instruments, lumps of a peculiar putty-like substance, were all most carefully arranged on shelves. And it was the contents of this table far more than any change of clothes that enabled him to make such extraordinary alterations in his personal appearance. Literally, when seated at that table, he could build himself a new face. He could change the colour of his eyes, he could alter the shape of his nose. A judicious stain could turn his normally perfect teeth into unpleasant, badly kept ones; whilst on the subject of dyes for hair and eyebrows he could have written a text-book.

It was three-quarters of an hour before the door opened again and the snuffling old German of the restaurant wagon emerged. Professor Scheidstrun was ready to discuss the atomic theory with Professor Goodman with special reference to carboniferous quartz. Outside the door a motor-car was standing with a large box on board containing his specimens, while by its side were two men who were to lift the box off the car, and in due course lift it on again. And the only other thing of interest which might be mentioned in passing is that if Frau Scheidstrun had happened to see him getting into the car wheezing peevishly in German, she would undoubtedly have wondered what on earth her husband was doing in London—so perfect was the make-up. But since that excellent woman was chasing the elusive mark in Dresden at the moment, there was but little fear of such an unfortunate contretemps.

It was at twenty past two that he arrived at Professor Goodman's house. As he stepped out of the car a man walked quietly towards him, a man who stopped to watch the big box being carefully lowered to the ground. He stopped just long enough to say, 'No one in the house except the servants,' and then he strolled on.

With great care the two men carried the box up the steps and, considering the contents were lumps of carboniferous quartz, the intense respect with which they handled it might have struck an onlooker as strange. But the parlourmaid, grown used through long experience to the sudden appearance of strange individuals at odd hours, merely led the way to the laboratory, and having remarked that the Professor might be back at three, or possibly not till six, according to whether he had remembered the appointment or not, she returned to her interrupted dinner.

'Get the box undone,' said Blackton curtly. 'But don't take anything out.'

The two men set to work, while he walked quickly round every corner of the room. Of necessity a little had had to be left to chance, and though he was perfectly capable of dealing with the unexpected when it arrived, he preferred to have things as far as possible cut and dried beforehand. And at the moment what he wanted to find was a cupboard large enough to accommodate a man. Not that it was absolutely necessary, but it would assist matters, especially in the event of the Professor bringing a friend with him. That was a possibility always present in his mind, and one which he had been unable to guard against without running the risk of raising the Professor's suspicions.

He found what he wanted in a corner—a big recess under the working bench screened by a curtain, and used for old retorts and test-tubes. It was ideal for his purpose, and with a nod of satisfaction he went over to the door. All was well—the key was on the inside; and with one final glance round the room the exponent of the new atomic theory sat down to wait.

Before him lay the riskiest thing he had ever done in all his risky career, but had anyone felt his pulse he would have found it normal. And it wasn't of the next hour that Mr Blackton was thinking so much, but of the future, when his coup had succeeded. That it would succeed was certain; no thought of failure was ever allowed to enter his mind.

Five minutes passed—ten—when the ringing of the front-door bell brought him back from dreams of the future. This must be Mr Lewisham, and with his arrival came the time for action. Blackton listened intently—would he be shown into the laboratory or into some other room? If the latter, it would necessitate getting him in on some pretext; but steps coming along the passage settled that point. Once more the door was flung open by the parlour-maid; once more she returned to better things in the servants' hall.

Lewisham paused, and glanced a little doubtfully at the old German in his dirty black clothes. Some chemical friend of the Professor's evidently; possibly it would be better to wait somewhere else. He half turned to the door as if to go out again, when suddenly he felt two hands like bars of steel around his throat. For a moment or two he struggled impotently; then he grew still. And after a while the limp body slipped to the floor and lay still.

'Underneath that bench with him,' snapped Blackton. 'Quick.'

He had opened the door an inch or two and was peering out. The passage was empty, and faint sounds were coming up the stairs from the servants' quarters.

'Stay where you are,' he said to the two men. 'I shall be back in a minute.'

He walked along the passage towards the front door, which he opened. Then he deliberately rang the bell, and stood for a few seconds peering out. And it was not until he heard the footsteps of the parlourmaid that he shut the door again with a bang, and advanced towards her, gesticulating wildly.

'Where is your master?' he cried. 'I must to my business get; I cannot here the whole day wait. That other gentleman—he does not wait. He go. I too—I follow him.' He glanced at the girl. 'Speak, woman.' He waved his arms at her, and she retreated in alarm. 'I will take my specimens, and I will go—like him.'

Still muttering horribly under his breath, he walked up and down the hall, while the parlourmaid endeavoured to soothe him.

'I expect the Professor will be back soon, sir,' she murmured.

'Soon,' he raved. 'I who have come from Germany him to see, and then I wait. He write to me: I write to him—and then I come with my specimens. And you say soon. *Nein*—I go. I go like that other.'

It was at that moment that the front door opened and Professor Goodman entered.

'A thousand apologies, my dear Professor,' he cried, hurrying forward. 'I fear I am late—very late. I hope I have not kept you waiting.'

He led the other towards the laboratory, and the parlourmaid made hurried tracks for safety.

'No wonder that there other one wouldn't wait,' she remarked to the cook. 'He's a holy terror—that German. Dirty old beast, with egg all over his coat, waving his arms at me. Old Goodman is a pretty fair freak, but he does wash. I 'opes he enjoys himself.'

Which was a kindly thought on the part of the parlourmaid. And the fact that it was expressed at the exact moment that Professor Goodman went fully under the influence of an anaesthetic may be regarded as a strange coincidence. For there was no time wasted in the laboratory that afternoon. Much had to be done, and hardly had the door closed behind the master of the house when he found himself seized and pinioned. One feeble cry was all he gave; then a pad soaked in ether was pressed over his nose and mouth, and the subsequent proceedings ceased to interest him.

Very interesting proceedings they were too—that went on

51

behind the locked door. Bursts of German loquacity with intervals of a voice astonishingly like Professor Goodman's would have convinced any inquisitive person listening outside the door that the two savants were in full blast. Not that anyone was likely to listen, but Blackton was not a man who took chances. And it takes time to change completely two men's clothes when one is dead and the other is unconscious. One hour it was, to be exact, before the body of Mr Lewisham, dressed in Professor Goodman's clothes, even down to his boots, was propped up in a chair against the bench, with various bottles and retorts in front of him. One hour and a quarter it was before a number of small packets had been taken from the big wooden case and stacked carefully on the bench so that they touched the dead man's chest. One hour and a half it was before the still unconscious Professor Goodman was placed as comfortably as possible—Mr Blackton had no wish to run any chances with *his* health—in the big wooden case, and nailed up. And during the whole of that hour and a half the discussion on carboniferous quartz had continued with unabated zest.

At last, however, everything was finished, and Blackton took from his pocket a little instrument which he handed very gingerly. He first of all wound it up rather as a Bee clock is wound, and when it was ticking gently he placed it in the centre of the heap of small packets. Then he unlocked the door.

'Put the box on the car,' he ordered. 'Then pick up Freyder, and go straight to the house.'

Once again the two men staggered down the passage with their load, while Blackton glanced at his watch. Just a quarter of an hour to put through—before things happened. He closed the door again, and once more his guttural voice was raised in wordy argument for the benefit of any possible audience. And in the intervals when he ceased only the faint ticking broke the silence. Everything had gone without a hitch, but there were still one or two small things to be done. And the first of these showed the amazing attention to detail which characterised all his actions. He took the key from the door and put it on the desk; a master-key of his own would enable him to lock the door from outside, whereas the presence of the key in the room would make it appear that it had been locked from within. And it was precisely that appearance which he wished given.

Once more he looked at his watch: ten minutes to go. Nervous work, that waiting; and even he began to feel the strain. But he daren't go too soon; he daren't leave too long a space of time between the moment he left the house and the moment when the ticking would cease. And he didn't want to go too late, because the last thing he desired was to be on, or even too near, the premises when the ticking ceased. Moreover, there was always the possibility of a flaw in the mechanism. Morelli was a wonderful craftsman, and he had staked his reputation on its taking exactly a quarter of an hour. But even so—it was nervous work, waiting.

Precisely five minutes later—and they were the longest five minutes Mr Blackton had ever spent in his life—he pressed the bell. His guttural voice was raised in expostulation and argument as the parlourmaid knocked at the door. Still talking, he opened it himself, and over his shoulder the girl got a fleeting glance of Professor Goodman engaged in one of his experiments to the exclusion of all else.

'My hat, girl,' cried the German, waving his arms at her. She went to get it, and from behind her back came the noise of a key turning. 'Ach! my friend—no one will disturb you,' rumbled the German. 'No need to your door lock.' Mechanically he took the hat the parlourmaid was holding out, while he still continued muttering to himself. 'What is the good? one mistake, and you will experiment no more. You and your house will go sky-high.'

Still waving his arms, he shambled off down the street, and the girl stood watching him. And it was just after he had turned the corner and she was expressing her opinion of his appearance to the cook, who was taking a breather in the area below, that she was hurled forward flat on her face. A terrific explosion shook the house; windows broke; plaster and pictures came crashing down. And if it was bad in the front, it was immeasurably worse at the back. A huge hole had been blown in the outside wall of what had once been the Professor's laboratory; the three inside walls had collapsed, and the ceiling had descended, bringing with it a bed, two wardrobes, and a washing-stand complete.

In fact there was every justification for the remark of the parlourmaid as she picked herself up.

'Lumme!' what's the old fool done now? I suppose he'll ring the bell in a minute and ask me to sweep up the mess.'

An hour later Edward Blackton was seated at his desk in the

house in the quiet square. Up to date his scheme had gone even more smoothly than he had expected, though there were still one or two small points to be attended to before he could retire from observation and devote himself to the Professor. There was bound to be an inquest, for instance, and he was far too big a man not to realise that it might be fatal for him not to attend it. Moreover, there was the little matter of that extra quarter of a million from the Metropolitan Syndicate.

But just at the moment Lewisham was occupying his mind. A note in cipher on the table in front of him from Freyder informed him that Henry Lewisham was a married man, and that he lived in South Kensington. And since the appearance of the late Mr Lewisham betokened his immense respectability, there was but little doubt that Mrs Lewisham would become seriously alarmed if her spouse absented himself for the night from the conjugal roof without any word to her.

Blackton pressed a bell on his desk twice, and a moment or two later the man who had been staring into the shop-window, and to whom he had spoken as he left the Metropolitan Syndicate earlier in the day, entered.

'That man you followed this morning—Lewisham: did he go home to lunch?'

'No, Chief. He had a chop in a restaurant in the city.'

'Did he use the telephone as far as you know?'

'I know he didn't use it. He was never out of my sight from the time he came into the street till he went into Goodman's house.'

Blackton nodded as if satisfied.

'Go to Euston, and send a wire to this address. "Called North on urgent business, Henry." Then go to the Plough Inn in Liverpool, and wait there for further orders. Draw fifty pounds for expenses' —he scribbled his signature on a slip of paper—'and it is possible you will have to start for South America at a moment's notice. If you do, it will be necessary for you to make yourself up to an approximate resemblance of Henry Lewisham, and your berth will be taken in his name.'

'I didn't have a chance of studying his face very closely, Chief,' said the man doubtfully.

Blackton waved his hand in dismissal.

'Approximate resemblance, I said,' he remarked curtly. 'You will receive full instructions later. Go.'

54

He lay back in his chair as the door closed behind the man, and pulled thoughtfully at his cigar. A merciful fact, he reflected, that it is not a police offence for a man to run away from his wife. In fact if Mrs Lewisham was anything like Mr Lewisham, it could hardly be regarded as an offence at all by any disinterested person, but rather as an example of praiseworthy discretion. A letter in due course from Liverpool stating his intention; a resemblance efficient to cope with a wireless description in case the lady should think of such a thing—and finally complete disappearance in South America. An easy place to disappear in—South America, reflected Mr Blackton; a fact he had made use of on several occasions, when the circumstances had been similar. And it was better for sorrowing relatives to picture their dear one alive and wandering through primeval forests in Brazil, or dallying with nitrates in Chile, than for them to realise that the dear one was very, very dead. It was also better for Mr Blackton.

He dismissed the unfortunate Lewisham from his mind, and produced from his pocket the papers he had taken from Professor Goodman before removing his clothes. The first thing he saw, to his intense satisfaction, was the warning typewritten letter, and holding a match under one corner of it he reduced it to ashes and finally to powder. Two or three private letters he treated similarly, and then he came to a dozen loose sheets of paper covered with incomprehensible scrawling hieroglyphics. These he carefully pinned together and put in his pocket, reflecting yet again on the extreme goodness of fate. And then for the second time he took from the drawer where he had placed it for safety the metal retort which apparently played such an important part in the process. He had found it standing on the electric furnace in the Professor's laboratory, and now he examined it curiously. It was about double the size of an ordinary tumbler, and was made of some dull opaque substance which resembled dirty pewter. And as Blackton looked at it and realised the incredible fortune that was soon to come to him out of that uninteresting-looking pot, his hand shook uncontrollably.

He replaced it in the drawer, as someone knocked on the door. It was the man who had spoken to him outside the Professor's house.

'They're all humming like a hive of bees, Chief,' he remarked. 'The police are in, and they've cleared away the débris. I managed to get in and have a look—and it's all right.'

'You're certain of that,' said Blackton quietly.

'There's nothing left of him, Chief, except a boot in one corner.'

Blackton rubbed his hands together.

'Excellent—excellent! You've done very well: cash this down-stairs.'

Again he scribbled his initials on a slip of paper, and pushing it across the table dismissed the man. Assuredly luck was in, though as a general rule Blackton refused to allow the existence of such a thing. The big man, according to him, made allowance for every possible contingency; only the fool ever trusted to luck if anything of importance was at stake. And in this case he only regarded his luck as being in because he would be able, as far as he could see, to carry on with the simplest of the three schemes which he had worked out to meet different emergencies should they arise. And though he had employed enough explosive to shatter ten men, no man knew better than he did how capricious it was in its action.

Now he was only waiting for one thing more—a telephone call from Freyder. He glanced at his watch: hardly time as yet, perhaps, for him to have reached his destination and to get through to London. In fact it was twenty minutes before the bell rang at his side.

'Everything gone without a hitch.'

Freyder was speaking, and with a gentle sigh of pure joy for work well and truly done Mr Blackton laid down the receiver.

Half an hour later he was strolling along Pall Mall towards his club. A newsboy passed him shouting. ' 'Orrible explosion in 'Ampstead,' and he paused to buy a copy. It had occurred to him that it is always a good thing to have something to read in the cooler rooms of a Turkish bath. And he never went into the hotter ones; there were peculiarities about Mr Edward Blackton's face which rendered great heat a trifle ill-advised.

CHAPTER 4

In Which Mr William Robinson Arrives at his Country Seat

The report made to Mr Blackton on the condition of the Professor's house was certainly justified. It looked just as if a heavy aeroplane bomb had registered a direct hit on the back of the premises. And the damage was continually increasing. The whole fabric of the house had been undermined, and it was only at considerable personal risk that the police pursued their investigations. Frequent crashes followed by clouds of choking dust betokened that more and more of the house was collapsing, and at length the Inspector in charge gave the order to cease work for the time. Half a dozen policemen kept the curious crowd away, whilst the Inspector retired to the front of the house, which had escaped the damage, to await the arrival of some member of the Professor's family. It was not a task that he relished, but it was his duty to make what inquiries he could.

In his own mind he felt pretty clear as to what had happened. The parlourmaid, who appeared a sensible sort of girl, had told him all she knew—particularly mentioning the German professor's remark as he left the house. And it seemed quite obvious that Professor Goodman had been experimenting with some form of violent explosive, and that, regrettable to say, the explosive had not behaved itself. When the débris had ceased to fall and it was safe to resume work, it might be possible to discover something more definite, but up to date the sole thing they had found of interest was one of the unfortunate savant's boots. And since that had already been identified by the parlourmaid as belonging to Professor Goodman, all the identification necessary for the inquest was there. Which from a professional point of view was just as well, since there was nothing else left to identify.

An open Rolls-Royce drew up outside, and the Inspector went to the window and looked out. From the driver's seat there descended a large young man, who said something to the two other occupants of the car, and then came rapidly up the short drive to the front door, where the Inspector met him.

57

'What on earth has happened?' he demanded.

'May I ask if you are a relative of Professor Goodman's?' said the Inspector.

'No; I'm not. My name is Drummond, Captain Drummond. But if you'll cast your eye on the back of my car you'll see his daughter, Miss Goodman.'

'Well,' said the Inspector gravely, 'I fear that I have some very bad news for Miss Goodman. There has been an accident, Captain Drummond—an appalling accident. The whole of the back of the house has been blown to pieces, and with it, I regret to say, Professor Goodman. There is literally nothing left of the unfortunate gentleman.'

'Good God!' gasped Algy, who had come up in time to hear the last part of the remark. 'Have you caught the swine . . .'

Hugh's hand gripped his arm in warning.

'How did it happen?' he asked quietly. 'Have you any ideas?'

The Inspector shrugged his shoulders.

'There is no doubt whatever as to how it happened,' he answered. 'The whole thing will, of course, be gone into thoroughly at the inquest, but it is all so obvious that there is no need for any secrecy. The unfortunate gentleman was experimenting with some form of high explosive, and he blew himself up and the house as well.'

'I see,' said Drummond thoughtfully. 'Look here, Algy—take Brenda back to my place, and tell the poor kid there. Turn her over to Phyllis.'

'Right you are, Hugh,' said Algy soberly. 'By God!' he exploded again, and once more Drummond's warning hand silenced him.

Without another word he turned and walked away. Brenda, in an agony of suspense, met him at the gateway and her sudden little pitiful cry showed that she had already guessed the truth. But she followed Algy back into the car, and it was not until it had disappeared that Drummond spoke again.

'You have no suspicions of foul play, I suppose?'

The Inspector looked at him quickly.

'Foul play, Captain Drummond? What possible reason could there be for foul play in the case of such a man as Professor Goodman? Oh! no. He was seen by the parlourmaid immersed in an experiment as she was letting some German professor out—a scientific acquaintance of the unfortunate gentleman. They had

58

been having a discussion all the afternoon, and not five minutes after his visitor left the explosion took place.'

Drummond nodded thoughtfully.

'Deuced agile fellow—the Boche. Did the hundred at precisely the right psychological moment. Would there be any objection, Inspector—as a friend of the family and all that—to my having a look at the scene of the accident? You see, there are only his wife and daughter left—two women alone; and Miss Goodman's fiancé —the man who took her off in the car—not being here, perhaps I might take it on myself to give them what information I can.'

'Certainly, Captain Drummond. But I warn you that there's nothing to see. And you'd better be careful that you don't get a fall of bricks on your head. I'll come with you, if you like.'

The two men walked round to the back of the house. The crowd, which by now had largely increased in size, surged forward expectantly as they disappeared through the shattered wall, and the Inspector gave an order to one of the constables.

'Move them along,' he said. 'There's nothing to be seen.'

'Good heavens!' remarked Drummond, staring round in amazement. 'This is what one used to expect in France. In fact I've slept in many worse. But in Hampstead . . .'

'I found this, sir, on the remains of the table,' said a sergeant, coming up to the Inspector with a key in his hand. 'It belongs to the door.'

The Inspector took the key and tried it himself.

'That confirms what the maid said.' He turned to Drummond. 'The door was locked on the inside. The maid heard him lock it as she showed the German out, which, of course, was a few minutes before the accident took place.'

Drummond frowned thoughtfully and lit a cigarette. That was a complication, and a very unexpected complication. In fact at one blow it completely shattered the idea that was already more than half formed in his mind—an idea which, needless to say, differed somewhat radically from the worthy Inspector's notion of what had happened.

'And what of the Professor himself?' he asked after a moment or two. 'Is the body much damaged?'

'There is nothing left of the body,' said the Inspector gravely. 'At least practically nothing.'

He crossed to the corner of the room by the door, where the

damage was least, and removed a cloth which covered some object on the floor.

'This is all we have found at present.'

'Poor old chap,' said Drummond quietly, staring at the boot. There was a patch on it—a rather conspicuous patch which he had noticed at lunch that day.

'It has been identified already by the parlourmaid as the Professor's boot,' said the Inspector, replacing the cloth. 'Not that there is much need for identification in this case. But it is always necessary at the inquest as a matter of form.'

'Of course,' answered Drummond absently, and once more fell to staring round the wrecked room. Three plain-clothes men were carefully turning over heaps of débris, searching for further traces of the dead scientist. But the task seemed hopeless, and after a while he said good-bye to the Inspector and started to walk back to Brook Street.

The whole thing had come with such startling suddenness that he felt shaken. It seemed incredible that the dear, absent-minded old man who had lunched with him only that day was dead and blown to pieces. Over and over again in his mind there arose the one dominant question—was it foul play, or was it not? If it wasn't, it was assuredly one of the most fortunate accidents for a good many people that could possibly have taken place. No longer any need to stump up a quarter of a million for the suppression of the Professor's discovery—no longer any need to worry. And suddenly Hugh stopped short in his tracks, and a thoughtful look came into his eyes.

'Great Scott!' he muttered to himself, 'I'd almost forgotten.'

His hand went to his breast-pocket, and a grim smile hovered for a moment or two round his mouth as he strolled on. Professor Goodman might be dead, but his secret wasn't. And if by any chance it had *not* been an accident . . . if by any chance this diamond syndicate had deliberately caused the poor defenceless old man's death, the presence of those papers in his pocket would help matters considerably. They would form an admirable introduction to the gentlemen in question—and he was neither old nor defenceless. In fact there dawned on his mind the possibility that there might be something doing in the near future. And the very thought of such a possibility came with the refreshing balm of a shower on parched ground. It produced in him a feeling of joy comparable only to that with which the hungry young view the advent of indigestible food. It radiated from his face; it enveloped him in a beatific glow. And he was still looking like a man who has spotted a winner at twenty to one as he entered his house.

His wife met him in the hall.

'Hugh, for goodness' sake, compose your face,' she said severely. 'Poor Mrs Goodman is here, and Brenda, and you come in roaring with laughter.'

'Good Lord! I'd forgotten all about 'em,' he murmured, endeavouring to assume a mournful expression. 'Where are they?'

'Upstairs. They're going to stop her tonight. Brenda telephoned through to her mother. Hugh—what an awful thing to have happened.'

'You're right, my dear,' he answered seriously. 'It is awful. The only comfort about it is that it must have been absolutely instantaneous. Where's Algy?'

'He's in your room. He's most frightfully upset, poor old thing, principally on Brenda's account.' She laid her hand on his arm. 'Hugh—he said something to me about it not being any accident. What did he mean?'

'Algy is a talkative ass,' answered her husband quietly. 'Pay no attention to him, and don't under any circumstances even hint at such a thing to Mrs Goodman or Brenda.'

'But you don't mean he killed himself?' said Phyllis in a horrified whisper.

'Good heavens! no,' answered Hugh. 'But there is a possibility, my dear, and more than a possibility that he was murdered. Now—not a word to a soul. The police think it was an accident; let it remain at that for the present.'

'But who on earth would want to murder the dear old man?' gasped his wife.

'The Professor had made a discovery, darling,' said Hugh gravely, 'which threatened to ruin everyone who was concerned in the diamond industry. He had found out a method of making diamonds artificially at a very low cost. To show you how seriously the trade regarded it, he was offered two hundred and fifty thousand pounds to suppress it. That he refused to do. This morning he received a letter threatening his life. This afternoon he died, apparently as the result of a ghastly accident. But—I wonder.'

'Does anybody know all this?' said Phyllis.

61

'A few very interested people who won't talk about it, and you and Algy and I who won't talk about it either—yet. Later on we might all have a chat on the subject, but just at present there's rather too much of the fog of war about. In fact the only really definite fact that emerges from the gloom, except for the poor chap's death, is this.'

He held out an envelope in his hand, and his wife looked at it, puzzled.

'That is the discovery which has caused all the trouble,' went on Hugh. 'And the few very interested people I was telling you about don't know that I've got it. And they won't know that I've got it either—yet.'

'So that's why you were looking like that as you came in.'

His wife looked at him accusingly, and Hugh grinned.

'Truly your understanding is great, my angel,' he murmured.

'But how did you get it?' she persisted.

'He gave it to me at lunch today,' said her husband. 'And in the near future it's going to prove very useful—very useful indeed. Why, I almost believe that if I advertised that I'd got it, it would draw old Peterson himself. Seconds out of the ring; third and last round; time.'

'Hugh—you're incorrigible. And don't do that in the hall—someone will see.'

So he kissed her again, and went slowly up the stairs to his own room. Most of the really brilliant ideas in life come in flashes, and he had had many worse than that last. There were times when his soul positively hankered for another little turn-up with Carl Peterson—something with a real bit of zip in it, something to vary his present stagnation. But he fully realised that a gentleman of Peterson's eminence had many other calls on his time, and that he must not be greedy. After all, he'd had two of the brightest and best, and that was more than most people could say. And perhaps there might be something in this present show which would help to keep his hand in. Sir Raymond Blantyre, the bird with the agitated eyeglass, for instance. He didn't sound much class—a bit of a rabbit at the game probably, but still, something might come of him.

He opened the door of his room, and Algy looked up from his chair.

'You don't think it was an accident, do you, Hugh?' he remarked quietly.

'I don't know what to think, old man,' answered Drummond. 'If it was an accident, it was a very remarkable and fortunate one for a good many people. But there is one point which is a little difficult to explain unless it was: Hannah, or Mary, or whatever that sweet woman's name is who used to breathe down one's neck when she handed you things at dinner, saw the old man at work through the open door. She heard him lock the door. Moreover, the key was found in the room—on the floor or somewhere; it was found while I was there. From that moment no one else entered the room until the explosion. Now, *you* haven't seen the appalling mess that explosion made. There must have been an immense amount of explosive used. The darned place looks as if it had had a direct hit with a big shell. Well, what I'm getting at is that it is quite out of the question that the amount of explosive necessary to produce such a result could have been placed there unknown to old Goodman. And that rules out of court this German bloke who spent the afternoon with him.'

'He might have left a bomb behind him,' said Algy.

'My dear boy,' exclaimed Hugh, 'you'd have wanted a bomb the size of a wheelbarrow. That's the point I've been trying to force into your skull. You can't carry a thing that size about in your waistcoat pocket. No—it won't work. Either the maid is talking through the back of her neck, or she isn't. And if she isn't, the old chap was dancing about in the room after the German left. Not only that, but he locked himself in. Well, even you wouldn't lock yourself in with a land-mine, would you? Especially one you'd just seen carefully arranged to explode in five minutes. Besides, he knew this German; he told me so at lunch today.'

'I suppose you're right,' grunted Algy. 'And yet it seems so deuced suspicious.'

'Precisely: it is deuced suspicious. But don't forget one thing, old boy. It is only suspicious to us because we've got inside information. It is not a bit suspicious to the police.'

'It would be if you told 'em about that letter he got.'

Hugh lit a cigarette and stared out of the window.

'Perhaps,' he agreed. 'But do we want to rouse their suspicions, old boy? If we're wrong—if it was a bonâ-fide accident—there's no use in doing so; if we're right, we might have a little game all on our own. I mean I was all in favour of the old boy going to the police about it while he was alive, but now that he's dead it seems a bit late in the day.'

'And how do you propose to make the other side play?' demanded Algy.

'Good Lord! I haven't got as far as that,' said Hugh vaguely. 'One might biff your pal with the eyeglass on the jaw, or something like that. Or one might get in touch with them through these notes on the Professor's discovery, and see what happens. If they then tried to murder me, we should have a bit of a pointer as to which way the wind was blowing. Might have quite a bit of fun, Algy; you never know. Anyway, I think we'll attend the inquest tomorrow; we might spot something if we're in luck. We will sit modestly at the back of the court, and see without being seen.'

But the inquest failed to reveal very much. It was a depressing scene, and more in the nature of a formality than anything else. The two young men arrived early, and wedged themselves in the back row, whence they commanded a good view of the court. And suddenly Algy caught Hugh's arm.

'See that little bird with the white moustache and the eyeglass in the second row,' he whispered. 'That's the fellow I was telling you about, who put up the offer of a quarter of a million.'

Hugh grunted non-committally; seen from that distance he seemed a harmless sort of specimen. And then the proceedings started. The police gave their formal evidence, and after that the parlourmaid was put into the box. She described in detail the events of the afternoon, and the only new point which came to light was the fact that another man beside the German professor had been to the house for a short time and left almost at once. First the German had arrived. No, she did not know his name—but his appearance was peculiar. Pressed for details, it appeared that his clothes were dirty, and his hands stained with chemicals. Oh! yes—she would certainly know him again if she saw him. A box had come with him which was carried into the laboratory by two men. They had brought it in a car, and had waited outside part of the time the German was there. Yes—she had talked to them. Had they said anything about the German? Surely they must have mentioned his name. No—they didn't even know it. The witness paused, and having been duly encouraged by the Coroner was understood to say that the only thing they had said about him was that he was a bit dippy.

The laughter in court having been instantly quelled, the witness proceeded. Just after the German had arrived another visitor came.

64

No—she didn't know his name either. But he was English, and she showed him into the laboratory too. Then she went down to finish her dinner.

About ten minutes later the front-door bell rang again. She went upstairs to find the German dancing about in the hall in his excitement. He wanted to know when Professor Goodman was returning. Said he had made an appointment, and that unless the Professor returned shortly he would go as the other visitor had gone.

Pressed on this point by the Coroner—she knew the second visitor had gone, as the only people in the laboratory as she passed it were the two men already alluded to. And just then Professor Goodman came in, apologised for having kept the German waiting, and they disappeared into the laboratory. For the next hour and a half she heard them talking whenever she passed the door; then the laboratory bell rang. She went up to find that the German was leaving. Through the open door she saw Professor Goodman bending over his bench hard at work; then just as she was halfway across the hall she heard the key turn in the door. And the German had waved his arms in the air, and said something about the house going sky-high. The motor had gone by that time, and the box and the two men. It was just before then that she'd spoken to them. And it was about four or five minutes later after the German had disappeared down the road that the explosion took place.

The witness paused, and stared into the court.

'There he is,' she cried. 'That's him—just come in.'

Drummond swung round in time to see the tall, ungainly figure of Professor Scheidstrun go shambling up the court. He was waving his arms, and peering short-sightedly from side to side.

'I hof just heard the dreadful news,' he cried, pausing in front of the Coroner. 'I hof it read in the newspaper. My poor friendt has himself blown up. But that I had gone he would myself have blown also.'

After a short delay he was piloted into the witness-box. His evidence, which was understood with difficulty, did, however, elucidate the one main fact which was of importance—namely, the nature of the explosive which had caused the disaster. It appeared that Professor Goodman had been experimenting for some time with a new form of blasting powder which would be perfectly harmless unless exploded by a detonator containing fulminate of mercury. No blow, no heat would cause it to explode. And when he left the house the Professor had in front of him numerous specimens of this blasting powder of varying quality. One only was the perfected article—the rest were the failures. But all were high explosive of different degrees of power. And then some accident must have happened.

He waved his arms violently in the air, and mopped his forehead with a handkerchief that had once been white. Then like a momentarily dammed stream the flood of verbosity broke forth again. The partially stunned court gathered that it was his profound regret that he had only yesterday afternoon called the deceased man a fool. He still considered that his views on the atomic theory were utterly wrong, but he was not a fool. He wished publicly to retract the statement, and to add further that as a result of this deplorable accident not only England but the world had lost one of its most distinguished men. And with that he sat down again, mopping his forehead.

It was then the Coroner's turn. He said that he was sure the bereaved family would be grateful for the kind words of appreciation from the distinguished scientist who had just given evidence—words with which he would humbly like to associate himself also. It was unnecessary, he considered, to subject Mrs Goodman to the very painful ordeal of identifying the remains, as sufficient evidence had already been given on that point. He wished to express his profound sympathy with the widow and daughter, and to remind them that 'Peace hath its victories no less renowned than War.'

And so with a verdict of 'Accidental Death caused by the explosion of blasting powder during the course of experimental work', the proceedings terminated. The court arose, and with the court rose Algy, to discover, to his surprise, that Hugh had already disappeared. He hadn't seen him go, but that was nothing new. For as Algy and everyone else connected with Hugh Drummond had discovered long ago, he had a power of rapid and silent movement which was almost incredible in such a big man. Presumably he had got bored and left. And sure enough when Algy got outside he saw Drummond on the opposite side of the street staring into the window of a tobacconist's. He sauntered across to join him.

'Well—that's that,' he remarked. 'Don't seem to have advanced things much.'

'Get out of sight,' snapped Drummond. 'Go inside and stop there. Buy matches or something.'

With a feeling of complete bewilderment Algy did as he was told. He went inside and he stopped there, until the proprietor began to eye him suspiciously. There had been two or three cases of hold-ups in the papers recently, and after he had bought several packets of unprepossessing cigarettes and half a dozen boxes of matches the atmosphere became strained. In desperation he went to the door and peered out, thereby confirming the shopman's suspicions to such good effect that he ostentatiously produced a dangerous-looking life-preserver.

Hugh had completely disappeared. Not a trace of him was to be seen, and feeling more bewildered than ever Algy hailed a passing taxi and drove off to Brook Street. Presumably Hugh would return there in due course, and until then he would have to possess his soul in patience.

It was two hours before he came in, and sank into a chair without a word.

'What's all the excitement?' demanded Algy eagerly.

'I don't know that there is any,' grunted Hugh. 'I'm not certain the whole thing isn't a false alarm. What did you think of the inquest?'

'Not very helpful,' said Algy. 'Seems pretty conclusive that it really was an accident.'

Once again Hugh grunted.

'I suppose you didn't notice the rather significant little point that your diamond pal Blantyre knew the old German.'

Algy stared at him.

'I happened to be looking at him as the German appeared, and I saw him give a most violent start. And all through the Boche's evidence he was as nervous as a cat with kittens. Of course there was no reason why he shouldn't have known him—but in view of what we know it seemed a bit suspicious to me. So I waited for them to come out of court. Sir Raymond came first and hung about a bit. Then came the old German, who got into a waiting taxi. And as he got in he spoke to Sir Raymond—just one brief sentence. What it was I don't know, of course, but it confirmed the fact that they knew one another. It also confirmed the fact that for some reason or other they did not wish to have their acquaintance advertised abroad. Now—why? That, old boy, is the question I asked myself all the way down to Bloomsbury in a taxi. I had one waiting too, and I followed the German. Why this mystery? Why should they be thus bashful of letting it be known that they had met before?'

'Did you find out anything?' asked Algy.

'I found out where the old German is staying. But beyond that nothing. He is stopping at a house belonging to a Mr Anderson—William Anderson, who, I gathered from discreet inquiries, is a gentleman of roving disposition. He uses the house as a sort of *pied-à-terre* when he is in London, which is not very often. Presumably he made the German's acquaintance abroad, and invited him to make use of his house.'

'Don't seem to be much to go on, does there?' said Algy disconsolately.

'Dam' little,' agreed Hugh cheerfully. 'In fact if you boil down to it, nothing at all. But you never can tell, old boy. I saw a baby with a squint this morning and passed under two ladders, so all may yet be well. Though I greatly fear nothing will come of it. I thought vaguely yesterday that we might get some fun by means of these notes of the old man's, but 'pon my soul—I don't know how. In the first place, they're indecipherable; and even if they weren't, I couldn't make a diamond in a thousand years. In the second place, they don't belong to us; and in the third it would look remarkably like blackmail. Of course, they're our only hope, but I'm afraid they won't amount to much in our young lives.'

He sighed profoundly, and replaced the envelope in his pocket.

'Oh! for the touch of a vanished hand,' he murmured. 'Carl—my Carl—it cannot be that we shall never meet again. I feel, Algy, that if only he could know the position of affairs he would burst into tears and fly to our assistance. He'd chance the notes being unintelligible if he knew what they were about. Once again would he try to murder me with all his well-known zest. What fun it would all be!'

'Not a hope,' said Algy. 'Though I must say I do rather wonder what the blighter is doing now.'

To be exact, he was just putting the last final touch on the aquiline nose of Edward Blackton, and remarking to himself that everything was for the best in the best of all possible worlds. Replaced carefully on their respective pegs were the egg-stained garments of Professor Scheidstrun; the grey wig carefully combed out occupied its usual head-rest.

And not without reason did Edward Blackton—alias Carl Peterson—alias the Comte du Guy, etc.—feel pleased with himself. Never in the course of his long and brilliant career had a coup gone with such wonderful success. It almost staggered him when he thought about it. Not a hitch anywhere; not even the suspicion of a check. Everything had gone like clockwork from beginning to end, thereby once again bearing out the main theory of his life, which was that the bigger the crop the safer it was. It is the bank clerk with his petty defalcations who gets found out every time; the big man does it in millions and entertains Royalty on the proceeds. But in his line of business, as in every other, to get big results the original outlay must be big. And it was on that point that Mr Blackton felt so particularly pleased. For the original outlay in this case had not only been quite small, but, in addition, had been generously found by the Metropolitan Diamond Syndicate. Which tickled his sense of humour to such an extent that once or twice it had quite interfered with the delicate operation of face-building.

But at last he had finished, and with his Corona drawing to his entire satisfaction he locked up his inner sanctuary and stepped into the room which served him as an office. At three o'clock he was to meet Sir Raymond Blantyre and receive from him the remaining quarter of a million in notes; at three-fifteen he would be on his way to the house Freyder had acquired for him to begin business in earnest. A note from Freyder received that morning had stated that Professor Goodman, though a little dazed, seemed in no way to have suffered from his uncomfortable journey, which was eminently satisfactory. For it was certainly no part of his play to treat his prisoner with anything but the utmost care and con-sideration, unless, of course, he should prove foolish. For a moment Blackton's eyes narrowed at the thought; then he gave the faintest possible shrug of his shoulders. Sufficient unto the day, and he had dealt with such cases before.

So after a final look round the room he carefully pulled down the blinds and went downstairs. Mr William Anderson was leaving London for another of his prolonged visits abroad.

His anticipations that there would be no trouble over the second payment were justified. Sir Raymond Blantyre and three other members of the syndicate were awaiting his arrival, and the expressions on their faces reminded him of young girls being introduced to a man who mother has told them is very wicked and not at all a nice person to know.

'Well, gentlemen,' he remarked affably, 'I trust you are satisfied. This—er—fortunate accident has settled things very pleasantly for all concerned, has it not?'

'It really was an accident?' said Sir Raymond, and his voice shook a little.

'Surely, Sir Raymond, your pitiable agitation in court this morning was not so great as to prevent your hearing the verdict? And that, I think, is all that concerns any of us; that, and the fact that Professor Goodman will not deliver his address to the Royal Society which was the *raison d'être* of our meeting. And so shall we terminate the business?'

In silence Sir Raymond handed over the notes, which Blackton carefully folded and placed in his pocket-book.

'Delightful weather, is it not?' he said courteously. 'My—ah—daughter tells me that Montreux has never been more lovely.'

'You are going back to Switzerland at once?' said Sir Raymond.

'Who knows?' answered the other. 'I am a man of moods.' He picked up his hat, and a faint smile hovered round his lips. 'But I certainly feel that I have earned a holiday. Well, gentlemen—I will say good-bye. Possibly we may meet again, though I doubt if I shall still be Mr Blackton. A pity, because I rather fancy myself like this. It is quite my best-looking rôle, so I am informed by competent judges. But change and novelty are essential in my work, as doubtless you can understand.'

He strolled towards the door, still smiling gently.

'One moment, Mr Blackton,' cried Sir Raymond. 'What about Mr Lewisham? His wife rang me up on the telephone this morning to say that he had not returned last night, and that she'd had a wire from Euston saying he'd been called North on business.'

Blackton studied the ash on his cigar.

'Really,' he murmured. 'You don't say so. However, I don't know that I'm greatly interested. He wasn't very entertaining, was he?'

'But that note,' cried Leibhaus—'the threatening note.'

'Destroyed by me personally. You may rest assured of that. And when you next see Mr Lewisham, please give him my kind regards. Doubtless an excellent man, though I thought him very quiet the last time I saw him. Dull—and overburdened with conscience.

A depressing mixture. Well, gentlemen, once again—good-bye. Or shall I say—au revoir?'

The door closed behind him a little abruptly. Just at the moment the topic of Mr Lewisham was not one he wished to go into in detail. Once he was on his way to Valparaiso it wouldn't matter so much—but at the moment, no. The subject failed to commend itself to him, and he dismissed it from his mind as he entered his waiting motor-car. It still remained the one weak link in the whole business, but nothing more could be done to strengthen it than he had already done. And that being the case, there was no object in bothering about it further. There were other things of more immediate importance in the near future to be decided, and it was of those he was thinking as the car spun smoothly along towards the luxurious house Freyder had acquired for him on the borders of the New Forest.

After mature thought he had decided to add a completely new character to his repertoire. At first he had considered the possibilities of being an ordinary English country gentleman, but he had very soon dismissed the idea. The gentleman part he could do—none better; even the English, but not the country. And he was far too clever not to realise his own limitations. Yet it was a pity, since no type is more inconspicuous in its proper place, and to be inconspicuous was his object in life. But it was too risky a rôle to play in the middle of the genuine article, and so he had reluctantly decided against it. And his intention now was to assume the character of an elderly recluse of eccentric habits and great wealth devoted to all sorts of scientific research work—particularly electrical and chemical. Most of his life had been spent abroad, and now, in his declining years, he had come back to the country of his birth partially from feelings of sentiment, but more particularly to look after his only brother, whose health and brain had been failing for some time. A part of the house was set apart for this brother, who was subject to delusions and saw no one.

Six months was the period he gave it before—in a last despairing effort to restore his brother's health—he took him for a cruise on a private yacht, and buried him quietly at sea. Possibly less; a great deal would depend on the rapidity with which the invalid produced the diamonds. For though he had no doubt as to his ability to learn the process in a very short time, the thought of mixing chemicals and getting electric shocks bored him excessively. Having got the dog, he had no intention of barking himself. No—six months was the period he had in his mind; after which the real game would begin. Again would an eminent savant approach Sir Raymond Blantyre and his syndicate and make diamonds artificially; again would the services of Mr Edward Blackton be requisitioned to deal with the situation. And as the gorgeous possibility of being paid a vast sum to kill himself dawned on him, as the endless vista of money, money, all the time stretched out before his imagination in all its wonderful simplicity, the charm of the countryside took on an added beauty. A glow of sublime benevolence flooded his soul; for one brief moment he took up the speaking-tube to stop the car. He felt he wanted to hear the birds sing; to put buttercups in his hair and dance with the chauffeur on the green sward. And since such a performance might have perplexed that worthy mechanic more than it enthralled him, it was just as well that at that moment the car swung through some massive gates and entered the drive of a largish house, which could be seen in the distance through the trees.

Mr William Robinson had reached his destination. For, quite rightly realising that shibboleth of our country life which concerns itself with whether a stranger belongs to the Leicestershire or the Warwickshire branch of the family, he had decided against calling himself De Vere Molyneux.

CHAPTER 5

In Which Mr William Robinson Loses his Self-control

He was met at the front door by Freyder, who led him at once to the room which he had set apart for his Chief's own particular and private use. In every house taken by Mr William Robinson—to adopt, at once, his new name—there was one such room into which no one, under any pretext whatever, might enter without his permission, once he was in residence. Freyder himself would not have dreamed of doing so; and even the girl, who was still enjoying the sunshine at Montreux, invariably knocked before she went into the holy of holies.

'Capital, Freyder,' he remarked, glancing round the room with a critical eye. 'And how is our friend?'

'Getting damned angry, Chief,' answered the other. 'Talking about legal proceedings and infamous conduct. The poor old bloke was wedged up against a nail in the packing-case, and it's made him as mad as the devil.'

'A pity,' murmured Mr Robinson. 'Still, I don't know that it matters very much. It would have been pleasanter, of course, if we could have kept the proceedings on an amicable basis, but I always had grave doubts. A pig-headed old man, Freyder; but there are ways of overcoming pig-headedness.' He smiled genially; he still felt he wanted to hear the birds sing. 'And now I will just make one or two alterations in my personal appearance. Then I will interview our friend.'

'Very good, Chief. By the way—the dynamo is installed, also the most modern brand of electric furnace. But, of course, I haven't been able to do anything with regard to the chemicals as yet.'

'Of course not. You've done extremely well, my dear fellow—extremely well. He will have to tell me what chemicals he requires this evening, and you will go up to London first thing tomorrow and obtain them.'

With a wave of his hand he dismissed his subordinate, and then for over an hour he occupied himself in front of a mirror. Mr William Robinson was being created. It was his first appearance in public, and so a little licence was allowable. There would be no one to point an accusing finger at his nose and say it had grown larger in the night or anything awkward of that sort. This was creation, pure and simple, giving scope to the creator's artistic mind. He could make what he would. Once made, a series of the most minute measurements with gauges recording to the hundredth of an inch would be necessary. Each would be entered up with mathematical precision in a book kept specially for the purpose, along with other details concerning the character. But that came later, and was merely the uninteresting routine work. The soul of the artist need not be troubled by such trifles.

And since the soul of the artist was gay within him, he fashioned a genial old man with twinkling eyes and mutton-chop whiskers. His nose was rather hooked; his horn spectacles reposed on his forehead as if they had been absent-mindedly pushed up from their proper position. His scanty grey hair was brushed back untidily (it

73

was the ruthless thinning out of his normal crop with a razor that he disliked most); his clothes were those of a man who buys good ones and takes no care of them. And, finally, his hands were covered with the stains of the chemist.

At length he had finished, and having surveyed himself from every angle he rang the bell for Freyder, who paused in genuine amazement at the door. Accustomed as he was to these complete metamorphoses of his Chief, he never ceased to marvel at them.

'How's that, Freyder?' demanded Mr Robinson.

'Wonderful, Chief,' said the other. 'Simply wonderful. I congratulate you.'

'Then I think I'll go and see our friend—my dear, dear brother. Doubtless a little chat will clear the air.'

With a curious shambling gait he followed Freyder up the stairs to the top of the house. Then rubbing his hands together genially, he entered the room which Freyder had pointed to and closed the door behind him.

Professor Goodman rose as he came in and took a step forward.

'Are you the owner of this house, sir?' he demanded angrily.

'Yes,' said the other. 'I am. I hope my servants have made you comfortable.'

'Then I demand to know by what right you dare to keep me a prisoner. How dare you, sir—how dare you? And where am I, anyway?'

With a sudden little gesture of weakness Professor Goodman sat down. He was still bewildered and shaken at his treatment, and Mr Robinson smiled affably.

'That's better,' he remarked. 'Let us both sit down and have a friendly talk. I feel that one or two words of explanation are due to you, which I trust, my dear Professor, you will receive in a friendly and—er—brotherly spirit. Brotherly, because you are my brother.'

'What the devil do you mean, sir?' snapped the Professor. 'I haven't got a brother; I've never had a brother.'

'I know,' murmured the other sadly. 'A most regrettable oversight on your parents' part. But isn't it nice to have one now? One, moreover, who will surround you with every care and attention in your illness.'

'But, damn you!' roared the unhappy man, 'I'm not ill.'

Mr Robinson waved a deprecating hand.

74

'I implore of you, do not excite yourself. In your weak mental state it would be most injurious. I assure you that you are my partially insane brother, and that I have taken this house entirely on your account. Could altruism go further?'

Professor Goodman was swallowing hard, and clutching the arms of his chair.

'Perhaps you'll say what you really do mean,' he muttered at length.

'Certainly,' cried Mr Robinson benevolently. 'It is for that express purpose that we are having this interview. It is essential that you should understand exactly where you are. Now, perhaps you are unaware of the fact that you died yesterday.'

'I did—what?' stammered the other.

'Died,' said Mr Robinson genially. 'I thought you might find that bit a little hard to follow, so I've brought you a copy of one of the early evening papers. In it you will find a brief account of the inquest—your inquest.'

With a trembling hand the Professor took the paper.

'But I don't understand,' he said after he had read it. 'For Heaven's sake, sir, won't you explain? I remember nothing from the time when I was chloroformed in my laboratory till I came to in a packing-case. It wasn't I who was blown up?'

'Obviously,' returned the other. 'But the great point is, Professor, that everyone thinks it was. The cream of the scientific world, in fact, will attend the burial of somebody else's foot, in the firm belief that they are honouring your memory. Whose foot it is you needn't worry about; I assure you he was a person of tedious disposition.'

'But I must go at once and telephone.' He rose in his agitation. 'It's the most dreadful thing. Think of my poor wife.'

'I know,' said Mr Robinson sadly. 'Though not exactly married myself, I can guess your feelings. But I'm afraid, my dear brother, that your wife must remain in ignorance of the fact that she is not a widow.'

Professor Goodman's face went grey. He knew now what he had only suspected before—that he was in danger.

'Possibly things are becoming clearer to you,' went on the other. 'The world thinks you are dead. No hue-and-cry will be raised to find you. But you are not dead—far from it. You are, as I explained, my partially insane brother, whom no one is allowed to see. I admit that you are not insane nor are you my brother—but

75

qu'importe. It is not the truth that counts, but what people think is the truth. I trust I make myself clear?'

Professor Goodman said nothing; he was staring at the speaker with fear in his eyes. For the mask of benevolence had slipped a little from Mr Robinson's face: the real man was showing through the assumed rôle.

'From your silence I take it that I do,' he continued. 'No one will look for you as Professor Goodman; no one will be permitted to see you as my brother. So—er—you will not be very much disturbed.'

'In plain language, you mean I'm a prisoner,' said the Professor. 'Why? What is your object?'

'You have recently, my dear Professor,' began Mr Robinson, 'made a most remarkable discovery.'

'I knew it,' groaned the other. 'I knew it was that. Well, let me tell you one thing, sir. If this infamous outrage has been perpetrated on me in order to make me keep silent about it—I still refuse utterly. You may detain me here in your power until after the meeting of the Society, but I shall give my discovery to the world all the same.'

Mr Robinson gently stroked his side whiskers.

'A most remarkable discovery,' he repeated as if the other had not spoken. 'I congratulate you upon it, Professor. And being a chemist in a small way myself, I am overcome with curiosity on the subject. I have therefore gone to no little inconvenience to bring you to a place where, undisturbed by mundane trifles, you will be able to impart your discovery to me, and at the same time manufacture diamonds to your heart's content. I should like you to make hundreds of diamonds during the period of your retirement; in fact, that will be your daily task. . . .'

'You want me to make them?' said the bewildered man. 'But that's the very thing Blantyre and those others didn't want me to do.'

Mr Robinson stroked his whiskers even more caressingly.

'How fortunate it is,' he murmured, 'that we don't all think alike!'

'And if I refuse?' said the other.

Mr Robinson ceased stroking his whiskers.

'You would be unwise, Professor Goodman—most unwise. I have methods of dealing with people who refuse to do what I tell them to do which have always succeeded up to date.'

His eyes were suddenly merciless, and with a sick feeling of fear the Professor sat back in his chair.

'A dynamo has been installed,' went on Mr Robinson after a moment or two. 'Also the most modern type of electric furnace. Here I have the retort which you use in your process'—he placed it on the table beside him—'and all that now remains are the necessary chemicals. Your notes are a trifle difficult to follow, so you will have to prepare a list yourself of those chemicals and they will be obtained for you tomorrow.'

He took the papers from his pocket and handed them to the Professor.

'Just one word of warning. Should anything go wrong with your process, should you pretend out of stupid obstinacy that you are unable to make diamonds—may God help you! If there is anything wrong with the apparatus, let me know, and it will be rectified. But don't, I beg of you, try any tricks.'

He rose, and his voice became genial again.

'I am sure my warning is unnecessary,' he said gently. 'Now I will leave you to prepare the list of the salts you require.'

'But these are the wrong notes,' said Professor Goodman, staring at them dazedly. 'These are my notes on peptonised proteins.'

Mr Robinson stood very still.

'What do you mean?' he said at length. 'Are those not the notes on your process of making diamonds?'

'Good gracious—no,' said the Professor. 'These have got nothing to do with it.'

'Are the notes necessary?'

'Absolutely. Why, I can't even remember all the salts without them—let alone the proportions in which they are used.'

'Do you know where they are?'

The Professor passed his hand wearily across his forehead.

'Whom was I lunching with?' he murmured. 'It was just before I went to meet Professor Scheidstrun, and I gave them to him to take care of. And by the way—what has happened to Scheidstrun? Surely it wasn't he who was killed.'

'Don't worry about Scheidstrun,' snarled Mr Robinson. 'Whom were you lunching with, you damned old fool?'

'I know—I remember now. It was Captain Drummond. I lunched at his club. He's got them. Good God! why are you looking like that?'

For perhaps the first time in his life every vestige of self-control had left the master-criminal's face and he looked like a wild beast.

'Drummond!' he shouted savagely. 'Not Captain Hugh Drummond, who lives in Brook Street?'

'That's the man,' said the Professor. 'Such a nice fellow, though rather stupid. Do you know him by any chance?'

How near Professor Goodman was to a violent death at that moment it is perhaps as well he did not know. In mild perplexity he watched the other man's face, diabolical with its expression of animal rage and fury, and wondered vaguely why the mention of Hugh Drummond's name should have produced such a result. And it was a full minute before Mr Robinson had recovered himself sufficiently to sit down and continue the conversation. Drummond again—always Drummond. How, in the name of everything conceivable and inconceivable, had *he* got mixed up in this affair? All his carefully worked out and brilliantly executed plan frustrated and brought to nothing by one miserable fact which he could not possibly have foreseen, and which, even now, he could hardly believe.

'What induced you to give the notes to him?' he snarled at length.

'He said he didn't think it was safe for me to carry them about with me,' said the other mildly. 'You see, I had received a threatening letter in the morning—a letter threatening my life . . .' He blinked apologetically.

So it was Lewisham's letter that had done it, and the only ray of comfort in the situation lay in the fact that at any rate he'd killed Lewisham.

'Did you give him any special instructions?' he demanded.

'No—I don't think so,' answered the Professor. 'I think he said something about handing them over to the bank.'

Mr Robinson rose and started to pace up and down the room. The blow was so staggering in its unexpectedness that his brain almost refused to work. That Drummond of all people should again have crossed his path was as far as his thoughts would go. The fact that Drummond was blissfully unaware that he had done so was beside the point; it seemed almost like the hand of Fate. And incredible though it may seem, for a short time he was conscious of a feeling of genuine superstitious fear.

But not for long. The prize, in this case, was too enormous for any weakness of that sort. If Captain Drummond had the notes, steps would have to be taken to make him give them up. The question was—what were those steps to be?

With an effort he concentrated on the problem. The thing must be done with every appearance of legality; it must be done naturally. From Drummond's point of view, which was the important one to consider, the situation would be a simple one. He was in the possession of valuable papers belonging to a dead man—papers to which he had no right; but papers to which he—being the type of person he was—would continue to stick to if he had the faintest suspicion of foul play. And since he had seen the threatening letter, those suspicions must be latent in his mind already. To keep them latent and not arouse them was essential.

And the second and no less important part of the problem was to ensure that once the notes had left Drummond's hands they should pass with a minimum of delay into his. The thought of anything happening to them or of someone else obtaining possession of them turned him cold all over.

He paused in his restless pacing up and down, and thoughtfully lit a cigar. His self-control was completely recovered; Mr William Robinson was himself again. A hitch had occurred in an otherwise perfect plan—that was all. And hitches were made to be unhitched.

'What is the name of your lawyer?' he said quietly.

'Mr Tootem of Tootem, Price, & Tootem,' answered Professor Goodman in mild surprise. 'Why do you want to know?'

'Never mind why. Now here's a pen and some paper. Write as I dictate. And don't let there be any mistake about the writing, my friend.

'DEAR DRUMMOND,

'I have been discussing things with my friend Scheidstrun this afternoon, and he agrees with you that it is better that I should not carry about the notes I gave you. So will you send them to Tootem, Price & Tootem. . . .

'What's the address? Austin Friars. Well—put it in.

'They will keep them for me until the meeting of the Royal Society. And if, as Scheidstrun humorously says, I shall have blown myself up before then with my new blasting powder, it is my wish that he should be given the notes. He is immensely interested in my discovery, and I know of no one to whom I would sooner bequeath it. But that, my dear Drummond, is not likely to occur.

Yours sincerely,

'Now sign your name.'

The Professor laid down his pen with a sigh.

'It is all very confusing,' he murmured. 'And I do hope I'm not going to get blood poisoning where that nail in the packing-case ran into my leg.'

But Mr Robinson evinced no interest in such an eventuality. He stood with the letter in his hand, pulling thoughtfully at his cigar, and striving to take into account every possible development which might arise. For perhaps a minute he remained motionless while Professor Goodman rubbed his injured limb; then he made a decisive little gesture oddly out of keeping with his benevolent appearance. His mind was made up; his plan was clear.

'Address an envelope,' he said curtly, 'to Captain Drummond.'

He took the envelope and slipped the letter inside. There was no time to be lost; every moment was valuable.

'Now, Professor Goodman,' he remarked, 'I want you to pay close attention to what I am going to say. The fact that you have not got the notes of your process constitutes a slight check in my plans. However, I am about to obtain those notes, and while I am doing so you will remain here. You will be well looked after, and well fed. A delightful bedroom will be placed at your disposal, and I believe, though I have not personally verified the fact, that there is a very good library below. Please make free use of it. But I must give you one word of warning. Should you make any attempt to escape, should you make the slightest endeavour even to communicate with the outside world, you will be gagged and put in irons in a dark room.'

Professor Goodman's hands shook uncontrollably; he looked what at the moment he was, a badly frightened old man.

'But, sir,' he quavered pitifully, 'won't you tell me where I am, and why all this is happening to me?'

'Finding the answer should give you some interesting mental recreation during my absence,' said Mr Robinson suavely.

'And my poor wife,' moaned the unhappy man.

'The pangs of widowhood are hard to bear,' agreed the other. 'But doubtless time will soften the blow. And anyway, my dear Professor, you died in the cause of duty. I can assure you that Professor Scheidstrun's peroration over your sole remaining boot brought tears to the eyes of all who heard it. Well, I will say au revoir. Ask for anything you require, but don't, I beg of you, try

80

any stupid tricks. My servants are rough fellows—some of them.'

With a genial smile he left the room and went downstairs. Whatever may have been his thoughts only the most perfect equanimity showed on his face. He possessed that most priceless asset of any great leader—the power of concealing bad news from his staff. In fact the tighter the corner the more calmly confident did this man always look. Nothing is more fatal to any enterprise than the knowledge on the part of subordinates that the man in charge is shaken. And though he would hardly admit it to himself, Mr William Robinson was badly shaken. In fact when he reached his own private sanctum he did a thing which in his whole long career of crimes he had done but twice before. From a small locked cabinet he took a bottle containing a white powder, and calmly and methodically he measured out a dose which he sniffed up his nose. And had anyone seen this secret operation, he would have realised that the man was the master and not the drug. Only one man in a million may employ cocaine as a servant and keep it in that position: Mr William Robinson was that one.

Deliberately he sat down to await the drug's action; then with a faint smile he rose and replaced the bottle in the cabinet. The nerve crisis had passed; the master-criminal was himself again.

'Freyder,' he remarked as that worthy entered the room in answer to the bell, 'a slight hitch has occurred in my scheme. The indecipherable notes which I so carefully extracted from our friend's pocket yesterday refer apparently to the prolongation of the lives of rabbits and other fauna. The ones we require are—er—elsewhere. I, naturally, propose to obtain them forthwith, but it will be necessary to proceed with a certain amount of discretion. Incredible to relate, they are in the possession of a young gentleman who we have come across before—one Drummond.'

Freyder's breath came in a sharp whistle.

'I see that you recall the name,' went on the other quietly. 'And I must say that when Professor Goodman informed me of the fact, I felt for the moment unreasonably annoyed. One cannot legislate for everything, and how any man out of an asylum could give that vast fool anything of importance to look after is one of those things which I confess baffle me completely. However, all that concerns us is that he has them at the moment: the problem is to remove them from his keeping as rapidly as possible. Under normal circumstances the solution of that problem would have presented no

81

difficulties, but Drummond, I am bound to admit, is not normal. In fact, Freyder, as you may remember, I have twice made the unforgivable mistake of underestimating him. This time, however, I have decided on a little scheme which, though a trifle complicated at first sight, is, in reality, profoundly simple. Moreover, it appeals to my sense of humour, which is a great point in its favour. You have your notebook? Then I will give you my instructions.'

They were clear and concise with no possibility of a misunderstanding, and, as Mr Robinson had said, they contained in them a touch of humour that was akin to genius. In fact, despite the seriousness of the situation, on two or three occasions Freyder broke into uncontrollable chuckles of laughter. The whole thing was so gloriously simple that it seemed there must be a flaw somewhere, and yet, try as he would, he could discover none.

'The essence of the whole thing is speed, Freyder,' said his Chief, rising at length. 'It is impossible to say what Drummond will do with those notes if he's left too long in undisturbed possession of them. He must know their value, but for all that he's quite capable of using them for shaving paper. The one thing, knowing him, which I don't think he will do is to take them to Scotland Yard. But I don't want to run any risks. To have to be content with a miserable half-million for this little affair would deprive me of my reason. I should totter to an early grave, as a grey-headed old man. So speed, don't forget—speed is absolutely essential.'

'I can make all arrangements tonight, Chief,' said Freyder, rising, 'and start at dawn tomorrow morning. Back tomorrow evening, and the whole thing can be done the day after.'

'Good,' answered the other. 'Then send for the car at once and we'll get off.'

And thus it happened that two hours after Mr Edward Blackton had arrived at his house on the borders of the New Forest, Mr William Robinson left it again. But on the return journey it is to be regretted that he no longer wished to hear the birds sing or put buttercups in his hair. He sat in his corner sunk in silence while the powerful limousine ate up the miles to London. And his companion Freyder knew better than to break that silence.

It was not until the tramlines at Hounslow were reached that he spoke.

'If I fail to settle accounts with Drummond this time, Freyder,

I'll do as he once recommended and take to growing tomatoes.'

Freyder grunted.

'The notes first, Chief, and after that the man. You'll win this time.' He spoke down the speaking-tube and the car slowed up. 'I'll get out here; our man is close-to. And I'll be back tomorrow evening.'

He gave the chauffeur the name of a residential hotel in a quiet part of Bayswater, and stood for a moment watching the car drive away. Then he turned and disappeared down a side-street, while Mr Robinson continued his journey alone. There was nothing more to be done now until Freyder returned, and so, in accordance with his invariable custom, he dismissed the matter from his mind.

To do in Rome as the Romans was another rule of his. And so after dinner at the quiet residential hotel Mr Robinson joined heartily in a merry round game which lacked much of its charm as two cards were missing from the pack. Then refusing with becoming modesty a challenge to take on the hotel champion at halma, he retired to his room and was asleep almost at once. And he was still peacefully sleeping at five o'clock the next morning, when Freyder, shivering a little in the morning air, drew his thick leather coat more closely around his throat. Below him lay the grey sea—hazy still, for the sun had no warmth as yet. In front the pilot was sitting motionless, and after a while the steady roar of the engine lulled him into a gentle doze. The aeroplane flew steadily on towards the east . . . and Germany.

CHAPTER 6

In Which Hugh Drummond Loses his Self-control

It must be admitted that there was an air of gloom over Hugh Drummond's house on the day following the inquest. Mrs Goodman and Brenda had not left their rooms, and somewhat naturally Phyllis was principally occupied in seeing what she could do for them in their terrible sorrow; while Algy Longworth, faced with the necessity of postponing the wedding, had relapsed into a condition of complete imbecility and refused to be comforted. In fact it was not an atmosphere conducive to thought, and Hugh was trying to think.

On the next day was the funeral. The whole thing had already dropped out of the public eye; Professor Goodman, having been neither a pugilist, film star, nor criminal, but merely a gentle old man of science, could lay no claim whatever to the slightest popular interest. But to Hugh he was something more than a gentle old man of science. He was a man who to all intents and purposes had appealed to him for help—a man whose life had been threatened, and who, within a few hours of receiving that threat, had died.

True, according to the verdict at the inquest, he would have died whether he had received that threat or not. But Hugh was still dissatisfied with that verdict. The proofs, the evidence, all pointed that way—but he was still dissatisfied. And coupled with his dissatisfaction was an uneasy feeling, which only grew stronger with time, that he had been wrong to suppress his knowledge of that letter from the police.

Now it was impossible to put it forward, but that made things no better. The only result in fact as far as he was concerned was that it hardened his resolve not to let the matter drop where it was. Until after the funeral he would say nothing; then he'd begin some inquiries on his own. And for those inquiries two obvious avenues suggested themselves: the first was Professor Scheidstrun, the second Sir Raymond Blantyre.

Once again he took the Professor's notes out of his pocket-book and studied them. He had already shown one sheet to a chemist in a neighbouring street in the hope that he might be able to decipher it, but with no result. The atrocious handwriting, coupled with the fact that, according to the chemist, it was written in a sort of code, made them completely incomprehensible to anyone save the man who wrote them. And he was dead. . . .

With a sigh he replaced the papers in his notecase and strolled over to the window. Brook Street presented a quiescent appearance due to the warmth of the day and the recent consumption by its dwellers of lunch. And Hugh was just wondering what form of exercise he could most decently take in view of Mrs Goodman's presence in the house, when he straightened up and his eyes became suddenly watchful. A wild, excited figure whom he recognised instantly was tacking up the street, peering with short-sighted eyes at the numbers of the houses.

'Algy!'

'What is it?' grunted Longworth, coming out of a melancholy reverie.

'Old Scheidstrun is blowing up the street. He's looking for a house. Surely he can't be coming here?'

Algy Longworth sat up in his chair.

'You mean the old bloke who gave evidence at the inquest?'

Hugh nodded.

'By Jove! he is coming here.' His voice held traces of excitement. 'Now, why the deuce should he want to see me?'

He went quickly to the door.

'Denny,' he called, and his servant, who was already on his way to the front door, paused and looked up. 'Show the gentleman outside straight up here to my room.'

He came back frowning thoughtfully.

'How on earth does he connect me with it, Algy?'

'It's more than likely, old man,' answered Longworth, 'that he may have heard that Mrs Goodman is here, and has come to shoot a card. Anyway, we'll soon know.'

A moment later Denny ushered Professor Scheidstrun into the room. Seen from close-to, he seemed more untidy and egg-stained than ever, as he stood by the door peering at the two young men.

'Captain Drummond?' he demanded in his hoarse, guttural voice.

'That's me,' said Hugh, who was standing with his back to the fireplace regarding his visitor curiously. 'What can I do for you, sir?'

The Professor waved his arms like an agitated semaphore and sank into a chair.

'Doubtless you wonder who I may be,' he remarked, 'and what for I come you to see.'

'I know perfectly well who you are,' said Drummond quietly, 'but I confess I'm beat as to why you want to see me. However, the pleasure is entirely mine.'

'So.' The German stared at him. 'You know who I am?'

'You are Professor Scheidstrun,' remarked Drummond. 'I was present at the inquest yesterday and saw you.'

'Goot.' The Professor nodded his head as if satisfied, though his brain was busy with this very unexpected item of news. 'Then I will proceed at once to the business. In the excitement of all this dreadful accident I had forgotten it until this moment. Then I remember and come to you at once.' He was fumbling in his pocket as he spoke. 'A letter, Captain Drummond, which my poor friend give to me to post—and I forgot it till an hour ago. And I say at once, I will go round myself and see this gentleman and explain.'

Drummond took the envelope and glanced at it thoughtfully, while Algy looked over his shoulder.

'That's Professor Goodman's writing.'

'Since he the letter wrote presumably it is,' remarked the German with ponderous sarcasm.

'You know the contents of this letter, Professor?' asked Drummond, as he slit open the envelope.

'He read it to me,' answered the other. 'Ach! it is almost incredible that what my dear friend should have said to me in jest—indeed that which he has written there in jest—should have proved true. Even now I can hardly believe that he is dead. It is a loss, gentlemen, to the world of science which can never be replaced.'

He rambled on while Drummond, having read the letter in silence, handed it to Algy. And if for one fleeting second there showed in the German's eyes a gleam of almost maniacal hatred as they rested on the owner of the house, it was gone as suddenly as it came. The look on his face was benevolent, even sad, as befitted a man who had recently lost a confrère and friend, when Drummond turned and spoke again.

'The letter is a request, Professor, that certain notes now in my possession should be handed over to you.'

'That is so,' assented the other. 'He to me explained all. He told me of his astounding discovery—a discovery which even now I can hardly believe. But he assured me that it was the truth. And on my shoulders he laid the sacred duty of giving that discovery to the world, if anything should happen to him.'

'Astounding coincidence that on the very afternoon he wrote this something did happen to him,' remarked Drummond quietly.

'As I haf said, even now I can hardly believe it,' agreed the Professor. 'But it is so, and there is no more to be said.'

'Rather astounding also that you did not mention this at the inquest,' pursued Drummond.

'Till one hour ago, my young friend, I forget I had the letter. I forget about his discovery—about the diamonds—about all. My mind was stunned by the dreadful tragedy. And think—five, ten

86

minutes more and I also to pieces would have been blown. *Mein Gott!* it makes me sweat.'

He took out a handkerchief and mopped his forehead.

'By the way, Professor,' said Drummond suddenly, 'do you know Sir Raymond Blantyre?'

For the fraction of a second Professor Scheidstrun hesitated. It was not a question he had been expecting and he realised that a lot might hinge on the answer. And then like a flash he remembered that on leaving the inquest he had spoken two or three words to Sir Raymond. Moreover, Drummond had been there himself.

'Sir Raymond Blantyre,' he murmured. 'He has a grey moustache and an eyeglass. Slightly I know him. He was—ja! he was at the inquest himself.'

It was glib, it was quick. It would have passed muster nine times out of ten as a spontaneous reply to a perfectly ordinary question. But it was made to a man who was already suspicious, and it was made to a man whose lazy eyes missed nothing. Drummond had noticed that almost imperceptible pause; what was more to the point, he had noticed the sudden look of wariness on the other's face. More a fleeting shadow than a look, but it had not escaped the lynx-eyed man lounging against the mantelpiece. And it had not tended to allay his suspicions, though his face was still perfectly impassive.

'I assume from what he has written here that Professor Goodman discussed with you the threatening letter he received,' he went on placidly.

'He mentioned it, of course.' The German shrugged his shoulders. 'But for me it seems a stupid joke. Absurd! Ridiculous! Who would be so foolish as to write such a thing if it was a genuine threat? It was—how do you say it—it was a hoax? *Nein—nein*—to that I paid no attention. It was not for that he this letter wrote. He told me of his discovery, and I who know him well, I say, "Where are the notes? It is not safe for you to carry them. You who lose everything —you will lose them. Or more likely still someone will your pocket pick. There are people in London who would like those notes." '

'There undoubtedly are,' agreed Drummond mildly.

'He tells me he give them to you. I say, "This young man—he too may lose them. Tell him to send them to your men of business." He says, "Goot—I will." And he write the letter there. Then he add, as he thinks, his little joke. My poor friend! My poor, poor friend!

For now the joke is not a joke. And on me there falls the sacred trust he has left. But his shall be the glory; all the credit will I give to him. And the world of science shall remember his name for ever by this discovery.'

Overcome by his emotion the Professor lay back in his chair breathing stertorously, while once again he dabbed at his forehead with his handkerchief.

'Very praiseworthy and all that,' murmured Drummond. 'Then I take it that your proposal is, sir, that I should hand these notes over to you here and now?'

The German sat up and shrugged his shoulders.

'It would save trouble, Captain Drummond. For me I wish to return to Germany after my poor friend's funeral tomorrow. Naturally I must with me take the notes. But if for any reason you would prefer to hand them to the good Mr Tootem of Austin Friars, then perhaps we could arrange to meet there some time tomorrow morning.'

He leaned back in his chair as if the matter was of no account, and Drummond, his hands in his pockets, strolled over to the window. On the face of it everything was perfectly above-board—and yet, try as he would, he could not rid himself of the feeling that something was wrong. Later, when he recalled that interview and realised that for half an hour on that warm summer's afternoon he had been in his own house with the man he knew as Carl Peterson sitting in his best chair, he used to shake with laughter at the humour of it. But at the time no thought of such a wildly amazing thing was in his mind; no suspicion that Professor Scheidstrun was not Professor Scheidstrun had even entered his head. It was not the German's identity that worried him, but his goodwill. Was he what he professed to be—a friend of the late Professor Goodman's? Did he intend to give this scientific discovery to the world as he had promised to do? Or had he deceived Professor Goodman? And if so, why? Could it be possible that this man was being employed by Sir Raymond Blantyre, and that he too was engaged in the conspiracy to destroy the results of the discovery for ever?

He turned and stared at the German, who, overcome by the heat, was apparently asleep. But only apparently. Behind that coarse face and heavy forehead the brain was very wide awake. And it would have staggered Drummond could he have realised how exactly his thoughts were being read. Not very extraordinary either, since the whole interview had been planned to produce those thoughts by a master of psychology.

Suddenly the German sat up with a start.

'It is warm; I sleep.' He extracted a huge watch from his pocket and gave an exclamation as he saw the time. 'I must go,' he said, scrambling to his feet. 'Well—how say you, Captain Drummond? Will you give me now the notes, or do we meet at the good Mr Tootem's?'

'I think, Professor,' said Drummond slowly, 'that I would sooner we met at the lawyer's. These notes were handed to me personally, and I should feel easier in my mind if I handed them over personally to the lawyer. Then my responsibility will end.'

'As you will,' remarked the German indifferently. 'Then we will say eleven o'clock tomorrow morning, unless I let you know to the contrary.'

He shambled from the room, and Drummond escorted him to the front door. Then, having watched him down the steps, he returned to his room.

'Seems a bonâ-fide show, Algy,' he remarked, lighting a cigarette.

'Will you give up the notes?' demanded his friend.

'My dear old thing, I must,' answered Hugh. 'You've seen the Professor's distinct instructions that jolly old Tootem & Tootem are to have 'em. I can't go against that. What the legal wallah does with them afterwards is nothing to do with me. Still, I wish I could feel more certain in my own mind. You see, the devil of it is, Algy, that even if that bloke is a stumer, our hands are tied. There are old Goodman's instructions, and the only thing I can do is to throw the responsibility on the lawyer's shoulders.'

He paced thoughtfully up and down the room, to stop suddenly and pick up his hat.

'It's worth trying,' he remarked half to himself, and the next moment Algy was alone. From the window he saw Hugh hail a taxi and disappear, and with a shrug of his shoulders he resumed his study of *Ruff's Guide*. At times the vagaries of his host were apt to be a little wearing.

And when some four hours later Hugh returned just in time for dinner, it certainly seemed as if he'd wasted his time.

'I've been watching Mr Atkinson's house, Algy,' he said despondently, 'you know the one I spotted after the inquest, where Scheidstrun is living. Went to ground in a house opposite. Said I

89

was a doctor looking for rooms. Thank heavens! the servant developed no symptoms requiring medical attention, because all I could have conscientiously recommended for anybody with a face like hers was a lethal chamber. However, as I say, I took cover in the parlour behind a bowl of stuffed fruit, and there I waited. Devil a thing for hours. Atkinson's house was evidently occupied; in fact, I saw him look out of the window once. A benevolent-looking old chap with mutton-chop whiskers. However, I stuck it out, and at last, just as I was on the point of giving it up, something did happen, though not much. A closed car drove up, and from it there descended old Scheidstrun, a youngish man, and an elderly woman. Couldn't see her very well—but she looked a typical Boche. Probably his wife, I should think.'

He relapsed into silence and lit a cigarette.

'An afternoon wasted,' he grunted after a while. 'I'm fed up with the whole dam' show, Algy. Why the devil didn't I give him the notes and be done with it when he was here? As it is, I've got to waste tomorrow morning as well fooling round in the city; and with the funeral in the afternoon the old brain will cease to function. Mix me a cocktail, like a good fellow. Everything is in the cupboard.'

And thus it came about that while two cocktails were being lowered in gloomy silence in Brook Street, a cheerful-looking old gentleman with mutton-chop whiskers entered his quiet residential hotel in Bayswater. There were no signs of gloomy silence about the old gentleman; in fact, he was almost chatty with the lounge-waiter.

'I think—yes, I think,' he remarked, 'that I will have a small cocktail. Not a thing I often do—but this evening I will indulge.'

'Spotted a winner, sir?' said the waiter, responding to the old gentleman's mood.

'Something of that sort, my lad,' he replied genially—'something of that sort.' And Mr William Robinson's smile was enigmatic.

He seldom remembered an afternoon when in a quiet way he had enjoyed himself so much. In fact, he was almost glad that Drummond had refused to hand over the notes: it would have been so inartistic—so crude. Of course it would have saved bother, but where is the true artist who thinks of that? And he had never really imagined that Drummond would; he knew that young gentleman far too well for that. Naturally he was suspicious: well, he would be more suspicious tomorrow morning. He would be so suspicious, in fact, that in all probability the worthy Mr Tootem would get the shock of his life. He chuckled consumedly, and departed so far from his established custom as to order a second Martini. And as he lifted it to his lips he drank a silent toast: he drank to the shrewd powers of observation of a beautiful girl who was even then watching orange change to pink on the snow-capped Dent du Midi from the balcony of her room in the Palace Hotel.

And so it is unnecessary to emphasise the fact that there were wheels destined to rotate within wheels in the comfortable room in Austin Friars where Mr Tootem senior discharged his affairs, though that pillar of the legal profession was supremely unaware of the fact. With his usual courtly grace he had risen to greet the eminent German savant Professor Scheidstrun, who had arrived at about ten minutes to eleven on the following morning. Somewhat to Mr Tootem's surprise, the Professor had been accompanied by his wife, and Frau Scheidstrun was now waiting in the next room for the business to be concluded.

'Most sad, Professor,' murmured Mr Tootem. 'An irreparable loss, as you say, to the scientific world—and to his friends.' He glanced at the clock. 'This young man—Captain Drummond—will be here, you say, at eleven.'

'That is the arrangement that I haf with him made,' answered the German. 'He would not to me quite rightly the notes hand over yesterday; but as you see from the letter, it was my dear friend's wish that I should haf them, and carry on with the great discovery he has made.'

'Quite so,' murmured Mr Tootem benevolently, wishing profoundly that Drummond would hasten his arrival. The morning was warm; the Professor's egg-stained garments scandalised his British soul to the core; and in addition, Mr Tootem senior had arrived at that ripe age when office hours were made to be relaxed. He particularly wished to be at Lord's in time to see Middlesex open their innings against Yorkshire, and only the fact that Professor Goodman had been a personal friend of his had brought him to the city at all that day.

At length with a sigh of relief he looked up. Sounds of voices outside betokened someone's arrival, and the business would be a short one.

'Is this the young man?' he said, rubbing his hands together.

But the Professor made no reply: he was watching the door

91

which opened at that moment to admit Drummond. And since Mr Tootem rose at once to greet him, the fact that he had not answered escaped the lawyer's attention. He also failed to notice that an unaccountable expression of uneasiness showed for a moment on the German's face, as he contemplated Drummond's vast bulk.

'Ah! Captain Drummond, I'm glad you've come,' remarked Mr Tootem. 'Let me see—you know Professor Scheidstrun, don't you?'

He waved Drummond to a chair.

'Yes, we had a little pow-wow yesterday afternoon,' said Drummond, seating himself.

The strained look had vanished from the Professor's face: he beamed cheerfully.

'In which I found him most suspicious,' he said in his guttural voice. 'But quite rightly so.'

'Exactly,' murmured Mr Tootem, again glancing at the clock. It would take him at least twenty minutes to get to Lord's. 'But I am sure he will not be suspicious of me. And since I have one or two important—er—business engagements, perhaps we can conduct this little matter through expeditiously.' He beamed benevolently on Drummond, who was leaning back in his chair regarding the Professor through half-closed lids.

'Now, I understand that my dear friend and client, the late Professor Goodman, handed over to you some very valuable papers, Captain Drummond,' continued Mr Tootem. 'A great compliment, I may say, showing what faith he placed in your judgment and trustworthiness. I have here—and I gather you have seen this letter—instructions that those papers should be handed over to me. You have them with you, I trust?'

'Oh! yes. I've got them with me,' said Drummond quietly, though his eyes never left the German's face.

'Excellent,' murmured Mr Tootem. At a pinch he might do Lord's in a quarter of an hour. 'Then if you would kindly let me have them, that will—ah—conclude the matter. I may say that I quite appreciate your reluctance to hand them to anyone but me . . .' The worthy lawyer broke off abruptly. 'Good heavens! Captain Drummond, what is the matter?'

For Drummond had risen from his chair, and was standing in front of the Professor.

'You're not the man who came to see me yesterday,' he said quietly. 'You're not Professor Scheidstrun at all.'

'But the man is mad,' gasped the German. 'You say I am not Scheidstrun—me.'

'You're made up to look exactly like him—but you're not Scheidstrun! I tell you, Mr Tootem'—he turned to the lawyer, who was staring at him aghast—'that that man is no more Scheidstrun than I am. The disguise is wonderful—but his hair is a slightly different colour. Ever since I came in I've been wondering what it was.'

'This young man is mad,' said the German angrily. 'The reason that it is a slightly different colour is that I wear a wig. I haf two: this morning I wear the other one to what I wear yesterday.'

But Drummond wasn't even listening. Like a bird fascinated by a snake he was staring at the Professor's left hand, beating an agitated tattoo on his knee. For a moment or two he was dazed, as the stupendous reality burst on his mind. Before him sat Carl Peterson himself, given away once again by that old trick which he could never get rid of, that ceaseless nervous movement of the left hand. It was incredible; the suddenness of the thing took his breath away. And then the whole thing became clear to him. Somehow or other Peterson had heard of the discovery; perhaps employed by Sir Raymond Blantyre himself. He had found out that the notes of the process were to be handed to Scheidstrun, and with his usual consummate daring had decided to impersonate the German. And the woman he had seen arriving the night before was Irma.

His thoughts were chaotic: only the one great thing stuck out. The man in front of him was Peterson: he knew it. And with one wild hoot of utter joy he leapt upon him.

'My little Carl,' he murmured ecstatically, 'the pitcher has come to the well once too often.'

Possibly it had; but the scene which followed beggared description. Peterson or not Peterson, his confession as to wearing a wig was the truth. It came off with a slight sucking noise, revealing a domelike cranium completely devoid of hair. With a wild yell of terror the unfortunate German sprang from his chair, and darted behind the portly form of Mr Tootem, while Drummond, brandishing the wig, advanced on him.

'Damn it, sir,' spluttered Mr Tootem, 'I'll send for the police, sir; you must be mad.'

'Out of the way, Tootles,' said Drummond happily. 'You'll scream with laughter when I tell you the truth. Though we'd best make certain the swab hasn't got a gun.'

With a quick heave he jerked the cowering man out from behind the lawyer, who immediately rushed to the door shouting for help.

'A madman,' he bellowed to his amazed staff. 'Send for a keeper, and a straight-jacket.'

He turned round, for a sudden silence had settled on the room behind. Drummond was standing motionless gripping both the Professor's arms, with a look of amazement slowly dawning on his face. Surely he couldn't be mistaken, and yet—unless Peterson had suffered from some wasting disease—what on earth had happened to the man? The arms he felt under the coat-sleeve were thin as match-sticks, whereas Peterson as he remembered of old was almost as strong as he was.

He stared at Professor Scheidstrun's face. Yes—surely that nose was too good to be true. He pulled it thoughtfully and methodically —first this way then that—while the unhappy victim screamed with agony, and the junior clerk upset the ink in his excitement at the untoward spectacle.

It was real right enough—that nose. At least nothing had come off so far, and a little dazedly Drummond backed away, still staring at him. Surely he hadn't made a mistake: the gesture—that movement of the left hand had been quite unmistakable. And the next instant a terrific blow on the right ear turned his attention to other things.

He swung round to find a monumental woman regarding him with the light of battle in her eyes.

'How dare you,' she boomed, 'the nose of my Heinrich pull?'

With great agility Drummond dodged a heavy second to the jaw, and it was now his turn to flee for safety. And it took a bit of doing. The lady was out for blood, as a heavy volume on the intricacies of Real Estate which missed Drummond's head by half an inch and broke a flower-vase clearly proved.

'He seize my wig; he try to pull off my nose,' wailed the Professor, as Mr Tootem, junior, attracted by the din, rushed in.

'And if I the coward catch,' bellowed his spouse, picking up a companion volume on Probate and Divorce, 'I will not try—I will succeed with this.'

'Three to one on the filly,' murmured young Tootem gracelessly,

94

as with a heavy crash Probate and Divorce shot through the window.

But mercifully for all concerned, especially the reputation of Tootem, Price & Tootem, it proved to be the lady's dying gasp. Completely exhausted she sank into a chair, and Drummond cautiously emerged from behind a table. He was feeling a little faint himself; the need for alcohol was pressing. One thing even to his whirling brain was beyond dispute. Impossible though it was that Peterson should have shrunk, it was even more impossible that Irma should have swollen. By no conceivable art of disguise could that beautiful and graceful girl have turned herself into the human monstrosity who was now regarding him balefully from her chair. Her arms were twice the size of his own, and unless Irma had developed elephantiasis the thing simply could not be. Of course she might have covered herself with india-rubber and blown herself out in some way; he didn't put anything beyond Peterson. But the thought of pricking her with a pin to make sure was beyond even his nerve. It was too early in the day to ask any woman to burst with a slow whistling noise. And if she was real . . . He trembled violently at the mere thought of what would happen.

No; incredible though it was, he had made a ghastly mistake. Moreover, the next move was clearly with him.

'I'm afraid I've made a bloomer,' he murmured, mopping his forehead. 'What about a small spot all round, and—er—I'll try to explain.'

It cannot be said that he found the process of explaining an easy one. The lady in particular, having got her second wind, seemed only too ready to cut the cackle and get down to it again; and, as Drummond had to admit even to himself, the explanation sounded a bit lame. To assault unmercifully an elderly German savant in a lawyer's office merely because he was drumming with his left hand on his knee was, as Mr Tootem junior put it, a shade over the odds. And his excuse for so doing—his description of the inconceivable villainies of Carl Peterson in the past—was received coldly.

In fact Hugh Drummond proceeded to spend an extremely unpleasant twenty minutes, which might have been considerably prolonged but for Mr Tootem senior remembering that the umpires were just about coming out at Lord's.

He rose from his chair pontifically.

'I think we must assume,' he remarked, 'that this misguided young man was actuated by worthy motives, even though his actions left much to be desired. His keenness to safeguard the valuable notes of my late lamented client no doubt inspired his amazing outburst. And since he has apologised so profusely to you, Professor—and also, my dear Madam, to you—I would suggest that you might see your way to accepting that apology, and that we—ah—might terminate the interview. I have no doubt that now that Captain Drummond has satisfied himself so—ah—practically that you are not—I forget his friend's name—he will have no hesitation in handing over the notes to me. Should he still refuse, I shall, of course, have no other alternative but to send for the police—which would cause a most unpleasant contretemps for all concerned. Especially on the very day of the—er—funeral.'

Drummond fumbled in his pocket.

'I'll hand 'em over right enough,' he remarked wearily. 'I wish I'd never seen the blamed things.'

He passed the sheets of paper across the desk to Mr Tootem.

'If I don't get outside a pint of beer soon,' he continued, reaching for his hat, 'there will be a double event in the funeral line.'

Once again he apologised profusely to the German, and staggered slightly in his tracks as he gazed at the lady. Then blindly he made his way to the door, and twenty minutes later he entered his house a comparatively broken man. Even Algy awoke from his lethargy and gazed at him appalled.

'You mean to say you pulled the old bean's nose?' he gasped.

'This way and that,' sighed Hugh. 'And very, very hard. Only nothing like as hard as his wife hit me. She's got a sweeping left, Algy, like the kick of a mule. Good Lord! what an unholy box-up. I must say if it hadn't been for old Tootem, it might have been deuced serious. The office looked like the morning after a wet night.'

'So you've handed over the notes?'

'I have,' said Hugh savagely. 'And as I told old Tootem in his office, I wish to heavens I'd never seen the bally things. Old Scheidstrun's got 'em, and he can keep 'em.'

Which was where the error occurred. Professor Scheidstrun had certainly got them—Mr Tootem senior had pressed them into his hands with almost indecent brevity the instant Drummond left the office—but Professor Scheidstrun was not going to keep them. At that very moment, in fact, he was handing them over to a benevolent-looking old gentleman with mutton-chop whiskers in a room in Mr Atkinson's house in the quiet square.

'Tell me all about it,' murmured the old gentleman, with a smile. 'You've no idea how interested I am in it. I would have given quite a lot to have been present myself.'

'*Mein Gott!*' grunted the Professor. 'He is a holy terror, that man. He tear off my wig; he try to tear off my nose.'

'And then I him on the ear hit,' boomed his wife.

'Splendid,' chuckled the other. 'Quite splendid. He is a violent young man at times is Captain Drummond.'

'It was that the colour of my wig was different that first made him suspect,' went on the German. 'And then I do what you tell me—I tap with my left hand so upon my knee. The next moment he jumps upon me like a madman.'

'I thought he probably would,' said the old gentleman. 'A very amusing little experiment in psychology. You might make a note of it, Professor. The surest way of allaying suspicions is to arouse them thoroughly, and then prove that they are groundless. Hence your somewhat sudden summons by aeroplane from Germany. I have arranged that you should return in the same manner to-morrow after the funeral—which you will attend this afternoon.'

'It was inconvenient—that summons,' said his wife heavily. 'And my husband has been assaulted . . .'

Her words died away as she looked at the benevolent old man. For no trace of benevolence remained on his face, and she shuddered uncontrollably.

'People who do inconvenient things, Frau,' he said quietly, 'and get found out must expect inconvenient calls to be made upon them.'

'How long is this to continue?' she demanded. 'How long are we to remain in your power? This is the second time that you have impersonated my husband. I tell you when I heard that young man speaking this morning, and knew how near he was to the truth—almost did I tell him.'

'But not quite. Not quite, Frau Scheidstrun. You are no fool; you know what would have happened if you had. I still hold the proofs of your husband's unfortunate slip a year or two ago.'

His eyes were boring into her, and once again she shuddered.

'I shall impersonate your husband when and where I please,' he continued, 'if it suits my convenience. I regard him as one of my most successful character-studies.'

His tone changed; he was the benevolent old gentleman again.

'Come, come, my dear Frau Scheidstrun,' he remarked affably, 'you take an exaggerated view of things. After all, the damage to your husband's nose is slight, considering the far-reaching results obtained by letting that young man pull it. All his suspicions are allayed; he merely thinks he's made a profound ass of himself. Which is just as it should be. Moreover, with the mark in its present depreciated state, I think the cheque I propose to hand to your husband for the trouble he has taken will ease matters in the housekeeping line.'

He rose from his chair chuckling.

'Well, I think that is all. As I said before, you will attend the funeral this afternoon. Such a performance does not call for conversation, and so it will not be necessary for me to prime you with anything more than you know already. Your brother-scientists, who will doubtless be there in force, you will know how to deal with far better than I, seeing that I should undoubtedly fail to recognise any of them. And should Drummond be there—well, my dear fellow, I leave it to your sense of Christian decency as to how you treat him. In the presence of—ah—death'—the old gentleman blew his nose—'a policy of kindly charity is, I think, indicated. Anyway, don't, I beg of you, so far forget yourself as to pull *his* nose. For without your wife to protect you I shudder to think what the results might be.'

He smiled genially as he lit a cigar.

'And you,' said the German, 'you do not the funeral attend?'

'My dear Professor,' murmured the other, 'you surprise me. In what capacity do you suggest that I should attend this melancholy function? Even the mourners might be a trifle surprised if they saw two of us there. And as Mr William Robinson—my present rôle—I had not the pleasure of the deceased gentleman's acquaintance. No; I am going into the country to join my brother—the poor fellow is failing a little mentally. Freyder will make all arrangements for your departure tomorrow, and so I will say good-bye. You have committed to memory—have you not?—the hours and days when you did things in London before you arrived? And destroyed the paper? Good; a document of that sort is dangerous. Finally, Professor, don't forget your well-known reputation for absent-mindedness and eccentricity. Should anyone ask you a question about your doings in London which you find difficult to answer, just give your celebrated imitation of a windmill and say nothing. I may remark that if Freyder's telephone report to me is satisfactory this evening, I shall have no hesitation in doubling the amount I suggested as your fee.'

With a wave of his hand he was gone, and Professor Scheidstrun and his wife watched the big car drive away from the door.

'*Gott im Himmel*,' muttered the German. 'But the man is a devil.'

'His money is far from the devil,' replied his wife prosaically. 'If he doubles it, we shall have five hundred pounds. And five hundred pounds will be very useful just now.'

But her husband was not to be comforted.

'I am frightened, Minna,' he said tremulously. 'We know not what we are mixed up in. He has told us nothing as to why he is doing all this.'

'He has told us all that he wishes us to know,' answered his wife. 'That is his way.'

'Why he is dressed up like that?' continued the Professor. 'And how did Goodman really die?' He stared fearfully at his wife. 'Blown up? Yes. But—by whom?'

'Be silent, Heinrich,' said his wife, but fear was in her eyes too. 'It is not good to think of these things. Let us have lunch, and then you must go to the funeral. And after that he will send us the money, as he did last time, and we will go back to Dresden. Then we will pray the good God that he will leave us alone.'

'What frightens me, Minna, is that it is I who am supposed to have been with Goodman on the afternoon it happened. And if the police should find out things, what am I to say? Already there are people who suspect—that big man this morning, for instance. How am I to prove that it was not I, but that devil made up to look like me? *Mein Gott*, but he is clever. I should not have hidden myself away as he told me to do in his letter.'

'He would have found out if you hadn't,' said his wife. 'He knows everything.'

'There was no one who saw us start,' went on the German excitedly. 'At least no one who saw me start. You they saw—but me, I was smuggled into the aeroplane. Everything is accounted for by that devil. It is impossible for me to prove an alibi. For four days I have concealed myself; our friends all think, as you told them, that I have gone to England. They think you follow, and they will see us return. Would anyone believe us if now we said it was all a lie? They would say—why did you remain hidden? What was the

99

object of all this deceit? And I—what can I say? That I am in the power of someone whom, to save my life, I cannot describe. No one would believe me; it would make my position worse.'

He grew almost hysterical in his agitation.

'There is one comfort, my dear,' said his wife soothingly. 'As long as everyone believes that it was you who was with Professor Goodman they are not likely to suspect very much. For foul play there must be a motive, and there could be no motive in your case. No, Heinrich, that devil has foreseen everything. No one was suspicious except the big man this morning, and now he is suspicious no longer. All that we have to do is just what we are told, and we shall be safe. But, *mein Gott*, I wish that we were on board that foul machine again, even though I shall assuredly be sick the whole way.'

The worthy woman rose and placed a hand like a leg of mutton on her husband's shoulder.

'Lunch,' she continued. 'And then you must go to the funeral, while I await you here.'

And so an hour later Professor Scheidstrun, fortified by a most excellent meal, chartered a taxi and drove off to attend the ceremony. After all, his wife was a woman of sound common sense, and there was much in what she said. Moreover, five hundred pounds was not obtained every day. With his usual diabolical cleverness that man, whose real name even he did not know, had so arranged things that his scheme would succeed. He always did succeed; this would be no exception. And provided the scheme was successful, he personally would be safe.

He stepped out at the church door and paid his fare. A celebrated Scotch chemist whom he knew, and who was entering the church at the same moment, stopped and spoke a few words with him, and for a while they stood chatting on the pavement outside. Then the Scotchman moved away, and the Professor was about to enter the church when someone touched him on the arm.

He turned to find a young man, wearing an eyeglass, whom he had never seen before in his life.

'Afternoon, Professor,' said the young man.

The Professor grunted. Who on earth was this? Some relative presumably of the dead man.

'You don't seem to remember me,' went on the young man slowly.

The fact was hardly surprising, but mindful of his instructions the German waved his arms vaguely and endeavoured to escape into the church. But the young man, whose eyes had narrowed suddenly, was not to be shaken off quite so easily.

'One moment, Professor,' he said quietly. '*Do* you remember me?'

Again the German grunted unintelligibly, but his brain was working quickly. Obviously this young man knew him; therefore he ought obviously to know the young man.

'Ja,' he grunted, 'I haf met you, but I know not where.'

'Don't you remember coming round to Captain Drummond's house yesterday afternoon?' went on the other.

'Of course,' said the Professor, beginning to feel firm ground again. 'It was there that we did meet.'

'That's it,' said the young man cheerfully. 'I was one of the four fellows there with Drummond.'

'It vos stupid of me to haf forgotten,' remarked the German, breathing an inward sign of relief. 'But so many were there, that must be my excuse.'

He escaped into the church, and Algy Longworth made no further attempt to detain him. Without thought, and as a mere matter of politeness, he had spoken to the Professor on seeing him, to be greeted with the blank stare of complete non-recognition. And now the German had concurred in his statement that there had been five of them in the room during the interview, whereas only Hugh and he himself had been present. The short service was drawing to a close, and Algy, who had not heard a word, still stared thoughtfully at the back of the Professor's head, two pews in front. He had noted the nods of greeting from several distinguished-looking old gentlemen as the German had entered the church; but five instead of two! Surely it was incredible that any man, however absent-minded and engrossed in other things, should have made such a mistake as that. Even poor old Goodman himself had not been as bad as that. Besides, he personally had spoken not once but several times to the German during the interview. He couldn't have forgotten so completely.

But the fact remained that after the service was over, Professor Scheidstrun chatted for some time with several other elderly men, who had apparently had no doubts as to his identity. In fact it was impossible to believe that the man was not what he professed to be, especially as he too, remembering what Hugh had said, had laid his hand on the German's arm outside the church and felt it. It was skinny and thin—and yet five instead of two! That was the thing that stuck in his gizzard.

If only he could think of some test question which would settle the matter! But he couldn't, and even if he had been able to there was no further chance of asking it. Professor Scheidstrun completely ignored his existence, and finally drove away without speaking to him again.

And it was a very puzzled young man who finally returned to Brook Street to find Hugh Drummond sunk in the depths of depression. He listened in silence to what Algy had to say, and then he shook his head.

'My dear old man,' he said at length, 'it cuts no ice. It's funny, I know. If you or I went round to have a buck with a fellow, we should remember whether the isolation was complete or whether we were crushed to death in the mob. But with these scientific blokes it's altogether different. He probably has completely forgotten the entire incident. And yet, Algy, the conviction is growing on me that I've been had for a mug. Somehow or other they've handed us the dirty end. I confess it's difficult to follow. I'm convinced that the man today in Tootem's office is the genuine article. And if he is it's almost impossible to believe that poor old Goodman's death was anything but an accident. Then where's the catch? That's what I've been trying to puzzle out for the last three hours, and I'm just where I was when I started.'

'You think that German is going to do what he said? Go back and carry on with Goodman's discovery?'

'I don't know what else to think.'

'Then I'll tell you one thing, Hugh,' said Algy thoughtfully. 'You'd have a death from heat-apoplexy if old Blantyre knew it. And he was showing no signs of a rush of blood to the face at the funeral today.'

Drummond sat up and stared at his friend.

'Which means either that he doesn't know anything about it and believes that the secret died with Goodman; or else, Algy, he's got at Scheidstrun. Somehow or other he's found out about that letter, and he's induced the German to part with the notes.'

He rose and paced up and down the room.

'Or else—Great Scott! Algy, can it be possible that the whole thing has been carefully worked from beginning to end? Blantyre went over to Switzerland—Toby told me that. He went over looking like a sick headache and came back bursting with himself.'

Drummond's face was hard.

'If I thought that that swine had deliberately hired the German to murder poor old Goodman . . .'

His great hands were clenched by his side, as he stared grimly out of the window.

'I made a fool of myself this morning,' he went on after a while. 'I suppose I've got Carl Peterson on the brain. But there are other swine in the world, Algy, beside him. And if I could prove . . .'

'Quite,' remarked Algy. 'But how the devil can you prove anything?'

Suddenly Drummond swung round.

'I'm going round to see Blantyre now,' he said decisively. 'Will you come?'

CHAPTER 7

In Which Drummond Takes a Telephone Call and Regrets It

Half an hour later Algy and he walked through the unpretentious door that led to the office of the Metropolitan Diamond Syndicate, to be greeted with a shout of joy from Toby Sinclair emerging from an inner room.

'You have come to ask me to consume nourishment at your expense,' he cried. 'I know it. I accept. I will also dine this evening.'

'Dry up, Toby,' grunted Hugh. 'Is your boss in?'

'Sir Raymond? Yes—why?'

'I want to see him,' said Hugh quietly.

'My dear old man, I'm sorry, but it's quite out of the question,' answered Toby. 'There's a meeting of the whole syndicate on at the present moment upstairs, and . . .'

'I want to see Sir Raymond Blantyre,' interrupted Hugh. 'And, Toby, I'm going to see Sir Raymond Blantyre. And if his darned syndicate is there, I'll see his syndicate as well.'

'But, Hugh, old man,' spluttered Toby, 'be reasonable. It's an important business meeting, and . . .'

Hugh laid his hands on Toby's shoulders and grinned.

'Toby, don't waste time. Trot along upstairs—bow nicely, and say "Captain Drummond craves audience". And when he asks what for, just say, "In connection with an explosion which took place at Hampstead." '

And of a sudden it seemed as if a strange tension had come into Toby Sinclair's room. For Toby was one of those who had hunted with Hugh in days gone by, and he recognised the look in the big man's eyes. Something was up—something serious, that he knew at once. And certain nebulous, half-formed suspicions which he had vigorously suppressed in his own mind stirred into being.

'What is it, old man?' he asked quietly.

'I'll know better after the interview, Toby,' answered the other. 'But one thing I will tell you now. It's either nothing at all, or else your boss is one of the most blackguardly villains alive in London today. Now go up and tell him.'

And without another word Toby Sinclair went. Probably not for another living man would he have interrupted the meeting upstairs. But the habits of other days held; when Hugh Drummond gave an order, it was carried out.

A minute later he was down again.

'Sir Raymond will see you at once, Hugh,' and for Toby Sinclair his expression was thoughtful. For the sudden silence that had settled on the room of directors as he gave the message had not escaped his attention. And the air of carefully suppressed nervous expectancy on the part of the Metropolitan Diamond Syndicate did not escape Drummond's attention either as he entered, followed by Algy Longworth.

'Captain Drummond?' Sir Raymond Blantyre rose, and indicated a chair with his hand. 'Ah! and Mr Longworth surely. Please sit down. I think I saw you in the distance at the funeral today. Now, Captain Drummond, perhaps you will tell us what you want as quickly as possible, as we are in the middle of a rather important meeting.'

'I will try to be as short as possible, Sir Raymond,' said Drummond quietly. 'It concerns, as you have probably guessed, the sad death of Professor Goodman, in which I, personally, am very interested. You see, the Professor lunched with me at my club on the day of his death.'

'Indeed,' murmured Sir Raymond politely.

'Yes—I met him in St James's Square, where he'd been followed.'

'Followed,' said one of the directors. 'What do you mean?'

'Exactly what I say. He was being followed. He was also in a very excited condition owing to the fact that he had just received a letter threatening his life, unless he consented to accept two hundred and fifty thousand pounds as the price for suppressing his discovery for manufacturing diamonds cheaply. But you know all this part, don't you?'

'I know nothing whatever about a threatening letter,' said Sir Raymond. 'It's the first I've heard of it. Of his process, of course, I know. I think Mr Longworth was present at the dinner on the night I examined the ornament Miss Goodman was wearing. And believing then that the process was indeed capable of producing genuine diamonds, I did offer Professor Goodman a quarter of a million pounds to suppress it.'

'Believing *then*?' said Drummond, staring at him.

'Yes; for a time I and my colleagues here did really believe that the discovery had been made,' answered Sir Raymond easily. 'And I will go as far as to say that even as it stands the process—now so unfortunately lost to science—produced most marvellous imitations. In fact'—he gave a deprecatory laugh—'it produced such marvellous imitations that it deceived us. But they will not stand the test of time. In some samples he made for us at a demonstration minute flaws are already beginning to show themselves—flaws which only the expert would notice, but they're there.'

'I see,' murmured Drummond quietly, and Sir Raymond shifted a little in his chair. Ridiculous though it was, this vast young man facing him had a peculiarly direct stare which he found almost disconcerting.

'I see,' repeated Drummond. 'So the system was a dud.'

'Precisely, Captain Drummond. The system was of no use. A gigantic advance, you will understand, on anything that has ever been done before in that line—but still, of no use. And if one may extract some little ray of comfort from the appalling tragedy which caused Professor Goodman's death, it surely is that he was at any rate spared from the laughter of the scientific world whose good opinion he valued so greatly.'

Sir Raymond leaned back in his chair, and a murmur of sympathetic approval for words well and truly uttered passed round the room. And feeling considerably more sure of himself, it dawned on the mind of the chairman that up to date he had done most of the talking, and that so far his visitor's principal contribution had been confined to monosyllables. Who was he, anyway, this Captain Drummond? Some friend of the idiotic youth with the eyeglass, presumably. He began to wonder why he had ever consented to see him.

'However, Captain Drummond,' he continued with a trace of asperity, 'you doubtless came round to speak to me about something. And since we are rather busy this evening . . .'

He broke off and waited.

'I did wish to speak to you,' said Drummond, carefully selecting a cigarette. 'But since the process is no good, I don't think it matters very much.'

'It is certainly no good,' answered Sir Raymond.

'So I'm afraid old Scheidstrun will only be wasting his time.'

For a moment it almost seemed as if the clock had stopped, so intense was the sudden silence.

'I don't quite understand what you mean,' said Sir Raymond, in a voice which, strive as he would, he could not make quite steady.

'No?' murmured Drummond placidly. 'You didn't know of Professor Goodman's last instructions? However, since the whole thing is a dud, I won't worry you.'

'What do you know of Scheidstrun?' asked Sir Raymond.

'Just a funny old Boche. He came to see me yesterday afternoon with the Professor's last will, so to speak. And then I interviewed him this morning in the office of the excellent Mr Tootem, and pulled his nose—poor old dear!'

'Professor Scheidstrun came to see you?' cried Sir Raymond, standing up suddenly. 'What for?'

'Why, to get the notes of the diamond process, which the Professor gave me at lunch on the day of his death.'

Drummond thoughtfully lit his cigarette, apparently oblivious of the fact that every man in the room was glaring at him speechlessly.

'But since it's a dud—I'm afraid he'll waste his time.'

'But the notes were destroyed.' Every vestige of control had left Sir Raymond's voice; his agitation was obvious.

'How do you know?' snapped Drummond, and the President of the Metropolitan Diamond Syndicate found himself staring almost fascinated at a pair of eyes from which every trace of laziness had vanished.

'He always carried them with him,' he stammered. 'And I—er—assumed . . .'

'Then you assumed wrong. Professor Goodman handed me those notes at lunch the day he died.'

'Where are they now?' It was Mr Leibhaus who asked the question in his guttural voice.

'Since they are of no use, what does it matter?' answered Drummond indifferently.

'Gentlemen!' Sir Raymond's peremptory voice checked the sudden buzz of conversation. 'Captain Drummond,' he remarked, 'I must confess that what you have told me this afternoon has given me a slight shock. As I say, I had assumed that the notes of the process had perished with the Professor. You now tell us that he handed them to you. Well, I make no bones about it that though—from a purely scientific point of view the process fails—yet—er—from a business point of view it is not one that any of us would care to have noised abroad. You will understand that if diamonds can be made cheaply which except to the eye of the most practical expert are real, it will—er—not be a good thing for those who are interested in the diamond market. You can understand that, can't you?'

'I tell you what I can't understand, Sir Raymond,' said Drummond quietly. 'And that is that you're a damned bad poker-player. If flaws—as you say—have appeared in the diamonds manufactured by this process, you and your pals here would not now be giving the finest example of a vertical typhoon that I've ever seen.'

Sir Raymond subsided in his chair a little foolishly; he felt at a complete loss as to where he stood with this astonishing young man. And it was left to Mr Leibhaus to make the next move.

'Let us leave that point for the moment,' he remarked. 'Where are these notes now?'

'I've already told you,' replied Drummond casually. 'The worthy Scheidstrun has them. And in accordance with Professor Goodman's written instructions he proposes to give the secret to the world of science at an early date. In fact he is going back to Germany tomorrow to do so.'

'But the thing is impossible,' cried Sir Raymond, recovering his speech. 'You mean to say that Professor Goodman left written instructions that the notes of his process were to be handed over to—to Scheidstrun?'

'I do,' returned Drummond. 'And if you want confirmation, you can ring up Mr Tootem of Austin Friars—Professor Goodman's lawyer. He saw the letter, and it was in his office the notes were handed over.'

'You will excuse me, Captain Drummond, if I confer for a few moments with my friends,' said Sir Raymond, rising.

The directors of the Metropolitan Diamond Syndicate withdrew to the farther end of the long room, leaving Drummond still sitting at the table. And to that gentleman's shrewd eye it was soon apparent that his chance arrow had hit the mark, though exactly what mark it was, was still beyond him. But the agitation displayed by the group of men in the window was too obvious to miss, and had he known all the facts he would have found it hardly surprising. The directors were faced unexpectedly with as thorny a problem as could well be devised.

Believing as they had that the notes had been destroyed—had not Mr Edward Blackton assured them of that fact?—they had unanimously decided to adopt the rôle that the process had proved useless, thereby removing any possible suspicion that might attach itself to them. And now they found that not only had the notes not been destroyed, but that they were in the possession of Blackton himself. And it needed but little imagination to realise that dangerous though the knowledge of the process had been in the hands of Professor Goodman, it was twenty times more so in the hands of Blackton if he meant to double-cross them.

That was the point: did he? Or had he discovered somehow or other that Drummond held the notes and taken these steps in order to get them?

And the second little matter which had to be solved was how much this man Drummond knew. If he knew nothing at all, why had he bothered to come round and see them? It was out of the question, surely, that he could have any inkling of the real truth concerning the bogus Professor Scheidstrun. Had not the impersonation deceived even London scientists who knew the real man at the funeral that afternoon?

For a while the directors conferred together in whispers; then Sir

Raymond advanced towards the table. The first thing was to get rid of Drummond.

'I am sure we are all very much obliged to you, Captain Drummond, for taking so much trouble and coming round to see us, but I don't think there is anything more you can do. Should an opportunity arise I will take steps to let Professor Scheidstrun know what we think——'

He held out a cordial hand to terminate the interview.

But it takes two people to terminate an interview, and Drummond had no intention of being the second. He realised that he was on delicate ground and that it behoved him to walk warily. But his conviction that something was wrong somewhere was stronger than ever, and he was determined to try to get to the bottom of it.

'It might perhaps be as well, Sir Raymond,' he remarked, 'to go round and tell him now. I know where he is stopping.'

Was it his imagination, or did the men in the window look at one another uneasily?

'As I told you, I pulled the poor old bean's nose this morning, and it seems a good way of making amends.'

Sir Raymond stared at him.

'May I ask you why you pulled his nose?'

And Drummond decided on a bold move.

'Because, Sir Raymond, I came to the conclusion that Professor Scheidstrun was not Professor Scheidstrun, but somebody else.' There was no mistaking the air of tension now. 'I may say that I was mistaken.'

'Who did you think he was?' Sir Raymond gave a forced laugh.

'A gentleman of international reputation,' said Drummond quietly, 'who masquerades under a variety of names. I knew him first as Carl Peterson, but he answers to a lot of titles. The Comte de Guy is one of them.'

And now the atmosphere was electric, a fact which did not escape Drummond. His eyes had narrowed; he was sitting very still. In the language of the old nursery game, he was getting warm.

'But I conclusively proved, gentlemen,' he continued, 'that the man to whom I handed those notes this morning was not the Comte de Guy. The Comte, gentlemen, has arms as big as mine. His physical strength is very great. This man had arms like walking-sticks, and he couldn't have strangled a mouse.'

One by one the men at the window had returned to their seats,

109

and now they sat in perfect silence staring at Drummond. What on earth was this new complication, or was this man deliberately deceiving them?

'Do you know the Comte de Guy well?' said Sir Raymond after a pause.

'Very well,' remarked Drummond. 'Do you?'

'I have heard of him,' answered the other.

'Then, as you probably know, his power of disguising himself is so miraculous as to be uncanny. He has one little mannerism, however, which he sometimes shows in moments of excitement whatever his disguise. And it has enabled me to spot him on one or two occasions. When therefore I saw that little trick of his in the lawyer's office this morning, I jumped to the conclusion that my old friend was on the war-path again. So I leaped upon him and the subsequent scene was dreadful. It was not my old friend at all, but a complete stranger with a vast wife who nearly felled me with a blow on the ear.'

He selected another cigarette with care.

'However,' he continued casually, 'it's a very good thing for you that the process is a dud. Because I am sure nothing would induce him to disregard Professor Goodman's wishes on the subject if it hadn't been.'

'You say you know where he is stopping?' said Sir Raymond.

'I do,' answered Drummond.

'Then I think perhaps that it would be a good thing to do as you suggest, and go round and see him now.' He had been thinking rapidly while Drummond was speaking, and one or two points were clear. In some miraculous way this young man had blundered on to the truth. That the man Drummond had met in the lawyer's office that morning was any other than Blackton he did not for a moment believe. But Blackton had bluffed him somehow, and for the time had thrown him off the scent. The one vital thing was to prevent him getting on to it again. And since there was no way of telling what Drummond would find when he went round to the house, it was imperative that he should be there himself. For if there was one person whom Sir Raymond did not expect to meet there, it was Professor Scheidstrun. And in that event he must be on hand to see what happened.

'Shall we go at once? My car is here.'

'By all means,' said Drummond, 'And if there's room we might

110

take Algy as well. He gets into mischief if he's left lying about.'

On one point at any rate Sir Raymond's expectations were not realised. Professor Scheidstrun was at the house right enough; in fact he and his wife had just finished their tea. And neither the worthy Teuton nor his spouse evinced the slightest pleasure on seeing their visitors. With the termination of the funeral they had believed their troubles to be over, and now this extremely powerful and objectionable young man had come to worry them again, to say nothing of his friend who had spoken to the Professor at the funeral. And what did Sir Raymond Blantyre want? Scheidstrun had been coached carefully as to whom and what Sir Raymond was, but what on earth had he come round about? Especially with Drummond?

It was the latter who stated the reason of their visit.

'I've come about those notes, Professor,' he remarked cheerfully. 'You know—the ones that caused that slight breeze in old Tootem's office this morning.'

'So,' grunted the Professor, blinking uneasily behind his spectacles. It struck him that the ground was getting dangerous.

'I feel,' went on Drummond affably, 'that after our unfortunate little contretemps I ought to try to make some amends. And as I know you're a busy man I shouldn't like you to waste your time needlessly. Now, you propose, don't you, to carry on with Professor Goodman's process, and demonstrate it to the world at large?'

'That is so,' said the German.

Out of the corner of his eye Drummond looked at Sir Raymond, but the President of the Metropolitan Diamond Syndicate was staring impassively out of the window.

'Well, I'm sorry to say the process is a dud; a failure; no bally earthly. You get me, I trust.'

'A failure. Ach! is dot so?' rumbled Scheidstrun, who was by this time completely out of his depth.

'And that being the case, Professor,' murmured Sir Raymond, 'it would be better to destroy the notes at once, don't you think? I was under the impression'—he added pointedly—'that they had already been destroyed in the accident.'

Strangely enough, the presence of Drummond gave him a feeling of confidence with Mr Edward Blackton which he had never experienced before. And this was a golden opportunity for securing the destruction of those accursed papers, and thus preventing any possibility of his being double-crossed.

'Shall we therefore destroy them at once?' he repeated quietly.

The German fidgeted in his chair. Willingly would he have destroyed them on the spot if they had still been in his possession. Anything to be rid of his visitors. He glanced from one to the other of them. Drummond was apparently staring at the flies on the ceiling; Sir Raymond was staring at him, and his stare was full of some hidden meaning. But since it was manifestly impossible for him to do as Sir Raymond suggested, the only thing to do was to temporise.

'I fear that to destroy them I cannot,' he murmured. 'At least—not yet. My duty to my dear friend . . .'

'Duty be damned!' snarled Sir Raymond, forgetting Drummond's presence in his rage. This swine *was* trying to double-cross him after all. 'You'll destroy those notes here and now, or . . .'

With a great effort he pulled himself together.

'Or what?' asked Drummond mildly. 'You seem strangely determined, Sir Raymond, that Professor Scheidstrun shouldn't waste his time. Deuced praiseworthy, I call it, on your part. . . . Interests of science and all that. . . .'

Sir Raymond smothered a curse, and glared still more furiously at the German. And suddenly Drummond rose to his feet, and strolled over to the open window.

'Well, I don't think there's much good our waiting here,' he remarked in a bored voice. 'If he wants to fool round with the process, he must. Coming, Sir Raymond?'

'In a moment or two, Captain Drummond. Don't you wait.'

'Right. Come on, Algy. Apologies again about the nose, Professor. So long.'

He opened the door, and paused outside for Algy to join him. And every trace of boredom had vanished from his face.

'Go downstairs noisily,' he whispered. 'Make a remark as if I was with you. Go out and slam the front door. Then hang about and wait for me.'

'Right,' answered the other. 'But what are you going to do?'

'Listen to their conversation, old man. I have an idea it may be interesting.'

Without a sound he opened the door of the next room and went in. It was a bedroom and it was empty, and Drummond heaved a sigh of relief. The window, he knew, would be open—he had seen that as he looked out in the other room. Moreover, the square was a quiet one; he could hear easily what was being said next door by leaning out.

And for the next five minutes he leaned out, and he heard. And so engrossed was he in what he heard that he quite failed to notice a dark-skinned, sturdy man who paused abruptly on the pavement a few houses away, and disappeared as suddenly as he had come. So engrossed was he in what he heard that he even failed to hear a faint click from the door behind him a few moments later.

All he noticed was that the voices in the next room suddenly ceased, but he had heard quite enough. There was not one Scheidstrun, but two Scheidstruns, and he had assaulted the wrong one. Of Mr Edward Blackton he had never heard; but there was only one man living who could have suggested that unmistakable trick with his hand—the man he knew as Carl Peterson. Somehow or other he had found out this mannerism of his and had used it deliberately to bluff Drummond, even as he had deliberately double-crossed the Metropolitan Diamond Syndicate. It was just the sort of thing that would appeal to his sense of humour.

So be it: they would crack a jest together over it later. At the moment he wanted a word or two with Sir Raymond Blantyre. He crossed to the door and tried to open it. But the door was locked, and the key was on the outside.

For a moment or two he stood staring at it. His mind was still busy with the staggering conversation he had been listening to, which had almost, if not quite, explained everything. Facts, disconnected before, now joined themselves together in a more or less logical sequence. Sir Raymond Blantyre's visit to Montreux to enlist the aid of this Mr Edward Blackton; the arrival in England of the spurious Professor Scheidstrun; the accident at Hampstead—all that part was clear now. And with regard to that accident, Drummond's face was grim. Cold-blooded murder it must have been, in spite of all Sir Raymond's guarded utterances on the subject.

For it had taken that gentleman ten minutes before he finally realised that the Scheidstrun he was talking to was the genuine article, and during that ten minutes he had spoken with some freedom. And then when he had finally realised it, and grasped the fact that he and his syndicate had been double-crossed, his rage had been terrible. Moreover, he had then said things which made matters even clearer to the man who was listening in the next room. Out of his own mouth he stood condemned as the instigator of an abominable crime.

But Sir Raymond could wait; there would be plenty of time later to deal with that gentleman and his syndicate. The man who called himself Edward Blackton was the immediate necessity, and Drummond had no illusions now as to his identity. It *was* Carl Peterson again, and with the faintest flicker of a smile he acknowledged the touch of genius that had caused him to pass on his little mannerism to the genuine Scheidstrun. It had had exactly the intended effect: certainty that they had again met in the lawyer's office, followed immediately by a crushing proof to the contrary—a proof so overwhelming that but for vague suspicion engendered by the Professor's non-recognition of Algy at the funeral he would have let the whole thing drop.

It was just like Peterson to bluff to the limit of his hand; moreover, it would have appealed to his sense of humour. And the point which was not clear to either Sir Raymond or the German was very clear to him. To them it had seemed an unnecessary complication to bring over the genuine Scheidstrun—but there Drummond could supply the missing link. And that link was his previous acquaintance with the arch-criminal. The combination of shrewd insight and consummate nerve which deliberately banked on that previous acquaintance and turned it to gain was Peterson all over— or rather Blackton, to give him his present name. Moreover, the advantage of having the genuine article at the funeral where he was bound to run into many friends and acquaintances was obvious. Most assuredly the touch of the master-hand was in evidence again, but where was the hand itself? It was that question which Sir Raymond, almost inarticulate with rage, had asked again and again; and it was the answer to that question which Professor Scheidstrun would not or could not give. Listening intently, Drummond had inclined to the latter alternative, though not being able to see the speaker's face, he had had to rely on inflection of voice. But it had seemed to him as if he was speaking the truth when he absolutely denied any knowledge whatever of Blackton's whereabouts. An old gentleman with mutton-chop whiskers—that was all he could say. But where he was, or what he was doing, he knew no more than Sir Raymond. He had left that morning with the notes in his possession, and that was all he could tell his infuriated questioner.

And then a sudden silence had fallen while Drummond still craned out of the window listening—a silence which endured so long that finally he stepped back into the room, only to discover that he was locked in. For a moment or two, as has been said, he stood staring at the door; then with a grunt he charged it with his shoulders. But the door was strong, and it took him three minutes before, with a final splintering crash, the door burst open, almost throwing him on his face. For a while he stood listening: the house was silent. And since in ordinary respectable houses the bursting open of a door is not greeted with absolute silence, Drummond's hand went automatically to his hip-pocket. Past association with Peterson accounted for the involuntary movement, but much water had flowed under the bridge since those happy days, and with a sigh he realised that he was unarmed. With his back to the wall he took careful stock of his surroundings. Every nerve was alert for possible eventualities; his arms, hanging a little forward, were tingling at the prospect of action.

Still there was no sound. The passage was deserted; all the doors were shut. And yet keys do not turn by themselves. Someone had locked him in: the question was, who had done it? And where was he? Or could it be a she? Could it be that monumental woman who had assaulted him only that morning? He turned a little pale at the thought; but with the knowledge that he now possessed of her husband's complicity in the affair he felt he could meet her on rather more level terms. And there was comfort in the knowledge that everyone in the house was so confoundedly crooked. The likelihood of their sending for the police to eject him from the premises was, to put it mildly, remote.

Silently as a cat, he took a quick step along the passage and flung open the door of the room in which he had left Sir Raymond Blantyre and the German. It was empty; there was no sign of either man. He crossed to one of the heavy curtains which was drawn back in the window behind the desk, and hit it a heavy blow with his fist. But the folds went back unresistingly; there was no one hiding behind it. And then swiftly and methodically he went from room to room, moving with that strange, silent tread which was one of his most marked peculiarities. No one ever heard Drummond coming; in the darkness no one ever saw him, if he didn't wish him

115

to. The first thing he knew of his presence was a pair of great hands which seemed to materialise out of the night, forcing his head backwards and farther back. And sometimes that was the last thing he knew as well. . . .

But there was no darkness in the house as he searched it from top to bottom—only silence. Once he thought he heard the sound of a step above him as he stood downstairs in the dining-room, but it was not repeated, and he decided it was only imagination—a board creaking, perhaps. He went into the kitchen and the scullery; the fire was lit in the range, but of cook or servant there was no sign.

And finally, he returned thoughtfully to the hall. There was no doubt about it, the house was empty save for himself. Sir Raymond and the German had gone during the period that he was locked in the room upstairs. And during that period the other occupants of the house, if any, had gone also.

He carefully selected a cigarette and lit it. The situation required reviewing.

Item one. Sir Raymond Blantyre was a consummate swine who had, by the grace of Allah, been stung on the raw by a hornet. Moreover, before Drummond had finished with him the hornets would have swarmed. But he could wait.

Item two. The genuine Professor Scheidstrun appeared to be a harmless old poop, who was more sinned against than sinning. And he certainly could wait.

Item three. The other Professor Scheidstrun—alias Blackton, alias Peterson, present address unknown—had got away with the goods. He was in full and firm possession of the momentous secret, which Blantyre had paid him half a million to destroy. And involuntarily Drummond smiled. How like him! How completely Peterson to the life! And then the smile faded. To get it, he had murdered a harmless old man in cold blood.

Item four. He himself was in undisputed possession of an empty house in which Peterson had been only that morning.

Could he turn item four to advantage in solving the address question in item three? Everything else was subservient to that essential fact: where was Peterson now? And from his knowledge of the gentleman it was unlikely that he had left directions for forwarding letters pasted conspicuously on the wall. He was one of those shy flowers that prefer to blush unseen. At the same time it was possible that an exhaustive search of the desk upstairs might

116

reveal some clue. And if it didn't, presumably the bird who had locked him in would return in due course to find out how he was getting on. Everything therefore pointed to a policy of masterly inactivity in the hopes that something or somebody would turn up.

He slowly ascended the stairs, and again entered the room where the interview had taken place. Time was of no particular object, and for a while he stood by the door turning over the problem in his mind. Then suddenly his eyes became alert: there was a door let into the wall which, by some strange oversight, he had not seen before. And in a flash he remembered the step which he thought he had heard while he was below. Was there someone in that room? and if so, who? Could it be possible—and a glow of wild excitement began to tingle in his veins at the mere thought—could it be possible that the solution of the problem lay close at hand? That here, practically in the same room with him, was Peterson himself?

With one bound he was across the room, and the door was open. One glance was sufficient to dash the dawning hope to the ground: the room was empty, like all the rest had been. But though it was empty it was not devoid of interest, and a faint smile came on Drummond's face as he surveyed the contents. Wigs, clothes, mirrors filled the place to overflowing, though there was no trace of untidiness. And he realised that he was in the inner sanctum where Peterson carried out his marvellous changes of appearance. And with a sudden grim amusement he recognised on a chair the identical egg-stained coat that the spurious Professor Scheidstrun had worn on his visit to him the preceding afternoon. In fact he was so interested in that and other things that he failed to notice a rather curious phenomenon in the room behind him. The heavy curtain which he had hit with his fist moved slightly as if blown by the wind. And there was no wind.

With genuine interest he examined the exhibits—as he called them in his own mind. It was the first time he had ever penetrated into one of Peterson's holy of holies, and though the proprietor was not there himself to act as showman, he was quite able to appreciate the museum without the services of a guide. The wigs—each one on its own head-rest—particularly appealed to him. In fact he went so far as to try some of them on. And after a time a feeling of genuine admiration for the wonderful thoroughness of the man filled his mind. Murderer, thief, forger, and blackguard generally—but what a brain! After all, he fought a lone hand, deliberately pitting himself against the whole of the organised resources of the world. With only the girl to help him he had fought mankind, and up to date he had won through. For both their previous battles had been drawn, and now that the third round was under way—or soon would be—he saluted his adversary in spirit as a foeman worthy of his steel. It was a good thing, after all, that he had not brought in the police. Peterson fought alone: so would he. As it had been in the past, so let it be this time. Their own particular pals on each side could join in the battle if and when occasion arose; but the principal combat must be between Peterson and him—no mercy given, no mercy asked. And this time he had a presentiment that it would be a fight to a finish. It required no stretch of imagination on his part to realise the enormous plum which the criminal had got hold of; it required no stretch of imagination to realise that he would fight as he had never fought before to retain it.

And once again there came up the unanswered question—where was he? It was even impossible to say if he was still in England.

Another thing occurred to Drummond also, as he strolled back into the other room and sat down at the desk. On this occasion the dice would be loaded more heavily in Peterson's favour than before. In the past the only method by which he had ever recognised him was by his strange but unmistakable little mannerism when excited —the mannerism which was innate and had persisted through all his disguises. And now he had discovered what it was; had actually told another man to employ the very trick to fool Drummond. And if he had discovered it, he would take very good care not to use it himself. He would keep his hand in his pocket or something of that sort.

Drummond lay back in his chair and stared at the ceiling, with his head almost touching the heavy curtains behind him. Life undoubtedly was good; but for the murder of Professor Goodman it would have been very good—very good indeed. And at that moment the telephone on the desk in front of him began to ring.

With a jerk Drummond sat up and looked at it—his mind recalled to the circumstances of the moment. Should he let it go on ringing till the operator gave up in despair, or should he take the call? One thing was obvious on the face of it: the call could not be for him. But that was no conclusive reason why he shouldn't take it. Monotonously, insistently, the instrument went on sounding in the silent room, and at last Drummond leaned forward and took

118

the receiver from the hook. And as he did so the curtain behind him stirred again and then was still. But whereas before it had hung in even, regular folds, now it did not. Outlined against it was the figure of a man—a man who inch by inch was pulling the curtain back, a man who held in his right hand a short, villainous-looking iron bar. And as Drummond leaned forward to be ready to speak into the mouthpiece, Freyder's hard eyes concentrated on the nape of his neck. He was an expert with a life-preserver. . . .

Julius Freyder had been anticipating that telephone call, which was why he had concealed himself behind the curtain. From the room which Drummond had overlooked until the end he had watched him strike that curtain with his fist, and had gambled on his not doing so again. Rarely had he received such a shock as when, rounding the corner of the street below, he had seen Drummond of all men leaning out of the window. For it showed conclusively that this accursed *bête noire* was on their heels again, though how he had managed to get there was a mystery. And when on entering the house he had heard, even before he mounted the stairs, the furious utterances of Sir Raymond Blantyre and had realised that Drummond must have heard them too, the need for instant action was obvious.

Julius Freyder was no fool, or he would not have occupied the position he did. And not only was he no fool, but he was also an extremely powerful and dangerous man. It was the work of a second to lock Drummond in, and rush the two excited gentlemen and everyone else in the house through a bolt-hole at the back into some old mews and thus away. But he had no delusions as to the efficacy of a mere bolt against Drummond, and the door was already beginning to crack and splinter as he hid himself amongst the clothes in the inner sanctum. What to do: that was the question. Powerful though he was, he would no more have dreamed of tackling Drummond single-handed than he would have thought of challenging the entire London police force. He would have lasted five seconds with luck. At the same time it was manifestly impossible to leave him in the house alone. Apart from the telephone call which he expected from the Chief at any moment, there might be incriminating documents in the desk. But it was the call that worried him most. Once Drummond got that, even if he didn't recognise the voice at the other end, he would be sure to ask exchange where it came from. And from that, to going down to the

119

New Forest to investigate for himself, probably supported by a bunch of his damned friends, would only be a question of hours. Which was the very last thing to be desired. Just as speed had been the essence of the game before, now it was secrecy. At all costs Drummond must be prevented from finding out the whereabouts of Mr William Robinson.

Perhaps he'd go—leave the house when he found it empty. But no such luck, and Freyder, ensconced behind the curtain, cursed savagely under his breath, as Drummond sat down not two feet from him. Once he was sorely tempted to use his life-preserver then and there, but caution prevailed. Perhaps the call would be delayed; perhaps he would get tired of waiting and go. That was all Freyder wanted—to get him out of the house. A stunned or wounded man at that stage of the proceedings would complicate matters terribly, and when that man was Drummond it could only be done as a last resource. But if it was done it would have to be done properly—no bungling, no faltering.

And then came the ring. Freyder gripped his life-preserver a little tighter and waited. He heard the click of the receiver being taken off the hook; he heard Drummond's preliminary 'Hullo'. And the next moment he struck. It was an easy mark, and, as has been said, he was an expert. With a little sighing grunt Drummond pitched forward and lay motionless, and Freyder picked up the receiver. From it came the Chief's voice vibrant with suspicion.

'What's happened? What was that I heard?'

'It's Freyder speaking, Chief. Drummond is here.'

'What?' It was almost a shout from the other end of the wire.

'He is asleep.' There was a peculiar inflection in Freyder's voice, and he smiled grimly as he heard the long-drawn sigh of relief. 'But I don't think it would be wise in his present condition of health to leave him here.'

'What does he know?'

'That it is impossible to say at present. But Sir Raymond Blantyre has found out a lot.'

The voice at the other end cursed thoughtfully.

'I *must* have at least twenty-four hours, Freyder; if possible more. I'd like three days, but two might do.' There was a pause. 'Will our friend sleep for long?'

'Quite a time, I think,' said Freyder. 'But I think he should be under supervision when he wakes. He might have concussion or be suffering from loss of memory.'

'Ah!' Again came that long-drawn sigh of relief. 'Then a sea voyage, Freyder, is clearly indicated. We will have two invalids instead of one. So bring our young friend here tonight.'

With a faint smile Freyder replaced the receiver on its hook and bent over the unconscious figure of Drummond as it sprawled over the desk.

'I trust you'll enjoy the trip, you young devil,' he snarled.

CHAPTER 8

In Which Drummond Plays a Little Game of Trains

The blow that Drummond had received would have broken the neck of any ordinary man. But not being an ordinary man he was only badly stunned. And he was still unconscious when he was carried out of a motor-car at Mr William Robinson's house in the New Forest. That his arrival was regarded as an important affair was evident from the fact that his host came himself to the front door to greet him. But from that moment it is to be feared that Mr Robinson's knowledge of those excellent books on etiquette which deal with the whole duty of a host towards those who honour his roof with their presence went under a slight eclipse. Regrettable to state, he did not escort his guest personally to the old oak bedroom complete with lavender-scented sheets; in fact, he even forgot himself so far as to leave him lying in the hall with his head in the coal-scuttle. But it is pleasant to state that not for long was he so remiss. At a sign from him two men picked up Drummond and carried him into his own private room, where they dropped him on the floor.

'I will make arrangements for the night later,' he remarked. 'Just at present I would like to look at him from time to time, so leave him here.'

The two men went out, leaving Freyder alone with his Chief. And though he had much to tell him of importance, for a while Freyder said nothing. For there was an expression of such incredible ferocity on the benign countenance of Mr Robinson as he stared at the motionless body on the floor that Freyder realised his presence was forgotten. For perhaps two minutes Mr Robinson's eyes never left Drummond's face; then he turned to his subordinate.

'I don't think I should ever have forgiven you, my dear Freyder,' he said softly, 'if you'd had the misfortune to kill him. That supreme joy must be mine and mine alone.'

With almost an effort he obliterated Drummond from his mind, and sat down at his desk.

'Business first; pleasure afterwards. Things have evidently been happening in London. Tell me everything.'

Clearly and concisely Freyder told him what had occurred, while Mr Robinson smoked his cigar in silence. Once or twice he frowned slightly, but otherwise he gave no sign of his feelings.

'You have no idea, then, as to how Drummond and Sir Raymond Blantyre found the house?' he asked as Freyder finished.

'Not the slightest, Chief,' he answered. 'All I know is that it was Drummond who found it, and not Blantyre. Sir Raymond told me that much as I was rushing him out of the house.'

'Did he make any objections to going?'

'Not the slightest. In fact, when he realised that what he had been saying to Scheidstrun had been overheard by Drummond, his one desire was to get away as fast as he could. He apparently thought Drummond had left the house a quarter of an hour before.'

Mr Robinson shrugged his shoulders.

'The point really is immaterial,' he murmured. 'That fool Blantyre dare not speak; Drummond can't. By the way, what has become of Scheidstrun?'

'I sent him and his wife off this evening,' said Freyder. 'The pilot said he could make Brussels tonight, and finish the journey to-morrow.'

'Excellent, Freyder—excellent,' said Mr Robinson. 'And the slight inconvenience of Blantyre knowing that I have not destroyed the notes is amply compensated for by the possession of our young friend here.'

'But it will mean altering our plans somewhat,' remarked Freyder doubtfully.

For a while Mr Robinson smoked in silence, gently stroking his mutton-chop whiskers.

'Yes,' he remarked at length, 'it will. Not the plans so much as the time-table. The advent of Drummond at this stage of the proceedings I must confess I did not contemplate. And since I am under no delusions as to his infinite capacity for making a nuisance of himself, the sooner he is finally disposed of the better.'

Freyder shrugged his shoulders.

'Well, Chief,' he said callously, 'there he is. And there's no time like the present.'

Mr Robinson raised a deprecating hand.

'How coarse, my dear Freyder!—how almost vulgar! My feelings against this young man are of a purely personal type. And I assure you they would not be gratified in the smallest degree by disposing of him when he was in the condition he is in now. One might just as well assault a carcase in a butcher's shop. No, no. It will be my earnest endeavour to restore Captain Drummond to perfect health before disposing of him. Or at any rate to such a condition that he realises what is taking place. But from my knowledge of him it is a matter that cannot be postponed indefinitely. As I said before, his capacity for making trouble when confined in any ordinary house is well-nigh unbelievable.'

'Then what do you propose to do, Chief?' asked Freyder.

Given his own way now that Drummond was safely out of London and in their power, he would have finished him off then and there. To his mind Drummond was one of those unpleasant individuals who can be regarded as really safe only when they're dead. And once granted that he was going to be killed in the near future, Freyder would have wasted no further time about it. But he knew the absolute futility of arguing with his Chief once the latter's mind was made up, so he resigned himself at once to the inevitable.

'You are certain that you were not followed here?' said Mr Robinson.

'As certain as anyone can ever be,' answered Freyder. 'Twice I stopped the car at the end of a long, straight stretch of road and turned into a lane. There was no sign of anyone. I didn't bother to change the tyres, since most of the road is tar macadam and there's been no rain. And really there are so many Dunlop Magnums about now, that it's only a waste of time.'

'And as far as I could make out, the telephone operator had no suspicions,' went on his Chief. 'You did it extremely skilfully and silently. So I think, Freyder, we can assume on twenty-four hours for certain before anyone even begins to take any notice. Drummond is a man of peculiar habits, and, somewhat naturally, when I realised he was coming here, I sent a letter in his writing to that inconceivable poop Longworth. A friend of his,' he explained, seeing the look of mystification on the other's face, 'who is engaged to Miss Goodman. It states that he is hot on the trail and the postmark will be Birmingham. So I think we can certainly rely on twenty-four hours, or even forty-eight before his friends begin to move. And that will give me plenty of time to ensure that our friend upstairs has not forgotten his process. Once I am assured of that, and he has written out in a legible hand the ingredients he uses, we will delay no longer. It's a nuisance—for I detest manual labour and smells in a laboratory. And but for Drummond, as you know, we would have remained on here for six months or so, and let the old fool make the stones himself, before disposing of him finally. But since this slight contretemps has occurred, I shall have, much as I regret it, to dispense with that part of the programme. Once I know for certain that I can do it myself—and I shall devote tomorrow to that exclusively—we will give up this house forthwith and go on board the yacht. A good idea of mine—that yacht, Freyder. There is nothing like dying convincingly to enable one to live in comfort.'

Freyder grinned as he watched Mr Robinson help himself to a mild whisky and soda: undoubtedly the Chief was in an excellent humour.

'We've run a pretty big risk this time, my dear fellow,' he went on thoughtfully. 'And sometimes it almost staggers me when I think how wonderfully we've succeeded. But I am under no delusions as to the abilities of the English police. Once they get on to a thing they never let go—and sooner or later they are bound to get on to this. Probably they will do it through Drummond's disappearance, and Scheidstrun. Sooner or later they will track our connection with this house, and the good ship *Gadfly*. And then when they find that *Gadfly* left England and has never been heard of again, with true British phlegm they will assume that she has sunk with all hands. And Sir Raymond Blantyre will breathe again—unless they've put the scoundrel in prison for having suggested such an abominable crime to me; in fact, everyone will breathe again except Drummond and our friend upstairs. Oh! and Mr Lewisham. Did you attend the obsequies on Mr Lewisham, Freyder?'

'I did not,' laughed Freyder; and Mr Robinson, contrary to his usual custom, helped himself to another whisky and soda.

124

'Yes,' he continued dreamily, 'it's a wonderful end to what I may claim without conceit has been a wonderful career. Henceforward, Freyder, my life will be one of blameless virtue.'

The other shook his head doubtfully.

'You'll find it a bit monotonous, Chief,' he said.

Mr Robinson smiled.

'Perhaps so—but I shall give it a trial. And whenever it becomes too monotonous, I shall merely remove more money from the pockets of those two villainous men Blantyre and Leibhaus. It almost makes one despair of human nature when one realises that such cold-blooded scoundrels exist.'

'And Drummond! Have you made up your mind yet as to how you intend to dispose of him?'

'Quite simply,' replied Mr Robinson genially. 'I shall merely attach some heavy weights to his feet and drop him overboard. I am not anxious that his body should be recovered, any more than that of our other friend. That part of the affair presents no difficulties.'

His eyes, grown suddenly hard and cruel, fastened on the motionless figure of Drummond, still sprawling on the floor. And suddenly he rose and bent over him with a look of anxiety on his face which changed to relief.

'For a moment I thought he was dead,' he remarked, resuming his seat. 'And that would have been a real grief to me. For him to die without knowing would rob this final coup of its crown. It is the one thing needed, Freyder, to make it perfect.'

The other looked at him curiously.

'How you must hate him, Chief!'

A strange look came into Mr Robinson's eyes, and involuntarily Freyder shuddered. Anger, rage, passion, he had seen on many men's faces, but never before such cold-blooded ferocity as that which showed on the face of the man opposite.

'We all have our weaknesses, Freyder, and I confess that Drummond is mine. And incredible though it may sound to you, if such a thing were possible as for me to have to choose between revenge on him and getting away with Professor Goodman's secret, I believe I would choose the former.'

For a while he sat silent; then with a short laugh he rose. Mr Robinson was his benevolent self once more.

'Happily the alternative is not likely to arise. We have both, my dear fellow—thanks largely to your quickness and skill. And now I

125

think I will go upstairs and see how our friend is getting on. By this time he should be very nearly ready to show me the result of his afternoon's labours.'

'And what about Drummond?' said Freyder, eyeing him professionally. 'I don't think he's likely to give us any trouble for the present, but it's just as well to be on the safe side.'

Mr Robinson turned the unconscious man over with his foot.

'Have him carried upstairs,' he ordered, 'and put in one of the bedrooms. And tell off someone to look after him.' He paused by the door as a thought struck him. 'And by the way—let me know the instant he recovers consciousness. I'd hate to postpone my first interview with the gentleman for one instant longer than necessary.'

'Well, if I'm any judge of such matters, Chief, you'll have to postpone it till tomorrow.'

'Then it will be a refreshing interlude in my period of tuition.'

And with a cheerful wave of his hand Mr Robinson made his way up the stairs. It was six hours since Professor Goodman had started, and by now the clinker in the metal retort should be quite cold enough to handle. Just at first the obstinate old fool had given a little trouble; in fact, he had even gone so far as to categorically refuse to carry out the experiment. But not for long—two minutes to be exact. At the end of that period a whimpering and badly hurt old man had started mixing the necessary ingredients under the watchful eye of Mr Robinson himself. And not till they were mixed and the retort placed in the electric furnace did he leave the room.

Twice during the two hours that followed did he come back again, unexpectedly. But the old scientist's feeble resistance was broken and the visits were unnecessary. Bent almost double he sat in his chair, with the white light from the glowing furnace falling on his face. And he was still in the same position when Mr Robinson opened the door and went in.

The heat in the room was stifling, though the furnace had now been out for two or three hours, and he left the door open. Then without a glance at the huddled figure he strode over to the table, his eyes gleaming with suppressed excitement. For there was the retort, and after cautiously testing it with his hand to discover the temperature, he picked it up and examined it curiously.

Though he had heard the experiment described in detail by Sir Raymond Blantyre, it was the first time he had actually seen it done. The retort, still warm, was full of an opaque, shaly substance

126

which he realised was the clinker. And inside that, like the stone inside a cherry, was the diamond. For a moment his hands shook uncontrollably; then with feverish excitement he started to chip the clinker away with a small chisel.

It broke up easily, coming off in great flakes. And as he got down deeper and deeper his excitement increased. Amongst his other accomplishments Mr Robinson was no bad judge of diamonds in the rough; in fact, if pushed to it, he could even cut and polish a stone for himself. Not, of course, with the wonderful accuracy of the expert, but sufficient to alter the appearance of any well-known historical diamond should it come into his possession. And in the past, it may be mentioned that many had. But in this case he had no intention of bothering over such trifles. Once satisfied that the diamond was there, and that Professor Goodman had forgotten nothing, he proposed to waste no time over that particular stone. Certainly he would put it aside for future use—but what was one paltry diamond to him? It was the process he wanted—and the certainty that he could carry out that process himself.

Deeper and deeper went the chisel, and gradually a dreadful suspicion began to grip him. Surely by now he ought to have struck the stone itself? More than half of the clinker had come away, and still there was no sign of it. Could it be possible that the accursed old fool had made a mistake?

Feverishly he went on chipping, and at length the suspicion became a certainty. There was no diamond in the retort; nothing but valueless grey powder. The experiment had failed.

For a moment or two Mr Robinson stood motionless, staring at the now empty retort. This was the one thing for which he had not legislated. That owing to the unusual conditions, and the strain to which Professor Goodman had been subjected, the stones might prove indifferent, he had been prepared for. But not total failure. His eyes rested thoughtfully on the huddled figure in the chair, but in them there was no trace of mercy. He cared not one whit for the obvious exhaustion of the weary old man; his sole thought was blind, overmastering rage at this further hitch in his scheme. Especially now that time had again become a dominant factor.

'This seems an unfortunate little effort on your part, my dear brother,' he remarked softly.

Professor Goodman sat up with a start.

'I beg your pardon,' he mumbled. 'I'm afraid I was asleep.'

'Then you would be well advised to wake up.' He crossed and stood in front of the Professor. 'Are you aware that your experiment has failed, and that there is no diamond in that retort?'

The old man sat up blinking.

'It is not my fault,' he said querulously. 'How can I be expected to carry out a delicate process under such conditions, and after the abominable way I have been treated?'

'May I point out,' pursued Mr Robinson, still in the same soft tone, 'that you assured me yourself that the conditions were in every way favourable? Further that you told me yourself, as you put the retort into the furnace, that everything was all right. Since then you have had to do nothing save regulate the heat of the electric furnace.' He paused, and a new note crept into his voice. 'Can it be, my dear brother, that you were lying to me?'

'It may be that the heat in the furnace was different from the one to which I have been accustomed,' answered the other, scrambling to his feet.

'May I point out that you assured me that the furnace was if anything better than your own? Further, you have a thermometer there by which to regulate the heat. So once again, dear brother, can it be that you were lying to me?' With a snarl he gripped the Professor by the arm, and shook him roughly. 'Speak, you miserable old fool—speak. And if you don't speak the truth, I'll torture you till you pray for death.'

He let go suddenly, and the Professor collapsed in his chair, only to stand up again and face the other bravely.

'A man can only die once,' he said simply. 'And men have been tortured in vain for other things besides religion. To me my science is my religion. I knew you would find no diamond in the retort—and you never will. You may torture me to death, you vile scoundrel—but never, never, never will I tell you my secret.'

Gently, almost caressingly, Mr Robinson stroked his mutton-chop whiskers.

'Is that so?' he murmured. 'Most interesting, my dear brother—most interesting.' With a benevolent smile he walked over to the bell and rang it.

'Most interesting,' he continued, returning to the other man, who was watching him with fear in his eyes. 'Brave words, in fact—but we will see. I think you remarked before you told me the truth, that it was possibly the fault of the electric furnace. A naughty fib, dear brother—and naughty fibs should always be punished. One presses this switch, I think, to start it. Yes—why, I feel the warmth already. And I see that the maximum temperature registered this evening was 2000° Centigrade. Is that you, Freyder?' he continued without turning his head, as someone entered the room.

'It is, Chief. What's the trouble?'

'The trouble, Freyder, is that this incredibly stupid old man refuses to carry out his process for me. He has wasted six valuable hours producing a nasty-looking mess of grey powder. He has also wasted a lot of expensive electric current. And we are now going to waste a little more. I can only hope that my experiment will prove more satisfactory than his, though I greatly fear, my dear brother, that you will find it rather more painful.'

'What are you going to do?' Professor Goodman's voice was shaking, as he looked first at his tormentor, and then at the furnace which was already glowing a dull red.

'I'm going to make quite certain,' remarked Mr Robinson affably, 'that these thermometers register correctly. I imagine that there must be a difference in the feeling of metal at 1000° and metal at 2000°, though both, I should think, would be most unpleasant. However, my dear Professor, you will know for certain very shortly. I see that it is just about 1000° now. The left arm, I think, Freyder—if you would be so good. And perhaps you had better turn up his sleeve: burning cloth gives such an unpleasant smell.'

A dreadful scream rang through the house, and Professor Goodman fell back in his chair almost fainting.

'Only half a second,' murmured Mr Robinson. 'And it will only be half a second at 2000°—this time. Then, dear brother, you will again carry out your process. If it succeeds—well and good. If it should fail again—I fear we shall have to make it a full second. And a second is a long time under certain conditions.'

Moaning pitifully, Professor Goodman lay back in his chair with his eyes closed.

'I won't,' he muttered again and again through clenched teeth, while the heat from the furnace grew greater and greater, and the dull red changed to white.

'Foolish fellow,' sighed Mr Robinson. 'However,' he added hopefully, 'it's only half a second this time. And as a special concession I'll let you off with only 1900°. Now, Freyder—we are quite ready.'

Freyder took a step forward, and at that moment it happened. He gave one agonised shout of terror, and then scream after scream of agony rang through the house. For it was not Professor Goodman's arm which touched the white-hot furnace, but Freyder's face—and to his Chief's horrified eyes it had seemed as if he had dived straight at it.

'My God!' he muttered foolishly, as Freyder, moaning horribly, dashed from the room. 'How did it happen?'

The words died away on his lips and he stood staring into the shadows beyond the light thrown by the furnace. Drummond was sitting on the floor grinning vacantly at space.

'Gug, gug, gug,' he burbled foolishly. 'Pretty light.'

Then, apparently bored with life in general, he returned with interest to his occupation.

'Puff—puff!' he cried happily. 'Puff—puff! Naughty man kicked train.'

And the train he was busily pushing along the floor consisted of his own shoes.

Once again Mr Robinson dashed to the bell and pealed it. His momentary shock at Freyder's ghastly accident had passed; his sole thought was that Drummond was no longer unconscious. And Drummond in full possession of his physical powers was a dangerous person to have about the place, even if his mind was wandering. But was it? That was the point. Or was he shamming? Such a possibility at once suggested itself to Mr Robinson's tortuous brain, and he was not a gentleman who took any unnecessary risks.

He had watched Professor Goodman totter from his chair with a look of wild hope in his face as he realised the unexpected presence of a friend; he had watched him sink back into it again with a groan as his cry for help was greeted with a vacuous grin from the man so happily playing on the floor. But still he was not satisfied, and a revolver gleamed ominously in his hand as he watched his enemy. His mind was made up on one point. Shamming or not shamming —mad or sane—at the slightest hint of trouble on Drummond's part he would kill him and be done with it. In fact he was sorely tempted to do so at once: it would save a lot of bother in the long run.

His finger tightened on the trigger, and he raised his revolver till it was pointing direct at Drummond's heart.

'I'm going to kill you, Drummond,' he said quietly.

But if he expected to discover anything by such a test he was doomed to disappointment. Still the same vacuous grin, still the same lolling head, and a jumble of incoherent words was all the result; and very slowly he lowered his weapon, as one of his men came rushing into the room, to stop abruptly at the door as his eyes fell on the figure on the floor.

He gave a sigh of relief.

'So there you are, my beauty,' he muttered.

'Was it you who was told off to look after Captain Drummond?' said Mr Robinson softly.

The man looked at the speaker with fear in his eyes.

'I put him on the bed, Chief,' he said sullenly, 'and he was unconscious. And I hadn't had any supper, so . . .'

'You went downstairs to get some,' Mr Robinson concluded his sentence for him. 'You went downstairs, you miserable fool, leaving him alone.' His eyes bored into the man's brain, and he shrank back against the wall. 'I will deal with you later,' continued Mr Robinson, 'and until then you will continue to look after him. If nothing further of this sort happens, it is possible that I may overlook your fault—so you had better see to it.'

'I'll swear it won't happen again, Chief,' said the man eagerly. 'It was only because I thought the young swine was stunned . . .'

With a gesture Mr Robinson cut him short.

'You're not paid to think, you're paid to do what you're told,' he remarked coldly. 'Go, now, and get one of the others. And bring some rope when you return.'

The man departed with alacrity, and once more Mr Robinson fell to staring at the man sitting on the floor. To Professor Goodman he paid not the slightest attention; all his thoughts were concentrated on Drummond. Was he shamming, or was he not? Had Freyder's blow on the head deprived him of his reason—or was it a wonderful piece of acting? And finally he decided on yet another test.

Still watching Drummond narrowly, he walked over to the door and affected to give an order to someone in the passage outside.

'Bring the girl Phyllis in here.'

Now surely there would be some tell-tale start if he was

shamming—some little movement that would give him away. But there was nothing—absolutely nothing—to show that Drummond had even heard. He was engrossed in some intricate shunting operations with his shoes, and after a time Mr Robinson came back into the room. Almost, if not quite, his mind was made up— Drummond was insane. Only temporarily possibly—but insane. The blow on the back of his head had caused something in his brain to snap, and the man he hated most on earth was just a babbling lunatic. Almost, if not quite, he was sure of it; for certain proof he would have to wait until he could examine him—and especially his eyes—more closely. And Mr Robinson had no intention of examining Drummond, sane or insane, closely until Drummond's arms were very securely lashed together.

'You'd better be very careful of him,' he remarked as the two men came in with rope. 'I am almost certain that he's got very bad concussion, but if you handle him roughly he may get angry. I shall be covering him the whole time with a revolver, but I want you to lash his wrists behind his back.'

They approached him cautiously, and Drummond smiled at them vacantly.

'All right, old chap,' murmured the first man ingratiatingly. 'Pretty train you've got there. Won't you shake hands?'

'Gumph,' remarked Drummond brightly, busily pushing his shoe.

'Get hold of his other hand,' said the first man tersely to his companion. 'Then we'll get them both behind his back, and I'll slip a running noose over them.'

Which was excellent in theory, but poor in execution. A loud crack was heard and the two men staggered back holding their heads, which had impinged with violence.

'Gumph,' again remarked Drummond. 'Puff—puff—puff.'

'Damn the swine!' snarled the man who had originally been told off to look after him, and Mr Robinson smiled gently. It was very obvious that, whatever his mental condition might be, Drummond's physical strength was unimpaired.

'I think, Chief,' said the second man, 'that we should do it better if we lashed his wrists in front of him to start with. It's being man-handled that he doesn't take to, and we might be able to slip the noose over his wrists without his realising what the game is.'

'Do it how you like,' snapped Mr Robinson, 'but do it quickly.'

Which again proved excellent in theory, but poor in execution. For it soon transpired that Drummond was far too happy playing trains on the floor to realise the desirability of having his hands lashed together. In fact the proceeding appeared to annoy him considerably. And it was not until another man had been summoned and Mr Robinson himself had joined in the fray that they finally got the noose over his wrists and drew it tight. And in the course of doing so two of the men had crashed heavily into the furnace, which, though cooling, was still unpleasantly hot.

But at last it was done, and four panting men stood round in a ring regarding him triumphantly as he rolled on the floor. And then after a while he lay still, with a foolish grin on his face.

'Gug-gug,' he burbled. 'Where's my train?'

'I'll gug-gug him,' snarled one of the men, kicking him heavily in the ribs. 'The young devil's a homicidal maniac.'

'Stop that!' said Mr Robinson savagely. 'All accounts with this young man are settled by me. Now stand by in case he struggles. I'm going to examine his eyes.'

They approached him cautiously, but for the moment the trouble seemed over. Like so many madmen, and people temporarily insane, his frenzied struggles of the last ten minutes had completely exhausted Drummond. And even when Mr Robinson raised his eyelids and stared into his eyes he made no attempt to move, but just lay there smiling stupidly. For a long while Mr Robinson examined him, and then with a nod of satisfaction he rose to his feet.

'Take him to his room, and see that he doesn't escape again. He's mad, but for how long he'll remain so I can't tell. If you see the faintest sign of his recovering his reason, come and tell me at once.'

He watched them pick up Drummond and carry him out. They took him into the next room and threw him on the bed, and Mr Robinson followed. For a moment or two he moved restlessly on the pillows—then he gave a strangled grunt and a snore.

'He's asleep, Chief,' said one of the men, bending over him.

'Good,' answered Mr Robinson. 'Let us trust he remains so for some time.'

Then with a look of cold determination on his face he returned to the room where Professor Goodman still sat huddled in his chair.

CHAPTER 9

In Which Professor Goodman Has a Trying Time

'And now, dear brother,' he remarked, gently closing the door, 'we will resume our little discussion where we left off. I was, if you remember just about to ask you to sample the temperature of the furnace at 2000° when the interruption occurred. Is it necessary that I should repeat that request, or was your experience at the lower temperature sufficient for you?'

Professor Goodman raised his haggard face and stared at his tormentor.

'What have you done to that poor young man, you devil?'

Mr Robinson smiled and stroked his whiskers.

'Well, really,' he answered mildly, 'I think the boot is on the other leg. The question is more what has he done to my unfortunate staff? Poor Mr Freyder I feel almost certain must be in great pain with his face, judging by the noise he made, and two of my other servants have very nasty burns.'

'I know all that,' said the other. 'But what has sent him insane?'

Mr Robinson smiled even more gently.

'As a scientist, dear brother, you should know the tiny dividing line between sanity and madness. One little link wrong in that marvellous mechanism of the brain, and the greatest thinker becomes but a babbling fool. Not that his best friends could ever have called poor Drummond a great thinker, but'—he paused to emphasise his words—'but, dear brother, he serves as a very good example of what might happen to one who is a great thinker.'

Professor Goodman shivered; there had been no need to emphasise the meaning underlying the words.

'You see,' continued Mr Robinson, 'Drummond very foolishly and very unfortunately for himself has again crossed my path. This time, as a matter of fact, it was by pure accident. Had you not lunched with him on the day of your death and given him the notes of your process, you may take it from me that this little interlude would never have occurred. But you did—and, well, you see what has happened to Drummond. The silly young fellow is quite mad.'

'You have done something to him to make him so,' said the other dully.

'Of course,' agreed Mr Robinson. 'Or to be strictly accurate, Freyder has.'

And suddenly Professor Goodman rose to his feet with a pitiful little cry.

'Oh! my God! I don't understand. I think I'm going mad myself.'

For a moment or two Mr Robinson looked at him narrowly. If such an appalling eventuality as that happened, the whole of his scheme would be frustrated. True, it was a common figure of speech, but Professor Goodman was a frail old man, accustomed to a sedentary life. And during the past two or three days his life had been far from sedentary. Supposing under the strain the old man's reason did snap. . . . Mr Robinson drew a deep breath: the mere thought of such a thing was too impossible to contemplate.

But it had to be contemplated, and it had to be taken into account in his immediate course of action. Whatever happened, Professor Goodman's intellect must be preserved at all costs. Even a nervous breakdown would constitute a well-nigh insuperable obstacle to his plans. And in spite of the seriousness of the position, Mr Robinson could hardly help smiling at the irony of the thing.

Here was he with the greatest prize of his career waiting to be picked up—almost, but not quite, within his grasp. All the difficult practical details, all that part of his scheme concerned solely with organisation, had gone without a hitch. And now he was confronted by something far smaller in comparison, and yet almost as important as all the rest put together—the state of the mind of an elderly scientist. It was a problem in psychology which in the whole of his career he had never had to face under exactly similar conditions.

There had been occasions when men's reasons had snapped under the somewhat drastic treatment with which Mr Robinson was wont to enforce his wishes. But on all those occasions a remarkable aptitude with the pen had enabled him to dispense with the formality of their signature. This time, however, his wonderful gifts as a forger were wasted. Knowledge of ancient cuneiform writing might have been of some use in enabling him to decipher the notes, he reflected grimly—but as it was they were hopelessly and utterly unintelligible. Only Professor Goodman could do it, and that was the problem which had just come home to him more acutely than ever. What was the best line to adopt with the old man? How far would it be safe to go in a policy of threats and force?

Or would apparent kindness do the trick better and quicker? Especially quicker—that was the important thing. It was a ticklish point to decide; but it was essential that it should be decided, and at once.

He glanced at the haggard, staring eyes of the man confronting him; he noted the twitching hands and he made up his mind. After all, it was easy to go from kindness to threats, whereas the converse was difficult. And though he had reluctantly to admit to himself that burning a man's arm on red-hot metal can hardly be regarded as the act of a personal friend, there was no good worrying about it. It had been done, and could not be undone. All that he could do now was to try to efface the recollection of it as far as possible.

'Sit down, Professor,' he said gently. 'I feel that I owe you some explanation.'

With a groan the other sank back into his chair.

'Will you have a cigar?' went on Mr Robinson easily, holding out his case. 'You don't smoke? You should. Most soothing to the nerves. In the first place I must apologise for not having made things clearer to you before, but this slight contretemps with Drummond has kept me rather fully occupied. Now I want you to recall to your mind the interviews that you had with Sir Raymond Blantyre.'

'I recall them perfectly,' answered the Professor, and Mr Robinson noted with quiet satisfaction that he seemed to be less agitated.

'He offered you, did he not? a large sum of money for the suppression of your secret, which you refused—and very rightly refused. But, my dear Professor, do you really imagine for a moment that an unscrupulous blackguard of his type was going to lie down and accept your refusal? If you chose to refuse the money, so much the better for him; but whether you refused or accepted, he intended to suppress you. And but for me'—he paused impressively—'he would have done.'

Professor Goodman passed a bewildered hand across his forehead.

'But for me,' repeated Mr Robinson, 'you would now be dead—foully murdered. You have never in your life—and I trust you never will again—been in such deadly peril as you were in a few days ago. Indeed, if it were known now that you were alive, I fear that even I would be powerless to save you.'

He drew carefully at his cigar; then he leaned forward and touched the Professor on the knee.

'Have you ever heard of a man called Peterson?'

'Never,' returned the other.

'No—probably not. You and he hardly move in the same circles. Peterson, of course, is only one of the many names by which that arch-devil is known. He is a King of Criminals—a man without mercy—a black-hearted villain.' Mr Robinson's voice shook with the intensity of his emotion. 'And to that man Sir Raymond Blantyre went with a certain proposal. Do you know what that proposal was? It concerned you and your death. You were to be murdered before you gave your secret to the world.'

'The villain!' cried Professor Goodman, in a shaking voice. 'To think that I've had him to dinner, and that his wife is a friend of ours.'

Mr Robinson smiled pityingly.

'My dear Professor,' he said, 'I'm afraid that your life has been lived far apart from the realities of the world. Do you really suppose that such a trifle as that would have weighed for one instant with Sir Raymond Blantyre? However, I will get on with my explanation. It matters not how I discovered these things: I will merely say that for twenty years now I have dogged this man Peterson as his shadow. He did me the greatest wrong one man can do another: I won't say any more.'

Mr Robinson choked slightly.

'I have dogged him, Professor,' he went on after a while, 'as I say, for twenty years, hoping—always hoping—that the time would come for my revenge. I have lived for nothing else; I have thought of nothing else. But one thing I was determined on—that my revenge when it did come should be a worthy one. A dozen times could I have given him away to the police, but I stayed my hand. When it came, I wanted the thing to be more personal. And at last the opportunity did come. It came with you.'

'With me?' echoed Professor Goodman. 'How can I have had anything to do with your revenge on this man?'

'That is what I am just going to explain to you,' continued Mr Robinson. 'In this man Peterson, Sir Raymond Blantyre had encountered a blackguard far more subtle than himself. Peterson was perfectly prepared to murder you—but he had no intention of murdering the secret of your process. That he proposed to keep for himself—so that he could continue blackmailing Sir Raymond. You see the manner of blackguard he is. It was a scheme after his own heart, and I made up my mind to strike at last. Apart from frustrating the monstrous crime of murdering you, I should achieve an artistic revenge.'

He again pulled thoughtfully at his cigar.

'Now pay close attention. Professor Scheidstrun the German scientist made an appointment to see you, didn't he?'

'He was with me when I was chloroformed,' cried the other.

Mr Robinson smiled.

'No, he wasn't. A man you thought was Scheidstrun was with you.'

'But—good heavens!' gasped the Professor. 'I met him in the hall. I was late, I remember . . .'

'And, as you say, you met him in the hall talking to your maidservant.'

'But how on earth did you know that?'

'Because the man you met in the hall was not Scheidstrun—but me.' He laughed genially at the amazement on the other's face. 'It's a shame to keep you mystified any further; I will explain everything. It was Peterson who made the original appointment with you, writing in Scheidstrun's hand. What he intended to do I know not; how he intended to murder you I am not prepared to say. But the instant I discovered about it, I realised that there was not a moment to be lost. So I took the liberty, my dear Professor, of posing over the telephone as your secretary. I rang up Peterson, and speaking in an assumed voice I postponed his appointment with you until the following day. And then I took his place. I may say that I am not unskilled in the art of disguise, and I knew I could make myself up to resemble Scheidstrun quite sufficiently well to deceive you.'

'But why on earth didn't you tell me at the time?' said Professor Goodman, peering at the speaker suspiciously.

Once again the other laughed.

'My dear fellow, surely Mrs Goodman must, during the course of your married life, have let you into the secret of one of your characteristics. Or has she been too tactful? You are, as I think you must admit yourself, a little obstinate, aren't you?' He dropped his tone of light banter, and became serious. 'I don't think—in fact, I know you don't realise the deadly peril you were in. Even had I

138

succeeded in convincing you on the matter, and you had agreed to come away and hide yourself, you would not have consented to the destruction of your laboratory. And that was essential. As long as Peterson thought you were alive he would have found you wherever you had hidden yourself. It was therefore of vital importance that he should think you dead—as he does now. Big issues, my dear Professor, require big treatments.'

Mr Robinson, having delivered himself of this profound utterance, leaned back in his chair and gazed at his listener. Bland assurance radiated from his mutton-chop whiskers, but his mind was busy. How was the old fool taking it? He still had his trump card to play, but he wanted that to win the game without possibility of failure. And as his mental metaphors grew a little mixed, he realised that it must fall on carefully prepared soil.

Professor Goodman stirred uneasily in his chair.

'I really can hardly believe all this,' he said at length. 'Why is all this deception necessary? Why have I to pose as your brother? And why, above all, have I to pose as your brother? And why, above all, have you tortured me?'

'Let me answer your last point first if I can,' said Mr Robinson. 'And yet I can't. Even if I can persuade you to forgive me, I never shall be able to forgive myself. Sudden anger, Professor, makes men do strange things—dreadful things. And I was furious with rage when I found that you had deliberately failed in the experiment. I realise now that I should have explained everything to you to start with. But I suppose my hatred of Peterson and my wish for revenge blinded me to other things. Everything, as I have told you, is subservient to that in my mind. Bringing you here, making you pose as my brother—what was all that done for except to throw that devil off the scent should he by any chance suspect? And at present he does not. He believes that the secret for which he would have given untold gold has perished with you. He is angry, naturally, at what he considers a buffet of fate, but that is no use to me as a revenge. He must know that it was not fate—but I who wrecked his scheme. He must know that not only has he lost the secret for ever—but that I have got it. There will be my revenge for which I have waited twenty years.' His eyes glistened, and he shook his fists in the air. 'And then and not till then will it be safe for you to go back and join your wife.'

Professor Goodman leapt from his chair.

'You mean that?' he cried. 'You will let me go?'

139

Mr Robinson gazed at him in pained surprise; then he bowed his head.

'I deserve it,' he said in a low voice. 'I deserve your bad opinion of me, firstly for not having told you, but especially for my vile and inexcusable loss of temper. But surely you can never have believed I was going to keep you here for good. Why'—he gave a little pained laugh—'it's almost as if you thought I was a murderer. Foolish I may have been, obsessed with one idea, but I never thought that you would think quite as badly of me as that. After all, believe me or not as you like, I saved your life.'

He rose from his chair and paced thoughtfully up and down the room.

'No, no, my dear fellow—please reassure yourself on that point. The very instant it is safe for you to do so, you shall return to your wife.'

'But when will it be safe?' cried the Professor excitedly.

'When Peterson knows that your secret is in my possession, and that therefore murdering you will avail him nothing,' answered Mr Robinson calmly.

'But how do I know you will keep your word?'

'You don't,' said the other frankly. 'You've got to trust me. At the same time I beg of you to use your common sense. Of what possible advantage is it to me to keep you here? I shall have to trust you to take no steps to incriminate me, and that I am fully prepared to do. My quarrel is not with you, Professor; nor is it with that young man Drummond. But quite by accident he got between me and my life's object—and he had to be removed. So is it fair to Mrs Goodman to keep her in this dreadful sorrow for one moment longer than is necessary? The very instant you have given me your secret, and your word of honour that you will say nothing to the police, you have my word of honour that you are free to go.'

'But what do you propose to do with my secret when you've got it?' asked the Professor. He was watching his captor with troubled eyes, wondering what to believe.

'Do with it?' cried the other exultantly. 'I propose to seek out Peterson and let him know that I have got what he has missed. And if you but knew the man, you would realise that no more wonderful revenge could be thought of.'

'Yes, yes—I see all that,' said the Professor irritably. 'But in the event of my giving the secret to the world—what then?'

Mr Robinson curbed a rising desire to throttle the old man in the chair. Never had his self-control been so severely tried as it was now; precious moments were flying when every one was of value. But true to his new policy he kept every hint of irritation out of his voice as he answered.

'I shall have to have your promise also on that point, Professor. For one year you will have to keep your discovery to yourself. That will be sufficient for my revenge.'

He realised that had he made no proviso of that sort it would have been enough to raise the other's suspicions, for Professor Goodman was no fool. He also realised that if he made the period too long the other's inherent pig-headedness might tempt him to refuse. So he compromised on a year, and to his intense relief it looked as if the old man was inclined to consider it favourably. He still sat motionless, but his brow was wrinkled in thought, and he drummed incessantly with his fingers on the arms of his chair.

'One year,' he said at length. 'For I warn you, sir, that all the Petersons in the world will not prevent me publishing my discovery then.'

'One year will be sufficient,' said Mr Robinson quietly.

'And will you on your side,' continued the Professor, 'promise not to publish it before that date?'

Mr Robinson concealed a smile.

'I undoubtedly will promise that,' he answered.

'And the instant you possess the secret I may go to my wife?'

Mr Robinson's pulse was beating a little quicker than normal. Could it be that he had succeeded in bluffing him?

'As soon as Peterson knows that the secret of the process is mine—and that will be very soon—you may go. Before that it would not be safe.'

'And if I refuse?'

For a moment or two Mr Robinson did not reply; he seemed to be weighing his words with care.

'Need we discuss that, Professor?' he said at length. 'I have already told you the main—almost the sole—object of my life: revenge on this man Peterson. Rightly or wrongly, I have decided that this is my opportunity for obtaining it. I have gone to an immensity of trouble and risk to achieve my object, and though, as I said, I have no quarrel with you, yet, Professor, you are an essential part of my scheme. Without you I must fail; I make no

141

bones about it. And I do not want to fail. So should you still refuse, your wife will go on thinking herself a widow until you change your mind. It rests with you and you alone.'

His eyes, shrewd and penetrating, searched the old man's face. Had he said enough, or had he said too much? Like an open book he read the other's mind: saw doubt, indecision, despair, succeed one another in rapid succession. And then suddenly he almost stopped breathing. For the Professor had risen to his feet, and Mr Robinson knew that one way or the other he had come to a decision.

'Very well, sir,' said the old man wearily. 'I give in. It seems that the only way of setting my poor wife's mind at rest as soon as possible is for me to trust you. I will tell you my process.'

Mr Robinson drew in his breath in a little whistling hiss, but his voice was quite steady as he answered.

'You have decided very wisely,' he remarked. 'And since there is no time like the present, I think we will have a bottle of champagne and some sandwiches to fortify us, and then get on with the experiment at once.'

'As you will,' said the Professor. 'And then perhaps tomorrow you will let me go.'

Mr Robinson glanced at his watch.

'Today, Professor,' he remarked jovially. 'It is past midnight. And I can promise you that should your experiment succeed, you will leave this house today.'

He watched the champagne bring back some colour to the other's cheeks, and then he produced his notebook.

'To save time,' he said, 'I propose to write down the name of each salt as you take it, and the amount you use. Does it make any difference in what order the salts are mixed?'

'None whatever,' answered the Professor. 'Provided they are all mixed properly. No chemical reaction takes place until the heat is applied.'

'And to make it perfectly certain, you had better give me the formula for each salt at the same time,' continued Mr Robinson.

At first the old man's fingers trembled so much that he could hardly use the balance, but Mr Robinson betrayed no impatience. And after a while the enthusiasm of the scientist supplanted everything else, and the Professor became absorbed in his task. Entry after entry was made in Mr Robinson's neat handwriting, and gradually the look of triumph deepened in his eyes. Success had come at last.

Of pity for the poor old man opposite he felt no trace; pity was a word unknown in his vocabulary. And so for an hour in the silent house the murderer and his victim worked on steadily, until, at length, the last salt was mixed, the last entry made. The secret was in Mr Robinson's possession. Not for another four hours would he be absolutely certain; the test of the electric furnace would furnish the only conclusive proof. But short of that he felt as sure as a man may feel that there had been no mistake this time, and his eyes were gleaming as he rose from the table.

'Excellent, my dear Professor,' he murmured. 'You have been lucidity itself. Now all that remains is to start up our current and await results.'

'The results will be there,' answered the other. 'That I know.'

He opened the furnace door and placed the retort inside; then, switching on the current, he sank wearily into his chair.

'You don't think it will be long, do you, before you can convince this man Peterson?' he said with a pathetic sort of eagerness.

'I can assure you that it won't be,' returned the other, with an enigmatic smile. 'I keep in very close touch with him.'

'Because I would be prepared to run any risk in order to let my dear wife know that I am alive as soon as possible.'

Mr Robinson nodded sympathetically.

'Of course you would, my dear fellow. I quite understand that. But I feel that I must safeguard you even against your own inclinations. The instant, however, that I consider it safe, you shall go back.'

'Can't I even write to her?' queried the other.

Mr Robinson affected to consider the point; then regretfully he shook his head.

'No—not even that,' he answered. 'I know this man Peterson too well. In fact, Professor, I am not even going to allow you to return to your wife from this house. It is better and safer for you that you should remain in ignorance of where you have been, and so I propose to take you for a short sea-voyage in my yacht and land you on another part of the coast. From the boat you will be able to radio to your wife, so that her mind will be set at rest. And then when you finally rejoin her, I would suggest your pleading sudden loss of memory to account for your mysterious disappearance.'

143

'But what on earth am I to say about the man who was buried?' And suddenly the full realisation of all that the question implied came home to him and he stood up. 'Who was that man?'

'An uninteresting fellow,' remarked Mr Robinson genially.

'But if you were the man I thought was Scheidstrun, you must—you must have murdered him.' The old man's voice rose almost to a scream. 'My God! I'd forgotten all about that.'

He shrank back staring at Mr Robinson, who was watching him narrowly.

'My dear Professor,' he said coldly, 'pray do not excite yourself unnecessarily. I have often thought that a society of murderers run on sound conservative lines would prove an admirable institution. After all, it is the majority who should be considered, and there are so many people who are better out of the way. However, to set your mind at rest,' he continued, 'it may interest you to know that the foot which was buried in your boot did not belong to a living man. There are methods of obtaining these things, as you are doubtless aware, for experimental purposes, if you possess a degree.'

There was no object, he reflected, in unnecessarily alarming the old man; it saves bother to get an animal to walk to the slaughter-house rather than having to drag it there. And he was likely to have all the dragging he wanted with Drummond, even though he was insane.

Professor Goodman, only half satisfied, sank back in his chair. Already the sweat was running down both their faces from the heat of the furnace, but Mr Robinson had no intention of leaving the room. He was taking no chances this time; not until the current was turned off and the furnace was cool enough to handle did he propose to go and rest. Then, once he was satisfied that the retort did contain diamonds, he would have some badly needed sleep in preparation for the work next night.

The yacht *Gadfly* was lying in Southampton Water, and he had decided to go on board in the late afternoon. His two invalids would be carried on stretchers; an ambulance was even now in readiness below to take them to the coast. They would both be unconscious—a matter which presented but little difficulty to Mr Robinson. And the Professor would never regain consciousness. He had served his purpose, and all that mattered as far as he was concerned was to dispose of him as expeditiously as possible. With Drummond things were a little different. In spite of what he had said to Freyder downstairs, the scheme was too big to run any unnecessary risks, and though it went against his grain to kill him in his present condition, he quite saw that he might have to. Drummond might remain in his present condition for months, and it was manifestly impossible to wait for that length of time to obtain his revenge. It might be, of course, that when he woke up he would have recovered his reason, and, if so . . . Mr Robinson's eyes gleamed at the thought. In anticipation he lived through the minute when he would watch Drummond, bound and weighted, slip off the deck into the sea.

Then with an effort he came back to the present. Was there anything left undone in his plans which would cause a check? Point by point he ran over them, and point by point he found them good. Their strength lay in their simplicity, and he could see nothing which was likely to go wrong before he was on board the *Gadfly*. Up to date no mention of Mr Lewisham's sudden disappearance had found its way into the papers; presumably, whatever Mrs Lewisham might think of the matter, she had not consulted the police. Similarly with regard to Drummond. No questions were likely to be asked in his case until long after he was safely out of the country. And after that, as he had said to Freyder, nothing mattered. The SY *Gadfly* would founder with all hands somewhere off the coast of Africa, but not too far from the shore to prevent Freyder and himself reaching it. That the crew, drugged and helpless, would go down in her he did not propose to tell them when he went on board. After all, there were not many of them, and it would be a pity to spoil their last voyage.

The heat from the furnace was growing almost insupportable, and he glanced at his watch. There was another hour to go, and with a sigh of impatience he sat back in his chair. Opposite him Professor Goodman was nodding in a kind of heavy doze, though every now and then he sat up with a jerk and stared about him with frightened eyes. He was muttering to himself, and once he sprang out of his chair with a stifled scream, only to sink back again as he saw the motionless figure opposite.

'I was dreaming,' he muttered foolishly. 'I thought I saw a man standing by the door.'

Mr Robinson swung round and peered into the passage; there was no one there. Absolute silence still reigned in the house. And then suddenly he rose and went to the door: it seemed to him as if something had stirred outside. But the passage was empty, and he resumed his seat. He felt angry with himself because his own nerves were not quite under their usual iron control. After all, what could possibly happen? It must be the strain of the last few days, he decided.

Slowly the minutes ticked on, and had anyone been there to see, it must have seemed like some ceremony of black magic. The furnace glowing white hot, and in the circle of light thrown by it two elderly men sitting in chairs—one gently stroking his mutton-chop whiskers, the other muttering restlessly to himself. And then outside the ring of light—darkness. Every now and then a sizzling hiss came from inside the furnace, as the chemical process advanced another stage towards completion—that completion which meant all power to one of the two who watched and waited, and death to the other. The sweat dripped down their faces; breathing was hard in the dried-up air. But to Mr Robinson nothing mattered: such things were trifles. Whatever might be the material discomfort, it was the crowning moment of his life—the moment when the greatest coup of his career had come to a successful conclusion.

And suddenly he shut his watch with a snap.

'Two hours,' he cried, and strive as he would he could not keep the exultation out of his voice. 'The time is up.'

With a start Professor Goodman scrambled to his feet, and mumbling foolishly he switched off the current. It was over; he had given away his secret. And all he wanted to do now was to get home as soon as possible. Two hours more to let it cool. . . .

He paused, motionless, his lips twitching. Great heavens! what was that in the door—that great dark shape. It was moving, and he screamed. It was coming into the circle of light, and as he screamed again, Mr Robinson leapt to his feet.

Once more the thing moved, and now the light from the furnace shone on it. It was Drummond, his arms still lashed in front of him. His face was covered with blood, but his eyes were fixed on Professor Goodman. And they were the eyes of a homicidal maniac.

For a moment or two Mr Robinson stood motionless, staring at him. Drummond's appearance was so utterly unexpected and terrifying that his brain refused to work, and before he realised what had happened, Drummond sprang. But not at him. It was Professor Goodman who had evidently incurred the madman's wrath, and the reason was soon obvious. Insane though he was, the one dominant idea of his life was still a ruling factor in his actions, though now it was uncontrolled by any reason. And that idea was Peterson.

Why he should imagine that Professor Goodman was Peterson it was impossible to say, but he undoubtedly did. Again and again he grunted the name as he shook the unfortunate scientist backwards and forwards, and for a while Mr Robinson wondered cynically whether he should let him go on in his delusion and await results. He was almost certain to kill the old man, which might save trouble. At the same time there was still the possibility of some mistake in the process which rendered it inadvisable to dispense with him for good quite yet.

An uproar in the passage outside took him to the door. Two of the three men who had been told off to guard Drummond were running towards him, and he cursed them savagely.

'Pull him off,' he roared. 'He'll murder the old man.'

They hurled themselves on Drummond, who had forced the Professor to his knees. And this time, strangely enough, he gave no trouble. He looked at them with a vacant stare, and then grinned placidly.

'Chief!' cried one of the men, 'he's murdered Simpson. He's lying there with his neck broken.'

Mr Robinson darted from the room, to return almost at once. It was only too true. The third man was lying across the bed dead.

'Where were you two imbeciles?' he snarled savagely.

'We were taking it in turns, boss,' said the one who had spoken, sullenly. 'The swine was asleep and his arms were bound. . . .'

He turned vindictively on Drummond, who grinned vacantly again.

'So you left him alone with only one of you,' Mr Robinson remarked coldly. 'You fools!—you triple-distilled damned fools. And then I suppose he woke and Simpson went to tuck him up. And Drummond just took him by the throat, and killed him, as he'd kill you or anyone else he got his hands on—bound or not.'

'Gug-gug,' said Drummond, sitting down and beaming at them. 'That man in there hit me in the face, when I took his throat in my hands.'

And suddenly the madness returned to his eyes, and his huge hands strained and wrestled with the rope that bound them. He grunted and cursed, and the two men instinctively backed away.

Only Mr Robinson remained where he was, and the light from the still glowing furnace glinted on the revolver which he held in his hand. This was no time for half-measures; there was no telling what this powerful madman might do next. If necessary, though he did not want to have to do it, he would shoot him where he sat. But the spasm passed, and he lowered his revolver.

'Just so,' he remarked. 'You might as well hit a steam-roller as hit Drummond, once he's got hold. And judging by his face, Simpson must have hit him hard and often before he died. Take him away; lash him up; and unless you want to join that fool Simpson, don't take it in turns to guard him—and don't get within range of his hands.'

The two men closed in warily on their prisoner, but he gave no further bother. Babbling happily he walked between them out of the room, and Mr Robinson suddenly remembered the unfortunate Professor.

'A powerful and dangerous young man,' he remarked suavely. 'I trust he hasn't hurt you, my dear Professor.'

'No,' said the other dazedly; 'he hasn't hurt me.'

'An extraordinary delusion of his,' pursued Mr Robinson. 'Fancy thinking that you, of all people, were that villain Peterson.'

'Most extraordinary!' muttered the Professor.

'And it's really quite amazing that he should have allowed himself to be separated from you so easily. His friends, I believe, call him Bulldog, and he has many of the attributes of that noble animal.' He peered at the Professor's throat. 'Why, he's hardly marked you. You can count yourself very lucky, believe me. Even when sane he's a terror—but in his present condition . . . However, such a regrettable contretemps will not occur again, I trust.'

He glanced at the furnace.

'Another hour, I suppose, before it will be cool enough to see the result of our experiment?'

'Another hour,' agreed the Professor mechanically.

And during that hour the two men sat in silence. Each was busy with his own thoughts, and it would be hard to say which would have received the greater shock had he been able to read the other's mind.

For Mr Robinson was thinking, amongst other things, of the approaching death of the Professor, which would scarcely have been comforting to the principal actor in the performance. And

Professor Goodman—who might have been expected to be thinking of nothing but his approaching reunion with his wife—had, sad
to relate, completely forgotten the lady's existence. His mind was
engrossed with something quite different. For when a man who is
undoubtedly mad—so mad, in fact, that in a fit of homicidal mania
he has just throttled a man—gets you by the throat, you expect to
experience a certain discomfort. But you do not expect to be
pushed backwards and forwards as a child is pushed when you play
with it—without discomfort or hurt. And above all you do not
expect that madman to mutter urgently in your ear, 'For God's
sake—don't give your secret away. Delay him—at all costs. You're
in the most deadly peril. Burn the house down. Do anything.'

Unless, of course, the madman was not mad.

CHAPTER 10

In Which Drummond Goes on Board the SY Gadfly

But however chaotic Professor Goodman's thoughts, they were
like a placid pool compared to Drummond's. He had first recovered
consciousness as he lay on the floor in the room below, and with
that instinctive caution which was second nature to him, he had
remained motionless. Two men were talking, and the sound of his
own name instinctively put him on his guard. At first he listened
vaguely—his head was still aching infernally—while he tried to
piece together in his mind what had happened. He remembered
taking the receiver off the telephone in the deserted house; he
remembered a stunning blow on the back of the head; and after
that he remembered nothing more. And since he realised that he
was now lying on the floor, it was obvious that an overwhelming
desire for his comfort was not a matter of great importance with the
floor's owner. The first point, therefore, to be decided was the
identity of that gentleman.

On that score he was not left long in doubt, and it needed all his
marvellous self-control to go on lying doggo when he realised who
it was. It was Peterson—and as he listened to the thoughtful
arrangements for his future it was evident that Peterson's feelings

for him were still not characterised by warm regard. He heard the other man pleasantly suggest finishing him off then and there; he heard Peterson's refusal and the reasons for it. And though his head was still swimming, and thinking was difficult, his subconscious mind dictated the obvious course. As long as he remained unconscious, Peterson's insensate hatred for him would keep him safe. So far, so good—but it wasn't very far. However, they couldn't sit there talking the whole night, and once they left him alone, or even with some man to guard him, he had ample faith in his ability to get away. And once out of the house he and Peterson would be on level terms again.

Once again he turned his attention to the conversation. Yacht—what was this about a yacht? With every sense alert he strove to make his throbbing brain take in what they were saying. And gradually as he listened the main outline of the whole diabolical scheme grew clear in all its magnificent simplicity. But who on earth was the man upstairs to whom Peterson kept alluding? Whoever he was, he was presumably completely unconscious of the fate in store for him. And it struck Drummond that he was going to complicate matters. It would mean intense rapidity of action on his part once he was out of the house if he was going to save the poor devil's life.

For one brief instant, as Peterson bent over him, he had a wild thought of bringing matters to a head then and there. To get his hands on the swine once more was an almost overmastering temptation, but he resisted it successfully. It would mean a fight and an unholy fight at that, and Drummond realised that conditions were all against him. His head, for one thing—and total ignorance of the house. And then, to his relief, Peterson sat down again. No—there was nothing for it but to go on shamming and take his chance later.

Up to date he had not dared to open his eyes for even the fraction of a second, so he had no idea in what guise Peterson was at present masquerading. Nor had he a notion as to what the second man looked like. All he knew about that sportsman was that he was the dealer of the blow that had stunned him. And Drummond had a rooted dislike for men who stunned him. His name he gathered was Freyder, so he added Mr Freyder to his mental black-list.

At last, to his relief, the conversation had ended, and he heard the orders given about his disposal for the night. Inert and sagging,

150

he had allowed himself to be carried upstairs, and thrown on the bed. And then in very truth nature had asserted herself. He ceased to sham and fell asleep. For how long he remained asleep he had no idea, but he awoke to find himself alone in the room. The door was open, and from outside there came the sound of voices. It seemed to him that it was now or never, and the next instant he was off the bed. He slipped off his shoes and stole into the passage.

The voices were coming from the next room, and the door of that was also open. He recognised Peterson and the man called Freyder, and without further delay he turned and went in the opposite direction, only to stop short in his tracks as a terrible scream rang out. It came from the room where Peterson was.

Like a shadow he stole back and looked in, and the sight he saw almost made him wonder if he wasn't delirious. For there, moaning pitifully in a chair, was Professor Goodman. That was the staggering fact which drummed in his brain—Professor Goodman was not dead, but alive. But—what to do: that was the point. They were going to torture the poor old man again, and he already heard steps in the hall.

And like a flash there came the only possible solution. Downstairs they had mentioned concussion: so be it—he would be concussed. It was the only hope, and the ease with which Freyder's face made contact with the electric furnace was a happy augury.

But he was under no delusions. From being a helpless log, he had suddenly become an obstreperous madman. It was going to make things considerably more difficult. And one thing it had definitely done—it had lessened any chance he had of escaping from the house. They would be certain to tie him up. Still, now that he had discovered the amazing fact about Professor Goodman, it would have been impossible for him to leave the house in any case, unless he could take the old man with him.

With his hands lashed together on the bed, and this time feigning sleep, he tried to see the way out. Three men were in the room with him now, and for a time he was inclined to curse himself for a fool. Better almost to have let the old man be burnt again—and got away himself for help. But no man—certainly not Drummond—could have allowed such a thing to take place if it was in his power to prevent it. Besides, Freyder's face was an immense compensation.

Why were they torturing him? There could only be one reason—

to compel him to do something which he didn't wish to. And what could that be except reveal to Peterson the secret of the process? The more he thought about it, the clearer it became. Once Peterson was in possession of the secret, any further necessity for keeping Goodman alive would have departed. Obviously he had deceived Peterson once—but would he have the pluck to do it again? That he was an obstinate old man at times, Drummond knew—but torture has a way of overcoming obstinacy. Especially Peterson's brand of torture.

For all that, however, torture would be better than death, and to give Peterson the secret would be signing his death-warrant. For hours he lay there trying to see a ray of light. That Peterson would try to restore him to sanity before killing him he knew, but, at the same time, it was not safe to bank on it absolutely. That Peterson would kill Goodman at the first moment possible he also knew. And that was the fact which tied his hands so completely.

If only he could get at Goodman—if only he could warn him not to give away his secret, whatever happened—there was hope. The Professor's life was safe till then; they might hurt him—but his life was safe. And if only he could get away, he might pull it off even now. The process, he knew, took six hours; if the Professor had the nerve to bluff Peterson twice more—twelve hours, say fourteen. . . . A lot could be done in fourteen hours.

And suddenly he lay very still—two of the men were leaving the room. Was this his chance? He stirred uneasily on the bed, as a sick man does who is asleep. Then he rolled over on his back breathing stertorously. It was all perfectly natural, and roused no suspicions in the mind of the remaining man. But it brought Drummond's hands into the position in which he wanted them.

Contemptuously the man came over and stared at him as he lay. It was a foolish thing to do, and it was still more foolish to lean down a little to see the patient better. For the next moment a pair of hands with fingers like steel hooks had fastened on his throat, and the sleeper was asleep no more. Gasping and choking, he beat impotently at the big man's face, striking it again and again, but he might as well have hit the wall for all the good he did. And gradually his struggles grew fainter and fainter till they ceased altogether.

Thus had Drummond got his message through to Professor Goodman. On the spur of the moment it had occurred to him that

152

by pretending to believe he was Peterson not only would it increase his chances of speaking to the Professor, but it would also tend to strengthen the belief that he was insane. An unexpected and additional help towards that end had been his appearance, though that he couldn't be expected to know. And now as once again he lay on the bed—bound this time hand and foot—he wondered desperately if he had succeeded.

Professor Goodman had got his whispered message—that he knew. But had he been in time? In addition, so far as he could tell, he had, up to the present, successfully bluffed Peterson and everyone else in the house as to his mental condition. But could he keep it up? And, anyway, trussed up as he now was, and as common sense told him he would continue to be until he was taken on board the yacht, what good would it do even if he could? It might save his life for the time being, but it wouldn't help his ultimate hopes of getting away. Nor the Professor's. Once they were on board he had to admit to himself that their chance of coming out alive was small. Anything can happen on a boat where the whole crew are unscrupulous. And even if the possibility arose of his getting away by going overboard and swimming, it was out of the question for the Professor. The chances were that the old man couldn't swim a stroke, and Drummond, powerful though he was in the water, was not such a fool as to imagine that he could support a non-swimmer for possibly several hours. Besides, it was not a matter of great difficulty to lower a boat, and an oar is a nasty thing to be hit on the head with, when swimming. No, the only hope seemed to be that Professor Goodman should hold out, and that by some fluke he should get away. Or send a message. But whom to?—and how? He didn't even know where he was.

And at that very moment the principal part of that forlorn hope was being dashed to the ground in the next room. Once again the benevolent Mr Robinson was chiselling out the clinker from the metal retort, while the Professor watched him wearily from his chair. There was no mistake this time; Drummond's warning had come too late. And with a cry of triumph Mr Robinson felt his chisel hit something hard: the diamond was there. He dug on feverishly, and the next minute a big uncut diamond—dirty still with the fragments of clinker adhering to it—lay in his hand. He gazed at it triumphantly, and for a moment or two felt almost unable to speak. Success at last: assured and beyond doubt. In his

153

notebook was the process; there was no need for further delay.

And then he realised that Professor Goodman was saying something.

'I have shown you as I promised.' His voice seemed very weary. 'That is the method of making the ordinary white diamond. To-morrow, after I have rested for a while, I will show you how to make one that is rose-pink.'

Mr Robinson hesitated.

'Is there much difference in the system?' he remarked thoughtfully.

The Professor's voice shook a little—but then it was hardly to be wondered at. He had had a trying evening.

'It will mean obtaining a somewhat rare strontium salt,' he answered. 'Also it has to be added to the other salts in minute doses from time to time to ensure perfect mixing. The heat also has to be regulated a little differently.'

His eyes searched the other's face anxiously. Delay him—at all costs. Drummond's urgent words still rang in his ears, and this seemed the only chance of doing so. The main secret he had already given away; there was nothing he could do or say to alter that. Only with Drummond's warning had he realised finally that he had been fooled; that in all probability the promise of rejoining his wife had been a lie from beginning to end. And the realisation had roused every atom of fight he had in him.

He was a shrewd old man for all his absentmindedness, and during the hour he had sat there while the furnace cooled his mind had been busy. How Drummond had got there he didn't know, but in Drummond lay his only hope. And if Drummond said delay, he would do his best to carry out instructions. Moreover, Drummond had said something else too, and he was a chemist.

'Where can you obtain this strontium salt?' asked Mr Robinson at length.

'From any big chemist in London,' replied the other.

Mr Robinson fingered the diamond in his hand. It would mean additional delay, but did that matter very much? Now that he was in possession of the secret he had half decided to get away early in the morning. The yacht was ready; he could step on board when he liked. But there were undoubted advantages in being able to make rose-pink diamonds as well as the ordinary brand, and it struck him that, after all, he might just as well adhere to his original plan.

Drummond was safe; there was nothing to fear from the old fool in the chair. So why not?

'Give me the name of the salt and it shall be sent for tomorrow,' he remarked.

'If you're sending,' said the Professor mildly, 'you might get some other salts too. By my process I can make them blue, green, black, or yellow, as well as red. Each requires a separate salt, though the process is basically the same.'

Once again Mr Robinson frowned thoughtfully, and once again he decided—why not? Blue diamonds were immensely valuable, and he might as well have the process complete.

'Make a list of everything you want,' he snapped, 'and I will get the whole lot tomorrow. And now, after you've done that, go to bed.'

He watched the old man go shambling along the passage to his room; then, slipping the diamond into his pocket, he went in to have a look at Drummond. He was apparently asleep, and for a while Mr Robinson stood beside him with a look of malignant satisfaction on his face. That his revenge on the man lying bound and helpless on the bed added to the risk of his plans, he knew; but no power on earth would have made him forgo it. In the eyes of the world Professor Goodman was already dead; in his case he would merely be confirming an already established fact. But with Drummond it was different. There would be a hue and cry: there was bound to be. But what did it matter? Was he not going to die himself—officially? And dead men are uninteresting people to pursue.

'Don't relax your guard for an instant,' he said to the two men. 'We shall be leaving here tomorrow afternoon.'

He left the room and went down to his own particular sanctum. He had made up his mind as to what he would do, and it seemed to solve all the difficulties in the most satisfactory way. These special salts should be sent direct to the yacht and Professor Goodman should initiate him into their mysteries on board. He would have the electric furnace taken from the house, and the experiments could be carried out just as easily at sea. And when finally he felt confident of making all the various colours, and not till then, he would drop the old fool overboard. Drummond also; the extra few days would increase the chance of his becoming sane again.

He suddenly bethought him of Freyder, and went into his room.

His face, even his eyes, were completely hidden by bandages, and Mr Robinson expressed his sympathy. In fact after Freyder had exhausted his vocabulary on the subject of Drummond, Mr Robinson even went so far as to promise his subordinate a special private chance of getting some of his own back.

'You may do anything you like to him, my dear fellow,' he said soothingly, 'save actually kill him. I shall watch it all with the greatest pleasure. I only reserve to myself the actual *coup de grâce*.'

He closed the door and, returning to his study, took the diamond out of his pocket. The tools at his disposal were not very delicate, but he determined, even at the risk of damaging the diamond, to work with them. He wanted to make assurance doubly sure, and it was not until the first faint streaks of dawn were coming through the window that he rose from his work with a sigh of satisfaction. On the table in front of him lay diamonds to the value of some six or seven thousand pounds; there had been no mistake this time. And with a sigh of satisfaction he placed them in his safe.

He felt suddenly tired, and glancing at his watch he found that it was already half-past three. A little rest was essential, and Mr Robinson went upstairs. He stopped by the Professor's room and looked in: the old man was fast asleep in bed. Then he went to see Drummond once more, and found him muttering uneasily under the watchful eyes of his two guards. Everything was correct and in order, and with another sigh of satisfaction he retired to his room for a little well-earned repose.

It was one of his assets that he could do with a very small amount of sleep, and eight o'clock the following morning found him up and about again. His first care were his two prisoners, and to his surprise he found the Professor already up and pottering about in the room where he had been working the night before. He seemed in the best of spirits, and for a moment or two Mr Robinson eyed him suspiciously. He quite failed to see what the old man had to be pleased about.

'One day nearer rejoining my dear wife,' he remarked as he saw the other standing in the doorway. 'You can't think how excited I feel about it.'

'Not being married myself,' agreed Mr Robinson pleasantly, 'I admit that I cannot enter into your joy. You're up early this morning.'

'I couldn't sleep after six,' explained the Professor. 'And so I decided to rise.'

Mr Robinson grunted.

'Your breakfast will be brought to you shortly,' he remarked. 'I would advise you to eat a good one, as we shall be starting shortly afterwards.'

'Starting?' stammered the Professor. 'But I thought you wished me to show you how to make blue diamonds. And the other colours too.'

'I do,' answered the other. 'But you will show me, Professor, on board my yacht. I trust that you are a good sailor, though at this time of year the sea should be calm.'

Professor Goodman stood by the electric furnace plucking nervously at his collar. It seemed as if the news of this early departure had given him a bit of a shock.

'I see,' he said at length. 'I did not understand that we were starting so soon.'

'You have no objections, I hope,' murmured Mr Robinson politely. 'The sooner we start, the sooner will come that delirious moment when you once more clasp Mrs Goodman in your arms. And now I will leave you, if you will excuse me. I have one or two things to attend to—amongst them our obstreperous young friend of last night.'

He strolled along the passage into the room where Drummond was. And though he realised that the idea was absurd, he felt a little throb of relief when he saw him still lying bound on the bed. Ridiculous, of course, that he should find anything else, and yet Drummond, in the past, had extricated himself from such seemingly impossible situations that the sight of him bound and helpless was reassuring. Drummond smiled at him vacantly, and with a shrug of his shoulders he turned to the two men.

'Has he given any trouble?' he asked.

'Not a bit, guv'nor,' answered one of them. 'He's as barmy as he can be. Grins and smiles all over his face, except when that old bloke next door comes near him.'

Mr Robinson stared at the speaker.

'What do you mean?' he said. 'Has the old man been in here this morning?'

'He came in about half an hour ago,' answered the other. 'Said he wanted to see how the poor fellow was getting on. And as soon as

Drummond saw him he started snarling and cursing and trying to get at him. I tell you we had the devil's own job with him—and then after a while he lay quiet again. Thinks he's some bloke of the name of Peterson.'

'How long was the old man here?' said Mr Robinson abruptly.

'About half a minute. Then we turned him out.'

'Under no circumstances is he to be allowed in here again.'

Mr Robinson again bent over Drummond and stared into his eyes. But no sign of reason showed on his face: the half-open mouth still grinned its vacant grin. And after a while Mr Robinson straightened up again. He had allowed himself to be alarmed unnecessarily: Drummond was still off his head.

'We are leaving at once after breakfast,' he remarked. 'He is to be put in the ambulance as he is. And if he makes any noise—gag him.'

'Very good, guv'nor. Is he to have anything to eat?'

'No—let the swine starve.'

Mr Robinson left the room without a backward glance, and the sudden desperate glint in Drummond's eyes passed unnoticed. For now indeed things did look utterly hopeless. The Professor's plan passed to him on a piece of paper and which he had conveyed to his mouth and swallowed as soon as read, even if it was a plan of despair, had in it the germ of success. It was nothing more nor less than to set fire to the house with chemicals that would burn furiously, and trust to something happening in the confusion. At any rate it might have brought in outside people—the police, the fire brigade. And Peterson could hardly have left him bound upstairs with the house on fire. Not from any kindly motives—but expediency would have prevented it. Only the chemicals had to come from London, and if they were starting at once after breakfast it was obvious that the stuff couldn't arrive in time.

The dear old Professor he took his hat off to. Tortured and abominably treated, he had kept his head and his nerve in the most wonderful way. For a man of his age and sedentary method of life not to have broken down completely under the strain was nothing short of marvellous. And not only had he not broken down, but he'd thought out a scheme and got it to Drummond wrapped round a Gillette razor-blade. It had taken a bit of doing to get the blade into his waistcoat pocket, and had his arms been bound to his body he couldn't have done it. But fortunately only his wrists were

158

lashed together, and he had managed it. And now it all seemed wasted.

He debated in his mind whether he would try to cut the ropes, and chance everything in one wild fight at once. But the two men eating their breakfast near the foot of his bed were burly brutes. And even if by twisting himself up he had been able to cut the cord round his legs without their noticing he would be at a terrible disadvantage, cramped after his confinement as he was. Besides, there was the Professor. Nothing now would have induced him to leave the old man. Whatever happened, he must stay beside him in the hopes of being able to help him. Because one thing was clear. Even if he personally escaped, unless he could get help before the yacht started—the Professor was doomed. The yacht was going down with all hands: there lay the devilish ingenuity of the scheme.

And even if he could have prevented the yacht sailing, he knew Peterson quite well enough to realise that he would merely change his plans at the last moment. As he had so often done in the past, he would disappear, with the secret—having first killed Professor Goodman.

No; the only possible chance lay in his going on the yacht himself and trusting to luck to find a way out. Incidentally it was perhaps as well that the only possible chance did lie in that direction, since, as far as Drummond could see, his prospects of not going on board were even remoter than his prospects of getting any breakfast.

A sudden shuffling step in the passage outside brought his two guards to their feet. They dashed to the door just as Professor Goodman appeared, and then they stopped with a laugh. For the old man was swaying backwards and forwards and his eyes were rolling horribly.

'I've been drugged,' he muttered, and pitched forward on his face.

Then the men sat down again, leaving him where he lay.

'That'll keep him quiet,' said one of them. 'It was in his tea.'

'If I had my way I'd put a bucket of it into the swab on the bed,' answered the other. 'It's him that wants keeping quiet.'

The first speaker laughed brutally.

'He won't give much trouble. Once we've got him on board, it'll be just pure joy to watch the fun. Freyder's like a man that's sat on a hornet's nest this morning.'

And at that moment Freyder himself entered the room. His face

159

was still swathed in bandages, and Drummond beamed happily at him. The sight of him provided the one bright spot in an otherwise gloomy horizon, though the horrible blow which he received on the mouth rather obscured the brightness, and gave him a foretaste of what he could expect from the gentleman. But true to his rôle, Drummond still grinned on, though he turned his head away to hide the smouldering fury in his eyes. In the past he had been fairly successful with Peterson's lieutenants, and he registered a mental vow that Mr Julius Freyder would not be an exception.

He watched him go from the room kicking the sprawling body of the Professor contemptuously as he passed, and once again he was left to his gloomy thoughts. It was all very well to register vows of vengeance, but to carry them out first of all entailed getting free. And then a sudden ray of hope dawned in his mind. How were they going to be got on board? Stretchers presumably, and that would be bound to attract attention if the yacht was lying in any harbour. But was she? She might be lying out to sea somewhere, and send a boat ashore for them in some deserted stretch of coast. That was the devil of it, he hadn't the faintest idea where he was. He might be in Essex; he might be on the South Coast; he might even be down on the Bristol Channel.

A little wearily he gave it up; after all, what was the good of worrying? He was bound and the Professor was drugged, and as far as he could see any self-respecting life insurance would hesitate at a ninety-five per cent premium for either of them. His principal desire at the moment was for breakfast, and as that was evidently not in the programme, all he could do was to inhale the aroma of eggs and bacon, and wonder why he'd been such a damned fool as to take that telephone call.

The tramp of footsteps on the stairs roused him from his lethargy, and he half-turned his head to look at the door. Two men were there with a stretcher, on which they were placing the Professor. Then they disappeared, to return again a few moments later with another, which they put down beside his bed. It was evidently his turn now, but, even bound as he was, they showed no inclination to treat him as unceremoniously as the Professor. His reputation seemed to have got abroad, and, though he smiled at them inanely and burbled foolishly, they invoked the assistance of the other two men, who had just finished their breakfast, before lifting him up and putting him on the stretcher.

In the hall stood Mr Robinson, who again peered at him intently as he passed, and then Drummond found himself hoisted into the back of a car which seemed to be a cross between an ambulance and a caravan. The back consisted of two doors instead of the conventional ambulance curtains, and on each side was a window covered with muslin blind. Two bunks, one on each side, stretched the full length of the car and a central gang-way, which had a little wash-basin at the end nearest the engine, separated them.

On one of these bunks lay Professor Goodman, breathing with the heavy, stertorous sounds of the drugged. The men pitched him on to the other, as Mr Robinson, who had followed them out, appeared.

'You have your orders,' he remarked curtly. 'If Drummond makes a sound—gag him. I shall be on board myself in about two hours.'

He closed the doors, leaving the two men inside, and the car started. It was impossible to see out of either window owing to the curtains, and the ostentatious production of a revolver by one of the men removed any thought Drummond might have had of trying to use the razor-blade. 'Mad or not, take no chances,' was the motto of his two guards, and when on top of everything else, though he hadn't made a sound, they crammed a handkerchief half-down his throat, he almost laughed.

He judged they had been going for about an hour, when the diminished speed of the car and the increased sounds of traffic indicated a town. It felt as if they were travelling over cobbles, and once they stopped at what was evidently a level crossing, for he heard a train go by. And then came the sound of a steamer's siren, to be followed by another and yet a third.

A seaport town obviously, he reflected, though that didn't help much. The only comfort was that a seaport town meant a well-used waterway outside. And if he could get free, if he could go over-board with the Professor, there might be a shade more of a chance of being picked up. Also there would almost certainly be curious loungers about as they were carried on board.

The car had stopped; he could hear the driver talking to someone. Then it ran forward a little and stopped again. And a moment or two later a curious swaying motion almost pitched him off the bunk. Surely they couldn't be at sea yet. The car dropped suddenly, and with a sick feeling of despair he realised what had happened.

The car had been hoisted bodily on board; his faint hope of being able to communicate with some onlooker had gone.

Once again the car became stationary, save for a very faint and almost imperceptible movement. From outside came the sounds of men heaving on ropes, and the car steadied again. They were actually on board, and the car was being made fast.

Still the two men sat there with the doors tight shut, and the windows hermetically sealed by the blinds. They seemed to be waiting for something, and suddenly, with a sigh of relief, one spoke.

'She's off.'

It was true: Drummond could feel the faint throb of the propeller.

'The specimens are aboard,' laughed the other man, 'and I guess it will be safe to open the doors in about a quarter of an hour or so, and get a bit of air. This damned thing is like a Turkish bath.'

He rose and peered cautiously through a slit in the curtain, but he made no movement to open the door until the throbbing of the propeller had ceased, and the harsh rattle of a chain showed that they were anchoring. Then and not till then did he open the doors with a sigh of relief.

Cautiously Drummond raised his head, and stared out. Where were they? He had followed every movement in his mind since he had come on board, but he was still as far as ever from knowing where they were. And luckily one glance was enough. It didn't even need the glimpse he got of a huge Cunarder about a half-mile away: he recognised the shore. They were in Southampton Water, and though the knowledge didn't seem to help very much, at any rate it was something to have one definite fact to start from.

Southampton Water! He managed to shift the sodden pocket-handkerchief into a more comfortable position, and his train of thought grew pessimistic. Why would men invent processes for making diamonds? he reflected morosely. If only the dear old blitherer still peacefully sleeping in the opposite bunk had stuck to albumenised food, he wouldn't have been lying trussed up like a Christmas turkey. Far from it: he would have been disporting himself on Ted Jerningham's governor's yacht at Cowes. Had not Ted expressly invited him—Ted, who had hunted Peterson with him in the past, and asked for nothing better than to hunt him again?

The irony of it! To think that Ted might even see the yacht go

162

by; might remark on the benevolence of the appearance of mutton-chop whiskers, if by chance he should be on deck. And he would never know. In all ignorance he would return to one of his habitual spasms of love, which always assailed him when afloat, with anyone who happened to be handy.

It was a distressing thought, and, after a while, he resolutely tried to banish it from his mind. But it refused to be banished. Absurd, of course, but suppose—just suppose he could communicate with Ted. Things were so desperate that he could not afford to neglect even the wildest chance. Ted's father's yacht generally lay, as he knew, not far from the outgoing waterway; he remembered sitting on deck with Phyllis and watching a Union Castle boat go by so close that he could see the passengers' faces on deck. What if he could shout or something? But Ted might not be on deck.

Eagerly he turned the problem over in his mind, and the more he thought of it the more it seemed to him to be the only possible way out. How to do it, he hadn't an idea—but at any rate it was something to occupy his thoughts. And when the benevolent face of Mr Robinson appeared at the door some hours later, he was still wrestling with the problem, though the vacant look in his eyes left nothing to be desired.

'Any difficulty getting on board?' asked Mr Robinson.

'None at all, boss,' answered the man who was still on guard. 'We gagged the madman to be on the safe side.'

Mr Robinson beamed.

'Take the old man below,' he remarked. 'He'll be coming round soon. I will stay with our friend here till you return.'

Thoughtfully he pulled the handkerchief out of Drummond's mouth and sat down on the opposite bunk.

'Still suffering from concussion,' he said gently. 'Still, we have plenty of time, Captain Drummond—plenty of time.'

'Gug-gug,' answered Drummond happily.

'Precisely,' murmured the other. 'I believe that men frequently say that when they drown. But I promise you we won't drown you at once. As I say—there is plenty of time.'

CHAPTER 11

In Which Drummond Leaves the SY Gadfly

Still smiling benevolently, Mr Robinson strolled away, and shortly afterwards a series of sharp orders followed by a faint throbbing announced that the voyage of the *SY Gadfly* had commenced. The Cunarder receded into the distance, and still Drummond lay on the bunk wrestling with the problem of what to do. He judged the time as being about six, so they would pass Ted Jerningham's yacht in daylight.

Apparently no guard was considered necessary for him now that the yacht was under way; after all, to watch a completely bound madman is a boring and uninteresting pastime. And with a feeling of impotent rage Drummond realised how easy it would be to cut the ropes and go quietly overboard. A swim of a mile or so meant nothing to him. If only it hadn't been for the Professor! . . .

No; the last hope—the only hope—lay in Ted Jerningham. Once that failed, it seemed to Drummond that nothing could save them. And it was perfectly clear that by no possibility could he hope to communicate with Ted from his present position. He must be free to use his limbs. And during the next ten minutes he discovered that the blade of a safety-razor is an unpleasant implement with which to cut half-inch rope, especially when one's wrists are bound.

But at last it was done, and he was free. No one had interrupted him, though once some footsteps outside had made him sweat with fear. But he was still no nearer to the solution of the problem. At any moment someone might come in and find him, and there would be no mistake about binding him the second time. Moreover, it would prove fairly conclusively that he was not as mad as he pretended.

Quickly he arranged the ropes with the cut ends underneath, so that to a cursory glance they appeared intact. Then he again lay still. That the glance would have to be very cursory for anyone to be deceived he realised, but it was the best he could do. And anyway he was free, even if only for the time. If the worst came to the worst he had no doubt as to his ability to fight his way to the side and go overboard; gun work is impossible in Southampton Water. But unless he did it near another ship, he feared that the delay before he

164

could do anything would be fatal to the Professor. Peterson would take no chances in this case; he would murder the old man out of hand, instead of postponing the event.

And then, suddenly, came the idea—Ted's motor-boat. How it was going to help he didn't see; he had no coherent plan. But with a sort of subconscious certainty he felt that in Ted's motor-boat lay the key to the problem. She was a wonderful machine, capable of doing her forty knots with ease, and she was the darling of Ted's heart. Her method of progress in the slightest swell resembled a continuous rush down the waterchute at Earl's Court; and her owner was wont to take whoever occupied his heart for the moment for what he termed 'a bit of a breather' on most evenings after dinner.

Ted's motor-boat was their hope, he decided; but how? How to get at Ted, how to tell him, was the problem. Methodically he thought things out; now that he had something definite in his mind to go on, his brain was cool and collected. And it seemed to him that the only way would be to go overboard as they passed Ted's yacht, and then follow the *Gadfly* at once while she was still close to land. There would be men on Ted's yacht, and they could board the *Gadfly* and hold her up. That there were difficulties he realised. It meant leaving the Professor for at least an hour even under the most favourable conditions. Further it would be getting dark when they overtook the *Gadfly*, and to board a yacht steaming her twelve to fifteen knots is not a simple matter when the crew of the yacht do not desire your presence, and await you with marline-spikes on deck. Besides, the guests on Ted's yacht might feel that as an evening's amusement 'hunt the slipper' won on points. Still, it seemed the only chance, and he decided on it unless something better turned up. Anyway, it was a plan with a chance of success, which was something.

He glanced through the open door to try to spot his position, and estimated that another half-hour at the rate they were going would just about bring them opposite Ted's yacht. Still no one came near him, though periodically he could see one of the sailors moving about the deck. As far as he could tell, he had been slung just aft of the funnel, though he dared not raise himself too much for fear of being seen.

The minutes passed, and his hopes began to rise. Could it be that luck was going to be on his side? Could it be that no one would come, and that in the failing light he might be able to slip over the side unperceived? If so, he might gain an invaluable half-hour; more—he might be able to get the motor-boat alongside the *Gadfly* later without the crew suspecting anything. It seemed too good to be true, and yet a quarter of an hour, twenty minutes, passed, and he was still alone.

He peered out again; they were getting very close. The deck was deserted, and suddenly he felt he could bear the strain no longer. He rose from the bunk and cautiously peered out of the door. And the sight he saw almost staggered him with his good fortune. If he had been walking about the deck instead of being cooped up under cover he could not have timed it more exactly. Not a hundred yards away to port lay Jerningham's yacht, with the motor-boat alongside the gangway.

Drummond glanced round; he could see no one. The structure in which he had been hoisted on board effectively screened him from the bridge; the sailors were apparently having their evening meal. And taking a quick breath he prepared to make a sprint for the side when he saw something which completely altered his plans. Leaning over the side of the yacht he was watching were a man and a woman. And the man was Ted Jerningham himself.

Drummond saw him focus a pair of field-glasses and turn them on the *Gadfly*. And then clear and distinct across the water he heard the amazed shout of 'Hugh'. Jerningham had seen him; the supreme chance had come, if only he wasn't interrupted. And it is safe to say that during the next minute a very astonished girl stood beside a man whom she almost failed to recognise as the Ted Jerningham of normal life.

'A pencil,' he snapped. 'Write as I spell out. Get a move on. Look out: he's beginning. D.A.N.G.E.R. F.O.L.L.O.W. I.N. M.O.T.O.R. B.O.A.T. P.E.T.E.R.S.O.N. U.R.G.E.N.T. That's all.'

She looked up: the huge man on board the passing yacht who had been standing outlined against the sky waving his arms had disappeared.

'What on earth was he doing?' she cried.

'Semaphoring,' answered Jerningham briefly.

'But I don't understand,' she said.

'Nor do I,' returned her companion. 'But that was Hugh Drummond. And what Hugh says—goes, if we follow for the whole night. Coming?'

'Rather. Who's Peterson?'

'A very dear old friend,' said Jerningham with a grim smile. 'But how the deuce . . .' He broke off, and stared after the retreating yacht. 'He loves me, because I emptied the entire sauce-boat over his shirt-front one night in Paris, when disguised as a waiter at the Ritz.'

'My dear Ted, are you mad?' laughed the girl, following him down the gangway into the waiting motor-boat.

'Oh! no—just fun and laughter. You wouldn't believe what a humorist old man Peterson is.'

A terrific explosion rent the air, followed by a cloud of blue smoke, and Jerningham took the tiller.

'Warm enough, Pat?' he asked. 'It may be a long show.'

'Quite, thanks,' she answered. 'Ted, why do you look so grave?'

'I'm just wondering, my dear, if I ought to take you.' His hand was still on the gangway, and he looked at her irresolutely.

'Why on earth not?'

'Because there may be very grave danger.'

The girl laughed.

'Get on with it while the going's good,' she said. 'That yacht will be past the Needles if you delay much longer.'

And so it came about that Drummond, watching feverishly from his bunk in the *Gadfly*, saw with a sigh of intense relief the motor-boat shoot out across the water. It was nearly a mile astern, but a mile was nothing to a boat of its great speed. Moreover, the distance was lessening, and he breathed a prayer that Ted wouldn't come too close. With the amount of traffic round and about Cowes at that time of year an odd motor-boat could raise no suspicion, but if he settled down to follow steadily at a hundred yards or so astern he would be bound to draw attention to himself.

He had not dared to send a longer message, and, of necessity, it had left a good deal to Ted's imagination. But of all the men who had followed him unhesitatingly in the past, Ted Jerningham had been always the quickest on the uptake, and he soon saw that his confidence had not been misplaced. Ted had evidently realised that to follow steadily would arouse suspicion, and was laying his plans accordingly. He overhauled them like an express train, passed forty yards to starboard, circled their bow, and came dashing back. Then away at a tangent for half a mile or so, only to shoot back and stop apparently with engine trouble.

The sea was like a millpond, and as the *Gadfly* passed the now silent motor-boat the sounds of a gramophone were plainly audible from it. Obviously someone with a racing motor-boat joy-riding with a girl, reflected the skipper as he paced the bridge; and forthwith dismissed the matter from his mind. He had other more important things to think of, and the first was the exact object of this trip. That the benevolent Mr Robinson had hired the *Gadfly* from its owner to take two invalids to Madeira he knew, but he wasn't quite satisfied. The method of bringing the invalids on board had seemed so unnecessarily secretive. However, as is the way of men who go down to the sea in ships, his nature was not curious. He was there to carry out orders, and mind his own business—not other people's. Still, he couldn't help wondering. And had he seen the occupation of one of those invalids at the moment he would have wondered still more. For Drummond, having found a cake of soap on the basin beside his bunk, was carefully cutting it into small cubes with the blade of a safety-razor. Though perhaps that is what one would expect from a madman.

A sudden hoarse scream of fear some five minutes later made the Captain jump to the side of the bridge. Two sailors were rushing along the deck as if pursued by the devil, and he roared an order at them. But they took no notice of him, and dashed below. For a moment the worthy skipper stood there dumbfounded; then, cursing fluently, he dashed after them, only to stop with a strange pricking feeling in his scalp as a huge and ghastly figure confronted him. A great mass of foam was round its mouth, and it was brandishing a marline spike and bellowing. A terrifying spectacle in the half-light of dusk—a spectacle to put the fear of God into any man. And then as suddenly as it appeared it was gone.

Terror is an infectious thing, and the infection spread in the good ship *Gadfly*. Within two minutes men were running in all directions, shouting that a homicidal maniac was loose on board. Below an appalling crash of breaking crockery and the sudden appearance on deck of a terrified steward told its own tale. The Captain was powerless; things had gone beyond him. He roared a futile order or two: no one paid the slightest attention to him. And then, quite suddenly, the pandemonium ceased—and men held their breath. How he had got there no one could say—but they all saw him outlined against the darkening sky.

The madman was in the stern, and in his arms he held the body of a man.

'At last,' they heard him shout, 'at last I've got you, Peterson. We die together—you devil. . . .'

'Stop them,' howled Mr Robinson, who had just dashed on deck, holding a limp right arm; but no man moved. Only a loud splash broke the silence, and the stern was empty.

'Man overboard. Lower a boat. Stop the yacht, you cursed fool,' snarled Mr Robinson to the Captain, and then he rushed to the stern. Dimly in the failing light he thought he could see two heads in the water, but it was a couple of minutes before a boat was lowered, and in that couple of minutes he heard the roar of an engine coming nearer. Then the engine ceased, and he saw the outline of a motor-boat.

'That boat may have picked 'em up, sir,' said the Captain, as Mr Robinson ran down the gangway into the waiting cutter.

'Give way all,' came the second officer's curt order. 'With a will, boys.'

The motor-boat, still motionless, loomed rapidly up, and Mr Robinson stood up.

'Ahoy there! Did you pick up those two men who fell overboard?'

'Two!' Ted Jerningham, a conspicuous figure in white flannels, stood up also. 'I heard the most infernal shindy on board your yacht and then a splash. Do you mean to say two men have fallen overboard?'

The yacht's boat was close to, the sailors resting on their oars.

'Yes. Have you seen 'em?' asked the second officer.

'Not a sign. And the water's like a duckpond too.'

The girl with him shuddered.

'How dreadful! You don't mean the poor fellows are drowned?'

'Afraid it looks like it, miss,' said the officer, staring round the water. 'Even in this light we'd see them with the sea as calm as it is.'

Mr Robinson whispered something in his ear, which he seemed to resent.

'Do what you're told,' snarled his master, and with a shrug he gave an order.

'Give way.'

The oars dipped in the water, and they passed astern of the motor-boat. And had Mr Robinson been watching Ted Jerningham instead of the water he might have seen a sudden strained look appear on that young gentleman's face, and his hand move instinctively towards the starting-switch. He might even have wondered why the girl, who had seemed so calm and unperturbed in the face of this dreadful tragedy, should suddenly give vent to a loud and hysterical outburst.

'It's dreadful,' she sobbed—'too dreadful! To think of those two poor men being drowned like that.'

But Mr Robinson was not concerned with the dreadfulness of the situation; all that mattered to him was whether it was true or not. From the moment when Drummond, foaming at the mouth, had dashed into the dining-saloon, Mr Robinson's brain had been working furiously. An attempt to intercept himself between Drummond and Professor Goodman had resulted in an appalling blow on his arm with a marline spike. And then, accustomed though he was to the rapidity of Drummond's movements, even he for a few seconds had been nonplussed. There had been something so diabolical about this huge man, bellowing hoarsely, who had, after that first blow, paid no more attention to him, but had hurled himself straight on the dazed Professor. And even when the Professor, squealing like a rabbit, had dashed on deck with Drummond after him, for an appreciable time Mr Robinson had remained staring stupidly at the door. Drummond sane was dangerous; Drummond mad was nerve-shattering. And then he had pulled himself together just in time to dash on deck and see them both go overboard.

Thoughtfully his eyes searched the water again; there was no trace of either man. Of a suspicious nature, he had examined both sides of the motor-boat; moreover, he had seen inside the motor-boat. And now as the girl's sobs died away he turned to the officer beside him.

'There can be no doubt about it, I fear,' he remarked with a suitable inflection of sorrow in his voice.

'None, sir, I'm afraid. Even if we couldn't see them, we could hear them. I'm afraid the madman's done the poor old gentleman in.'

'Sink in a brace of shakes with a holy terror like that 'anging round yer neck,' said one of the sailors, and a mutter of agreement came from the others.

'Yes, I'm afraid there can be no possibility of saving them now.' Ted Jerningham took out his cigarette-case, only to replace it hurriedly as he remembered the dreadful tragedy they had just witnessed. 'Doubtless, however, their bodies will be washed ashore in time.'

'Er—doubtless,' murmured Mr Robinson. That aspect of the case had already struck him, and had not pleased him in the slightest degree. Had he been able to conform with his original plan, neither body would have ever been seen again. However, he had not been able to conform to that plan, so there was no more to be said about it. The main point was that both of them were drowned.

'Doubtless,' he repeated. 'Poor fellows!—poor fellows! Two neurasthenic patients of mine, sir. . . . How sad!—How terribly sad! However, I fear there is no good wasting any more time. I can only thank you for your prompt assistance, and regret that, through no fault of yours, it was not more effective.'

Jerningham bowed.

'Don't mention it, sir—don't mention it,' he murmured. 'But I think, as I can do no more, that I will now get back. The tragedy, as you will understand, has somewhat upset this lady.'

He put his finger on the starting-switch, and the quiet of the night was broken by the roar of the engine. And as the sailors dipped in their oars to row back to the yacht, the motor-boat circled slowly round.

'Good night, sir.' Mr Robinson waved a courteous hand. 'And again a thousand thanks.'

'And again don't mention it,' returned Jerningham, sitting down by the tiller. 'You can take your wrap off his hand now, Pat,' he whispered. 'They can't see.'

A vast hand grasping the gunwale was revealed as she did so, and an agonised whisper came from the water.

'Hurry, old man, for the love of Pete. Unless we can hold the old man upside-down soon to drain the water out of him, he'll drown.'

'Right-oh! Hugh. Can you hold on for a couple of hundred yards? I'll go slow. But they may have a searchlight on the yacht, and we're still very close to her.'

'All right, Ted. I leave it to you.'

'I'll still keep broadside on, old man; though I don't think he had any suspicions.'

He nosed the motor-boat through the water, and a few moments later the necessity of his precaution was justified. A blinding light flickered across the water, found them, and held steady: it was the *Gadfly*'s searchlight. Jerningham rose and waved his hand, and after a while the beam passed on searching the sea. One final attempt evidently to try to spot the victims of the tragedy, rewarded by empty water. And at last the light went out; all hope had been abandoned.

'Quick, Hugh,' cried Jerningham. 'Get the old boy on board.'

With a heave the almost unconscious form of Professor Goodman was hoisted into the boat, to be followed immediately by Drummond himself.

'Lie down, old man—lie down in case they use that searchlight again.'

The engine roared and spluttered, and two black mountains of water swirled past the bows.

'Forty-five on her head, Hugh,' shouted Ted. 'Incidentally, what's this particular brand of round game?'

'The largest drink in the shortest time, old son,' laughed the other. 'And for the Professor—bed, quick.'

He turned to the girl.

'My dear soul,' he said, 'you were magnificent. If you hadn't had hysteria when I began to sneeze it was all up.'

'But what could he have done?' cried the girl. 'And he looked such a nice old man.'

Drummond laughed grimly.

'Did you recognise him, Ted?' Once again he turned to the girl. 'If he'd known that we were in the water, that nice old man would have had no more compunction in shooting you and Ted and dropping your bodies overboard than I shall have in drinking that drink. It's been the biggest coup of his life, Ted—but it's failed. But, by Jove, old man, it's been touch and go, believe me.'

The roar of the engine made conversation difficult, but after covering the dripping form of the Professor with a dry rug they fell silent. Astern the lights of the *Gadfly* were growing fainter and fainter in the distance; ahead lay Cowes and safety. But Drummond's mind, now that the immediate danger was over, had jumped ahead to the future. To restore the Professor to the bosom of his family was obviously the first thing to be done; but—after that?

The engine ceased abruptly, and he realised they had reached the yacht. Leaning over the side were some of the guests, and as he and Ted lifted the body of the Professor up the gangway a chorus of excited questioning broke out, a chorus which was interrupted by the amazed ejaculation of an elderly man.

'God bless my soul,' he cried incredulously, as the light fell on the Professor's face, 'it's old Goodman's double!'

'Not exactly,' answered Drummond. 'It's Professor Goodman himself.'

'Damme, sir,' spluttered the other, 'I was at his funeral a week ago. He was blown up in his house in Hampstead doing some fool experiment.'

'So we all thought,' remarked Drummond quietly. 'And as it happened we thought wrong. Get him below, Ted—and get him to bed, or we really shall be attending his funeral. He's swallowed most of the English Channel as it is. Though I can assure you, sir,' he addressed the elderly man again, 'that he possesses a vitality which turns Kruschen salts a pale pink. Within the last week he's been blown up; his remains, consisting of one boot, have been buried; he's been bounced on a white-hot electric furnace to keep his circulation going; he's had his breakfast doped; and last, but not least, he's gone backwards and forwards under Ted's motor-boat. And now if someone will lead me to a whisky-and-soda of vast dimensions, I'll——My God! what's that?'

It was very faint, like the boom of a distant heavy gun, but he happened to be looking towards the Needles. And he had seen a sudden deep orange flash, in the water against the sky—the flash such as in old days an aeroplane bomb had made on bursting. The others swung round and stared seawards, but there was nothing more to be seen.

'It sounded like a shell,' said one of the men. 'What did you think it was?'

He turned to Drummond, but he had disappeared, only to dash on deck a moment or two later with Ted behind him.

'Every ounce you can get out of her, Ted. Rip her to pieces if necessary—but get there. That infernal devil has blown up the yacht.'

The motor-boat spun round, and like a living beast gathered speed. The bow waves rose higher and higher, till they stood four feet above the gunwales, to fall away astern into a mass of seething white.

'I'll never forgive myself,' shouted Drummond in Ted's ear. 'I knew he was going to blow her up, but I never thought he'd do it so soon.'

Quivering like a thing possessed, the boat rushed towards the scene of the explosion. The speedometer needle touched—went back—touched again—and then remained steady at fifty.

'Go to the bows,' howled Ted. 'Wreckage.'

With a nod Drummond scrambled forward, and lying between the two black walls of water, he slowly swung the headlight backwards and forwards over the sea in front. To hit a piece of floating wreckage at the speed they were travelling would have ripped them open from stem to stern. Other craft attracted to the spot loomed up and dropped back as if stationary, and then suddenly Drummond held up his hand. In front was a large dark object with two or three men clinging to it, and as he focused the headlight on them he could see them waving. The roar of the engine died away, and timing it perfectly Jerningham went full speed astern.

The thing in the water was one of the large wooden lockers used for storing life-belts, and they drew alongside just in time. It was waterlogged, and the weight of the men clinging to it was more than it could stand. Even as the last of them stepped into the boat, with a sullen splash the locker turned over and drifted away only just awash.

'Yer'd better mind out,' said one of the men. 'There's a lot of that about.'

'Go slow, Ted,' cried Drummond. Then he turned to the men. 'What happened?'

'Strike me pink, governor, I'm damned if I know. We've had a wonderful trip, we 'ave—you can take my word. Fust a ruddy madman jumps overboard with another bloke—and they both drowns. Then half an hour later there comes the devil of an explosion from below; the 'ole deck goes sky 'igh, and the skipper he yells, "We're sinking." It didn't require for 'im to say that; we all knew we was. We 'eeled right over, and in 'alf a minute she sank.'

'Anybody else saved?' asked Drummond.

'I dunno, governor,' answered the man. 'There wasn't no women and children on board, so I reckons it was everyone for himself.'

'Any idea what caused the explosion?'

'I 'aven't, governor—that's strite. But I knew as no good was a-going to come of this trip, as soon as that there madman went and drowned hisself.'

Drummond stared silently ahead. In the dim light he had no fear of being recognised, even if any of the three men they had saved had seen him. And his mind was busy. He had not the slightest doubt that Peterson had caused the explosion; he had even less doubt that Peterson, at any rate, was not drowned. But why had he taken the appalling risk of doing such a thing in so populous a waterway?

He went back to the stern and sat down beside Ted, who was nosing the boat gently through the water. Masses of débris surrounded them, and it was necessary to move with the utmost caution.

'What made him risk it here, Ted?' he whispered.

'Obvious, old man,' returned the other in a low voice. 'He thought your bodies would be washed ashore; he had no means of telling when. He knew they would be identified; he further knew that I would at once say what had happened. From that moment he would be in deadly danger; wireless would put every ship at sea wise. And to do a little stunt of this sort, if he was to escape, it was imperative he should be near land. So, as Peterson would do, he didn't hesitate for a moment, but put the job through at once.'

Drummond nodded thoughtfully.

'You're right, Ted—perfectly right.'

'And unless I'm very much surprised, our friend at the present moment is stepping out of his life-belt somewhere on the beach in Colwell Bay. Tomorrow, I should imagine, he will cross to Lymington—and after that you possibly know what his moves will be. I certainly don't—for I'm completely in the dark over the whole stunt.'

'It's too long a story to tell you now, old man,' said Drummond. 'But one thing I do know. Whoever else may be picked up, our friend will not be amongst the survivors. He's run unheard-of risks to pull this thing off, including a cold-blooded murder. And now officially he's going to die himself in order to throw everyone off the scent.' He laughed grimly. 'Moreover, he'd have done what he set out to do if you hadn't been leaning over the side of your governor's yacht.'

'But what's the prize this time?'

'Old Goodman's secret for making artificial diamonds—that was the prize, and Peterson has got it.'

Ted whistled softly.

'I heard something about it from Algy,' he remarked. 'But it seems to me, Hugh, that if that is the case, he's won.'

Drummond laughed.

'You were a bit surprised, Ted, when I refused to allow you to pull us on board your boat. Of course I knew as well as you did that with your speed we could have got clean away from them. But don't you see, old man, the folly of doing so? He would have spotted at once that we were not drowned; he would further have spotted that I was not as mad as I made out. Chewing soap is the hell of a game,' he added inconsequently. Then he went on again, emphasising each point on his fingers.

'Get me so far? Once he knew we were alive, it would have necessitated a complete alteration of his plans. He'd probably have put straight into some place on the south coast; gone ashore himself and never returned. And then he'd have disappeared into the blue. Maybe he'd have had another shot at murdering old Goodman; however, that point doesn't arise. The thing is he'd have disappeared.'

'Which is what he seems to have done now,' remarked Ted.

Again Drummond laughed.

'But I think I know where he'll turn up again. In what form or guise remains to be seen: our one and only Carl is never monotonous, to give him his due. You see, Ted, you don't seem to realise the intense advantage of being dead. I didn't till I heard him discussing it one night in his study. And now I'm dead, and the Professor's dead, and dear Carl is dead. That's why I bumped the poor old man's head on the barnacles underneath your boat, as we changed sides. It's a gorgeous situation.'

'Doubtless, old man,' murmured the other. 'Though you must remember it's all a little dark and confusing to me. And anyway, where do you think he'll turn up again so that you can recognise him?'

'My dear man, our little Irma, or Janet, or whatever name the sweet thing is masquerading under this time, is a powerful magnet. And I am open to a small bet that at the moment she is taking the air in Switzerland: Montreux to be exact. What more natural, then, that believing himself perfectly safe, our one and only Carl will return to the arms of his lady—if only for a time.'

'And you propose to fly there also?'

'Exactly. I want the notes of that process, and I also want a final reckoning with the gentleman.'

'Final?' said Ted, glancing at Drummond thoughtfully.

'Definitely final,' answered Drummond quietly. 'This time our friend has gone too far.'

Jerningham looked at the numerous other boats which, by this time, had arrived at the scene of the disaster. Then he swung his helm hard round.

'That being so,' he remarked, 'since our presence is no longer needed here, I suggest that we get a move on. From my knowledge of Montreux, old man, it is getting uncomfortably hot just now. Deauville will be more in Irma's line. If I were you, I'd get out there, and do it quick. Joking apart, you may be right and, of course, I don't know all the fact of the case. But from what I've guessed, I think friend Peterson will cover all his tracks at the first possible moment.'

'He may,' agreed Drummond. 'And yet—believing that the Professor and I are both dead—he may not. You see,' he repeated once again, 'he thinks he's safe. Therein lies the maggot in the Stilton.'

With which profound simile he relapsed into silence, only broken as once more the boat drew up alongside the yacht.

'He thinks he's safe, which is where he goes into the mulligatawny up to his neck. Put these fellows on shore, Ted, give me a change of clothes, and then run me over to Lymington.'

CHAPTER 12

In Which he Samples Mr Blackton's Napoleon Brandy

That Drummond was no fool his intimate friends knew well. He had a strange faculty for hitting the nail on the head far more often than not. Possibly his peculiarly direct method of argument enabled him to reach more correct conclusions than someone subtler-minded and cleverer could achieve. His habit of going for essentials and discarding side issues was merely the mental equivalent of those physical attributes which had made him a holy terror in the ring. Moreover, he had the invaluable gift of being able to put himself in the other man's place.

But it may be doubted if in any of his duels with Peterson he had ever been more unerringly right than in his diagnosis of the immediate future. It was not a fluke; it was in no sense guesswork. He merely put himself in Peterson's place, and decided what he would do under similar circumstances. And having decided on that, he went straight ahead with his own plans, which, like all he made, were simple and to the point. They necessitated taking a chance, but, after all, what plan doesn't?

He had made up his mind to kill Peterson, but he wanted to do it in such a manner that it would appeal to his sense of art in after-life. And with Drummond the sense of art was synonymous with the sense of fair play. He would give Peterson a fair chance to fight for his life. But in addition to that his ambition went a little farther. He felt that this culminating duel should be worthy of them both. The mental atmosphere must be correct, as well as the mundane surroundings. That that was largely beyond his control he realised, but he hoped for the best. The sudden plunging of Peterson from the dizzy heights of success into the valley of utter failure must not be a hurried affair, but a leisurely business in which each word would tell. How dizzy were the heights to which Peterson thought he had attained was, of course, known only to Peterson. But, on that point, he need not have worried.

For Mr Edward Blackton, as he stepped out of the train at Montreux station at nine o'clock on a glorious summer's evening, was in a condition in which even a request for one of his three remaining bottles of Napoleon brandy might have been acceded to. True, his right arm pained him somewhat; true, he was supremely unaware that at seven o'clock that morning Drummond had descended from the Orient express on to the same platform. What he was aware of was that in his pocket reposed the secret which would make him all-powerful; and in his hand-bag reposed an English morning paper giving the eminently satisfactory news that only six survivors had been rescued from the *SY Gadfly*, which had mysteriously blown up off the Needles. Moreover, all six had combined in saying that the temporary owner of the yacht—a Mr Robinson—must be amongst those drowned.

The hotel 'bus drew up at the door of the Palace Hotel, and Mr Blackton descended. He smiled a genial welcome at the manager, and strolled into the luxurious lounge. In the ballroom leading out of it a few couples were dancing, but his shrewd glance at once found whom he was looking for. In a corner sat Irma talking to a young Roumanian of great wealth, and a benevolent glow spread over him. No more would the dear child have to do these fatiguing things from necessity. If she chose to continue parting men from their money as a hobby it would be quite a different thing. There is a vast difference between pleasure and business.

He sauntered across the lounge towards her, and realised at once that there was something of importance she wished to say to him. For a minute or two, however, they remained there chatting; then with a courteous good night they left the Roumanian and ascended in the lift to their suite.

'What is it, my dearest?' he remarked, as he shut the sitting-room door.

'That man Blantyre is here, Ted,' said the girl. 'He's been asking to see you.'

He sat down and pulled her to his knee.

'Blantyre,' he laughed. 'Sir Raymond! I thought it possible he might come. And is he very angry?'

'When he saw me he was nearly speechless with rage.'

'Dear fellow! It must have been a dreadful shock to him.'

'But, Ted,' she cried anxiously, 'is it all right?'

'Righter even than that, *carissima*. Blantyre simply doesn't come into the picture. All I trust is that he won't have a fit in the room or anything, because I think that Sir Raymond in a fit would be a disquieting spectacle.'

There was a knock at the door, and the girl got quickly up. 'Come in.'

Mr Blackton regarded the infuriated man who entered with a tolerant smile.

'Sir Raymond Blantyre, surely. A delightful surprise. Please shut the door, and tell us to what we are indebted for the pleasure of this visit.'

The President of the Metropolitan Diamond Syndicate advocated slowly across the room. His usually florid face was white with rage, and his voice, when he spoke, shook uncontrollably.

'You scoundrel—you infernal, damned scoundrel!'

Mr Blackton thoughtfully lit a cigar; then, leaning back in his chair, he surveyed his visitor benignly.

'Tush, tush!' he murmured. 'I must beg of you to remember that there is a lady present.'

Sir Raymond muttered something under his breath; then, controlling himself with an effort, he sat down.

'I presume it is unnecessary for me to explain why I am here,' he remarked at length.

'I had imagined through a desire to broaden our comparatively slight acquaintance into something deeper and more intimate,' said Mr Blackton hopefully.

'Quit this fooling,' snarled the other. 'Do you deny that you have the papers containing Goodman's process?'

'I never deny anything till I'm asked, and not always then.'

'Have you got them, or have you not?' cried Sir Raymond furiously.

'Now I put it to you, my dear fellow, am I a fool or am I not?' Mr Blackton seemed almost pained. 'Of course I have the papers of the process. What on earth do you suppose I put myself to the trouble and inconvenience of coming over to England for? Moreover, if it is of any interest to you, the notes are no longer in the somewhat difficult calligraphy of our lamented Professor, but in my own perfectly legible writing.'

'You scoundrel!' spluttered Sir Raymond. 'You took our money —half a million pounds—on the clear understanding that the process was to be suppressed.'

Mr Blackton blew out a large cloud of smoke.

'The point is a small one,' he murmured, 'but that is not my recollection of what transpired. You and your syndicate offered me half a million pounds to prevent Professor Goodman revealing his secret to the world. Well, Professor Goodman hasn't done so—nor will he do so. So I quite fail to see any cause for complaint.'

The veins stood out on Sir Raymond's forehead.

'You have the brazen effrontery to sit there and maintain that our offer to you did not include the destruction of the secret? Do you imagine we should have been so incredibly foolish as to pay you a large sum of money merely to transfer those papers from his pocket to yours?'

Mr Blackton shrugged his shoulders.

'The longer I live, my dear Sir Raymond, the more profoundly do I become impressed with how incredibly foolish a lot of people are. But, in this case, do not let us call it foolishness. A kinder word is surely more appropriate to express your magnanimity. There are people who say that business men are hard. No—a thousand times, no. To present me with the secret was charming; but to force upon me half a million pounds sterling as well was almost extravagant.'

'Hand it over—or I'll kill you like a dog.'

Mr Blackton's eyes narrowed a little; then he smiled.

'Really, Sir Raymond—don't be so crude. I must beg of you to put that absurd weapon away. Why, my dear fellow, it might go off. And though I believe capital punishment has been abolished in most of the cantons in Switzerland, I don't think imprisonment for life would appeal to you.'

Slowly the other man lowered his revolver.

'That's better—much better,' said Mr Blackton approvingly. 'And now, have we anything further to discuss?'

'What do you propose to do?' asked Sir Raymond dully.

'Really, my dear fellow, I should have thought it was fairly obvious. One thing you may be quite sure about: I do not propose to inform the Royal Society about the matter.'

'No, but you propose to make use of your knowledge yourself?'

'Naturally. In fact I propose to become a millionaire many times over by means of it.'

'That means the ruin of all of us.'

'My dear Sir Raymond, your naturally brilliant brain seems amazingly obtuse this evening. Please give me the credit of knowing something about the diamond market. I shall place these stones with such care that even you will have no fault to find. It will do me no good to deflate the price of diamonds. Really, if you look into it, you know, your half-million has not been wasted. You would have been ruined without doubt if Professor Goodman had broadcast his discovery to the world at large. Every little chemist would have had genuine diamonds the size of tomatoes in his front window. Now nothing of the sort will happen. And though I admit that it is unpleasant for you to realise that at any moment a stone worth many thousands may be put on the market at the cost of a fiver, it's not as bad as it would have been if you hadn't called me in. And one thing I do promise you: I will make no attempt to undersell you. My stones will be sold at the current market price.'

Sir Raymond stirred restlessly in his chair. It was prefectly true what this arch-scoundrel said: it was better that the secret should be in the hands of a man who knew how to use it than in those of an unpractical old chemist.

'You see, Sir Raymond,' went on Mr Blackton, 'the whole matter is so simple. The only living people who know anything about this process are you and your syndicate—and I. One can really pay no attention to that inconceivable poop—I forget his name. I mean the one with the eyeglass.'

'There's his friend,' grunted Sir Raymond—'that vast man.'

'You allude to Drummond,' said Mr Blackton softly.

'That's his name. I don't know how much he *knows*, but he suspects a good deal. And he struck me as being a dangerous young man.'

Mr Blackton smiled sadly.

'Drummond! Dear fellow. My darling,' he turned to the girl, 'I have some sad news for you. In the excitement of Sir Raymond's visit, I quite forgot to tell you. Poor Drummond is no more.'

The girl sat up quickly.

'Dead! Drummond dead! Good heavens! how?'

'It was all very sad, and rather complicated. The poor dear chap went mad. In his own charming phraseology he got kittens in the granary. But all through his terrible affliction, one spark of his old life remained: his rooted aversion to me. The only trouble was that he mistook someone else for your obedient servant, and at last his feelings overcame him. I took him for a short sea-voyage, with the gentleman he believed was me, and he rewarded me by frothing at the mouth, and jumping overboard in a fit of frenzy, clutching this unfortunate gentleman in the grip of a maniac. They were both drowned. Too sad, is it not?'

'But I don't understand,' cried the girl. 'Good heavens! what's that?'

From a large cupboard occupying most of one wall came the sound of a cork being extracted. It was unmistakable, and a sudden deadly silence settled on the room. The occupants seemed temporarily paralysed: corks do not extract themselves. And then a strange pallor spread over Mr Blackton's face, as if some ghastly premonition of the truth had dawned on him.

He tottered rather than walked to the cupboard and flung it open. Comfortably settled in the corner was Drummond. In one hand he held a corkscrew, in the other a full bottle of Napoleonic brandy, which he was sniffing with deep appreciation.

'I pass this, Carl,' he remarked, 'as a very sound liqueur brandy. And if you would oblige me with a glass, I will decide if the taste comes up to the bouquet. A tooth-tumbler will do excellently, if you have no other.'

The pallor grew more sickly on Blackton's face as he stared at the speaker. He had a sudden sense of unreality; the room was spinning

182

round. It was untrue, of course; it was a dream. Drummond was drowned: he knew it. So how could he be sitting in the cupboard? Manifestly the thing was impossible.

'Well, well,' said the apparition, stretching out his legs comfortably, 'this is undoubtedly a moment fraught with emotion and, I trust I may say, tender memories.' He bowed to the girl, who, with her hands locked together, was staring at him with unfathomable eyes. 'Before proceeding, may I ask the correct method of addressing you? I like to pander to your foibles, Carl, in any way I can, and I gather that neither Mr Robinson nor Professor Scheidstrun is technically accurate at the moment.'

'How did you get here?' said Blackton in a voice he hardly recognised as his own.

'By the Orient express this morning,' returned Drummond, emerging languidly from the cupboard.

'My God! you're not human.'

The words seemed to be wrung from Blackton by a force greater than his own, and Drummond looked at him thoughtfully. There was no doubt about it—Peterson's nerve had gone. And Drummond would indeed not have been human if a very real thrill of triumph had not run through him at that moment. But no trace showed on his face as he opened his cigarette-case.

'On the contrary—very human indeed,' he murmured. 'Even as you, Carl—you'll excuse me if I return to our original nomenclature: it's so much less confusing. To err is human—and you erred once. It's bad luck, because I may frankly say that in all the pleasant *rencontres* we've had together nothing has filled me with such profound admiration for your ability as this meeting. There are one or two details lacking in my mind—one in particular; but on what I do know, I congratulate you. And possessing, as I think you must admit, a sense of sportsmanship, I feel almost sorry for that one big error of yours, though it is a delightful compliment to my histrionic abilities. How's Freyder's face?'

'So you hadn't got concussion?' said the other. His voice was steadier now; he was thinking desperately.

'You've hit it, Carl. I recovered from my concussion on the floor of your room, and listened with interest to your plans for my future. And having a certain natural gift for lying doggo, I utilised it. But if it's any gratification to you, I can assure you that I very nearly gave myself away when I found who it was you had upstairs.

183

You will doubtless be glad to hear that by this time Professor Goodman is restored to the bosom of his family.'

A strangled noise came from behind him, and he turned round to find Sir Raymond Blantyre in a partially choking condition.

'Who did you say?' he demanded thickly.

'Professor Goodman,' repeated Drummond, and his voice was icy. 'I haven't got much to say to you, Sir Raymond—except that you're a nasty piece of work. Few things in my life have afforded me so much pleasure as the fact that you were swindled out of half a million. I wish it had been more. For the man who carried this coup through one can feel a certain unwilling admiration; for you, one can feel only the most unmitigated contempt.'

'How dare you speak like that!' spluttered the other, but Drummond was taking no further notice of him.

'That was your second error, Carl. You ought to have come into the motor-boat. I assure you I had a dreadful time dragging that poor old chap underneath it, as you crossed our stern. His knowledge of swimming is rudimentary.'

'So that was it, was it?' said Blackton slowly. His nerve had completely recovered, and he lit a cigar with ease. 'I really think it is for me to congratulate you, my dear Drummond. Apart, however, from this exchange of pleasantries—er—what do we do now?'

'You say that Professor Goodman is still alive?' Sir Raymond had found his voice again. 'Then who—who was buried?'

'Precisely,' murmured Drummond. 'The one detail in particular in which I am interested. Who was the owner of the boot? Or shall I say who was the owner of the foot inside the boot, because the boot was undoubtedly the Professor's?'

'The point seems to me to be of but academic interest,' remarked Mr Blackton in a bored voice. '*Nil nisis bonum*'—you know the old tag. And I can assure you that the foot's proprietor was a tedious individual. No loss to the community whatever.'

And suddenly a light dawned on Sir Raymond Blantyre.

'Great heavens! it was poor Lewisham.'

Absorbed as he had been by other things, the strange disappearance of his indiscreet fellow-director, the peculiar radiogram from mid-Atlantic and subsequent silence, had slipped from his mind. Now it came back, and he stared at Blackton with a sort of fascinated horror. The reason for Lewisham's visit to Professor Goodman was clear, and he shuddered uncontrollably.

184

'It was Lewisham,' he repeated dully.

'I rather believe it was,' murmured Blackton, dismissing the matter with a wave of his hand. 'As I said before, the point is of but academic interest.' He turned again to Drummond. 'So Professor Goodman is restored to his family once more. I trust he has suffered no ill-effects from his prolonged immersion.'

'None at all, thank you,' answered Drummond. 'Somewhat naturally, he is angry. In fact, for a mild and gentle old man, he is in what might be described as the devil of a temper.'

'But if he's back in London,' broke in Sir Raymond excitedly, 'what about his secret? It will be given to the world, and all this will have been in vain.'

Mr Blackton thoughtfully studied the ash on his cigar, while Drummond stared at the speaker. And then for one fleeting instant their eyes met. Sworn enemies though they were, for that brief moment they stood on common ground—unmitigated contempt for the man who had just spoken.

'From many points of view, Sir Raymond, I wish it could be given to the world,' said Drummond. 'I can think of no better punishment for you, or one more richly deserved. Unfortunately, however, you can set your mind at rest on that point. Professor Goodman no longer possesses his notes on the process.'

'Precisely,' murmured Mr Blackton. 'It struck me that one copy was ample. So I destroyed his.'

'But for all that,' continued Drummond, noting the look of relief that spread over Sir Raymond's face, 'I don't think you're going to have a fearfully jolly time when you return to London. In fact, if I may offer you a word of advice, I wouldn't return at all.'

'What do you mean?' stammered the other.

'Exactly what I say, you damned swine,' snapped Drummond. 'Do you imagine you can instigate murder and sudden death, and then go trotting into the Berkeley as if nothing had happened? You're for it, Blantyre; you're for it—good and strong. And you're going to get it. As I say, the Professor is angry and he's obstinate—and he wants your blood. My own impression is that if you get off with fifteen years, you can think yourself lucky.'

Sir Raymond plucked at his collar feverishly.

'Fifteen years! My God!' Then his voice rose to a scream. 'But it was this villain who did it all, I tell you, who murdered Lewisham, who . . .'

With a crash he fell back in the chair where Drummond had thrown him, and though his shaking lips still framed words, no sound came from them. Blackton was still critically regarding the ash on his cigar; Drummond had turned his back and was speaking again.

'Yes, Carl,' he was saying, 'the Professor and I will deal with Sir Raymond. Or if anything should happen to me, then the Professor is quite capable of doing it himself.'

'And what do you anticipate should happen to you?' asked Blackton politely.

'Nothing, I trust. But there is one thing which I have never done in the past during all our games of fun and laughter. I have never made the mistake of underrating you.'

Blackton glanced at him thoughtfully.

'We appear,' he murmured, 'to be approaching the sixpence in the plum-pudding.'

'We are,' returned Drummond quietly. 'Sir Raymond is the Professor's portion; you are mine.'

A silence settled on the room—a silence broken at length by Blackton. His blue eyes never left Drummond's face; the smoke from his cigar rose into the air undisturbed by any tremor of his hand.

'I am all attention,' he remarked.

'There is not much to say,' said Drummond. 'But what there is, I hope may interest you. If my memory serves me aright, there was one unfailing jest between us in the old days. Henry Lakington did his best to make it stale before he met with his sad end; that unpleasant Count Zadowa let it trip from his tongue on occasions; in fact, Carl, you yourself have used it more than once. I allude to the determination expressed by you all at one time or another to kill me.'

Blackton nodded thoughtfully.

'Now you speak of it, I do recall something of the sort.'

'Good,' continued Drummond. 'And since no one could call me grudging in praise, I will admit that you made several exceedingly creditable attempts. This time, however, the boot is on the other leg; it's my turn to say—snap. In other words, I am going to kill you, Carl. At least, lest I should seem to boast, I'm going to have a damned good attempt—one that I trust will be even more creditable than yours.'

Once again a silence settled, broken this time by an amused laugh from the girl.

'Adorable as ever, my Hugh,' she murmured. 'And where shall I send the wreath?'

'Mademoiselle,' answered Drummond gravely, 'I propose to be far more original than that. To do your—er—father—well, we won't press that point—to do Carl justice, his attempts were most original. You were not, of course, present on the evening at Maybrick Hall, when that exceedingly unpleasant Russian came to an untimely end. But for the arrival of the Black Gang, I fear that I should have been the victim—and Phyllis. However, let me assure you that I have no intention whatever of doing you any harm. But I should like you to listen—even as Phyllis had to listen—while I outline my proposals. Carl ran over his that night for my benefit, and I feel sure he would have fallen in with any proposals I had to make. Similarly, believe me, I shall be only too charmed to do the same for him.'

Sir Raymond Blantyre sat up and pinched himself. Was this some strange jest staged for his special benefit? Was this large young man who spoke with a twinkle in his eyes the jester? And glancing at the two men, he saw that there was no longer any twinkle, and that Blackton's face had become strangely drawn and anxious. But his voice when he spoke was calm.

'We appear to be in for an entertaining chat,' he murmured.

'I hope you will find it so,' returned Drummond gravely. 'But before we come to my actual proposal, I would like you to understand quite clearly what will happen if you refuse to fall in with it. Outside in the passage, Carl, are two large, stolid Swiss gendarmes: men of sterling worth, and quite unbribable. They don't know why they are there at present; but it will not take long to enlighten them. Should you decide, therefore, to decline my suggestion, I shall be under the painful necessity of requesting them to step in here, when I will inform them of just so much of your past history as to ensure your sleeping for the next few nights in rather less comfortable quarters. Until, in fact, extradition papers arrive from England. Do I make myself clear?'

'Perfectly,' answered the other. 'That will occur if I do not fall in with your suggestion. So let us hear the suggestion.'

'It took a bit of thinking out,' admitted Drummond. 'I haven't got your fertile brain, Carl, over these little matters. Still, I flatter myself it's not bad for a first attempt. I realised somewhat naturally the drawbacks to shooting you on sight—besides, it's so bad for the carpet. At the same time I have come to the unalterable conclusion that the world is not big enough for both of us. I might—you will justly observe—hand you over anyway to those stolid warriors outside. And since you would undoubtedly be hanged, the problem would be solved. But unsatisfactorily, Carl—most unsatisfactorily.'

'We are certainly in agreement on that point,' said the other.

'We have fought in the past without the police; we'll finish without them. And having made up my mind to that, it became necessary to think of some scheme by which the survivor should not suffer. If it's you—well, you'll get caught sooner or later; if it's me, I certainly don't propose to suffer in any way. Apart from having just bought weight-carrying hunters for next winter, it would be grossly unfair that I should.'

He selected a cigarette with care and lit it.

'It was you, Carl, who put the idea into my head,' he continued, 'so much of the credit is really yours. Your notion of making my death appear accidental that night at Maybrick Hall struck me as excellent. Worthy undoubtedly of an encore. Your death, Carl—or mine—will appear accidental, which makes everything easy for the survivor. I hope I'm not boring you.'

'Get down to it,' snarled Blackton. 'Don't play the fool, damn you!'

'As you did, Carl, that night at Maybrick Hall.' For a moment the veins stood out on Drummond's neck as the remembrance of that hideous scene came back to him; then he controlled himself and went on. 'At first sight it may seem absurd—even fanciful—this scheme of mine; but don't judge it hastily, I beg you. Know anything about glaciers, Carl?'

He smiled at the look of blank amazement on the other's face.

'Jolly little things, my dear fellow, if you treat 'em the right way. But dangerous things to play tricks with. There are great cracks in them, you know—deep cracks with walls of solid ice. If a man falls down one of those cracks, unless help is forthcoming at once, he doesn't live long, Carl; in fact, he dies astonishingly quickly.'

Blackton moistened his lips with his tongue.

'People fall down these cracks accidentally sometimes,' continued Drummond thoughtfully. 'In fact there was a case once—I won't vouch for its truth—but I'm sure you'd like to hear the story. It occurred on the glacier not far from Grindelwald—and it's always tickled me to death. It appears that one of the local celebrities went out to pick edelweiss or feed the chamois or something equally jolly, and failed to return. He'd gone out alone, and after a time his pals began to get uneasy. So they instituted a search-party, and in due course they found him. Or rather they saw him. He had slipped on the edge of one of the deepest crevasses in the whole glacier, and there he was about fifty feet below them wedged between the two walls of ice. He was dead, of course—though they yodelled at him hopefully for the rest of the day. A poor story, isn't it, Carl?—but it's not quite finished. They decided to leave him there for the night, and return next day and extract him. Will you believe it, Mademoiselle, when they arrived the following morning, they couldn't get at him. The old glacier had taken a heave forward in the night, and there he was wedged. Short of blasting him out with dynamite he was there for keeps. A terrible position for a self-respecting community, don't you think? To have the leading citizen on full view in a block of ice gives visitors an impression of carelessness. Of course, they tried to keep it dark; but it was useless. People came flocking from all over the place. Scientists came and made mathematical calculations as to when he'd come out at the bottom. Every year he moved on a few more yards; every year his widow—a person now of some consequence—took her children to see father, and later on her grandchildren to see grandfather. Forty years was the official time—and I believe he passed the winning-post in forty-one years three months: a wonderful example of pertinacity and dogged endurance.' Drummond paused hopefully. 'That's a pretty original idea, Carl, don't you think?'

Sir Raymond gave a short, almost hysterical laugh, but there was no sign of mirth on the faces of the other two.

'Am I to understand,' said Blackton harshly, 'that you propose that one or other of us should fall down a crevasse in a glacier? I've never heard anything so ridiculous in my life.'

'Don't say that,' answered Drummond. 'It's no more ridiculous than braining me with a rifle-butt, as you intended to do once. And a great deal less messy. Anyway, that is my proposal. You and I, Carl, will go unarmed to a glacier. We will there find a suitably deep crevasse. And on the edge of that crevasse'—his voice changed suddenly—'we will fight for the last time, with our bare hands. It will be slippery, which is to your advantage, though the fact that I am stronger than you cannot be adjusted at this late hour. It's that—or the police, Peterson: one gives you a chance, the other gives you none. And if, as I hope, you lose—why, think of your triumph. The leading detectives of four continents will be dancing with rage on the top of the ice watching you safely embalmed underneath their feet.'

'I refuse utterly,' snarled the other. 'It's murder—nothing more nor less.'

'A form of amusement you should be used to,' said Drummond. 'However, you refuse. Very good. I will now send for the police.'

He rose and went to the door, and Blackton looked round desperately.

'Wait,' he cried. 'Can't we—can't we come to some arrangement?'

'None. Those are my terms. And there is one other that I have not mentioned. You said that two copies of the Professor's notes were excessive. I agree—but I go farther: one is too much; that process is altogether too dangerous. If the police take you—it doesn't matter; but if you accept my terms, you've got to hand that copy over to me now. And I shall burn it. I don't mind running the risk of being killed; but if I am, you're not going to get away with the other thing too.' Drummond glanced at his watch. 'I give you half a minute to decide.'

The seconds dragged by and Blackton stared in front of him. Plan after plan flashed through his mind, only to be dismissed as impossible. He was caught—and he knew it. Once the police had him, he was done for utterly and completely. They could hang him ten times over in England alone. Moreover, anything in the nature of personal violence under present circumstances was out of the question. Powerful though he was, at no time was he a match for Drummond in the matter of physical strength; but here in the Palace Hotel it was too impossible even to think of. Almost as impossible as any idea of bribery.

He was caught: not only had this, his greatest coup, failed, but his life was forfeit as well. For he was under no delusions as to what would be the result of the fight on the glacier.

He heard the snap of a watch closing.

'Your half-minute is up, Peterson.' Drummond's hand was on the door. 'And I must say—I thought better of you.'

'Stop,' said the other sullenly. 'I accept.'

Drummond came back into the room slowly.

190

'That is good,' he remarked. 'Then—first of all—the notes of Professor Goodman's process.'

Without a word Blackton handed over two sheets of paper, though in his eyes was a look of smouldering fury.

'You fool!' he snarled, as he watched them burn to ashes. 'You damned fool!'

'Opinions differ,' murmured Drummond, powdering the ash on the table. 'And now to discuss arrangements. We start early to-morrow morning by car. I have been to some pains to examine the time-table—I mention this in case you should try to bolt. There is nothing that will do you any good either in the Lausanne direction or towards Italy. Behind you have the mountain railways, which don't run trains at night; in front you have the lake. Below two very good friends of mine are waiting to assist if necessary—though I can promise you they will take no part in our little scrap. But you're such an elusive person, Peterson, that I felt I could take no chances. To the best of my ability I've hemmed you in for the few hours that remain before we start. And then you and I will sit on the back seat and discuss the view. I feel the precautions seem excessive, but I have not the advantage of a specially prepared house—like you have always had in the past.'

'And until we start?' said Blackton quietly.

'We remain in this room,' answered Drummond. 'At least—you and I do. Mademoiselle must please herself.'

The girl looked at him languidly.

'You don't mind if I leave you?' she remarked. 'To tell you the truth, *mon ami*, you're being a little tedious this evening. And since I am going to Evian-les-Bains for the waters tomorrow, I think I'll retire to bed. Do you know Evian?'

'Never heard of it, I'm afraid,' said Drummond. 'My geography was always rotten.'

He was lighting a cigarette, more to conceal his thoughts than for any desire to smoke. That she was a perfect actress he knew, and yet it seemed impossible to believe that her composure was any-thing but natural. He glanced at Peterson, who was still sitting motionless, his chin sunk on his chest. He glanced at the girl, and she was patting a stray tendril of hair in front of a mirror. He even glanced at Sir Raymond, but there was nothing to be learned from that gentleman. He still resembled a man only partially recovered from a drugged sleep. Was it conceivable that he had left a loophole in his scheme? Or could it be that she had ceased to care for Peterson?

She had turned and was regarding him with a faint smile.

'I fear I shan't be up before you go tomorrow,' she murmured. 'But whoever does not go into cold storage must come and tell me about it. And there are a lot of other things, too, I want to hear about. Why Carl, for instance, ought to have looked in the motor-boat, and how you got concussion.'

Drummond looked at her steadily.

'I find you a little difficult to understand, Mademoiselle. I trust you are under no delusions as to whether I am bluffing or not. You can, at any rate, settle one point in your mind by glancing outside the door.'

'To see the two large policemen,' laughed the girl. 'La, la, my dear man—they would give me what you call a nightmare. I will take your word for it.'

'And any appeal for help will result somewhat unfortunately for Carl.'

She shrugged her shoulders irritably.

'I know when the game is up,' she remarked. Then abruptly she turned on the man who had been her companion for years. 'Bah! you damned fool!' she stormed. 'Every time this great idiot here does you down. Not once, but half a dozen times have you told me "Drummond is dead", and every time he bobs up again like a jack-in-the-box. And now—this time—when you had everything—everything—everything—you go and let him beat you again. You tire me. It is good that we end our partnership. You are imbecile.'

She raged out of the room, and Carl Peterson raised his haggard eyes as the door closed. His lips had set in a twisted smile, and after a while his head sank forward again, and he sat motionless, staring at the table in front of him. His cigar had long gone out; he seemed to have aged suddenly. And into Drummond's mind there stole a faint feeling of pity.

'I'm sorry about that, Peterson,' he said quietly. 'She might at least have seen the game out to the end.'

The other made no reply—only by a slight shake of his shoulders did he show that he had heard. And Drummond's feeling of pity increased. Scoundrel, murderer, unmitigated blackguard though he knew this man to be, yet when all was said and done he was no weakling. And it wasn't difficult to read his thoughts at the moment—to realise the bitterness and the fury that must be possessing him. Half an hour ago he had believed himself successful beyond his wildest dreams; now—— And then for the girl to go back on him at the finish.

Drummond pulled himself together; such thoughts were dangerous. He forced himself to remember that night when it had been the question of seconds between life and death for Phyllis; he recalled to his mind the words he had listened to as he lay on the floor in the house to which Freyder had brought him while still unconscious.

'I think if it was a question between getting away with the process and killing Drummond—it would be the latter.'

If the positions were reversed, would one thought of mercy have softened the man he now held in his power? No one knew better than Drummond himself that it would not. He was a fool even to think about it. The man who hated him so bitterly was in his power. He deserved, no man more so, to die; he was going to die. Moreover he was going to have a sporting chance for his life into the bargain. And that was a thing he had never given Drummond. And yet he could have wished the girl had not proved herself so rotten.

The lights went out on the long terrace fronting the lake, and he glanced at his watch. It was twelve o'clock: in another three hours it would be light enough to start. Through Château d'Oex to Interlaken—he knew the way quite well. And then up either by train or car to Grindelwald. It would depend on what time they arrived as to the rest of the programme. And as he saw in his mind's eye the grim struggle that would be the finish one way or the other—for Peterson was no mean antagonist physically—Drummond's fists tightened instinctively and his breathing came a little quicker. Up above the snow-line they would fight, in the dusk when the light was bad, and there would be no wandering peasant to spread awkward stories.

Peterson's voice cut in on his thoughts.

'You are quite determined to go through with this?'

'Quite,' answered Drummond. 'As I told you, I have definitely come to the conclusion that the world is not big enough for both of us.'

Peterson said no more, but after a while he rose and walked into the glassed-in balcony. The windows were open, and with his hands in his pockets he stood staring out over the lake.

'I advise you to try nothing foolish,' said Drummond, joining him. 'The Swiss police are remarkably efficient, and communication with the frontiers by telephone is rapid.'

'You think of everything,' murmured Peterson. 'But there are no trains, and it takes time to order a car at midnight. And since it is beyond my powers to swim the lake, there doesn't seem much more to be said.' He turned and faced Drummond thoughtfully. 'How on earth do you do it, my young friend? Are you aware that you are the only man in the world who has ever succeeded in doing me down? And you have done it not once—but three times. I wonder what your secret is.' He gave a short laugh, then once again stared intently out of the window. 'Yes, I wonder very much. In fact I shall really have to find out. Good God! look at that fool Blantyre.'

Drummond swung round, and even as he did so Peterson hit him with all his force under the jaw. The blow caught him off his balance, and he crashed backwards, striking the back of his head against the side of the balcony as he fell. For a moment or two he lay there half-stunned. Dimly he saw that Peterson had disappeared, then, dazed and sick, he scrambled to his feet and tottered to the window. And all he saw was the figure of a man which showed up for a second in the light of a street-lamp and then disappeared amongst the trees which led to the edge of the lake.

Desperately he pulled himself together. The police outside; the telephone; there was still time. He could hear the engine of a motor-boat now, but even so there was time. He rushed across the room to the door; outside in the passage were the two gendarmes.

They listened as he poured out the story, and then one of them shook his head a little doubtfully.

'It is perfectly true, Monsieur,' he remarked, 'that we can communicate with the gendarmes of all the Swiss towns *au bord du lac*—and at once. But with the French towns it is different.'

'French?' said Drummond, staring at him. 'Isn't this bally lake Swiss?'

'*Mais non*, monsieur. Most of it is. But the southern shore from St Gingolph to Hermance is French. Evian-les-Bains is a well-known French watering-place.'

'Evian-les-Bains!' shouted Drummond—'Evian-les-Bains! Stung!—utterly, absolutely, completely stung! And to think that that girl fixed the whole thing under my very nose.'

For a moment he stood undecided; then at a run he started along the corridor.

'After 'em, *mes braves*. Another motor-boat is the only chance.'

There was another moored close inshore, and into it they all tumbled, followed by Ted Jerningham and Algy Longworth, whom they had roused from their slumbers in the lounge. Ted, as the authority, took charge of the engine—only to peer at it once and start laughing.

'What's the matter?' snapped Drummond.

'Nothing much, old man,' said his pal. 'Only that there are difficulties in the way of making a petrol engine go when both sparking-plugs have long been removed.'

And it seemed to Drummond that, at that moment, there came a faint, mocking shout from far out on the darkness of the lake.

'Mind you wear hob-nailed boots on the glacier.'

CHAPTER 13
_____

In Which Drummond Receives an Addition to his Library

It was four days later. During that four days Drummond's usual bright conversational powers had been limited to one word—'Stung'. And now as he drew his second pint from the cask in the corner of his room in Brook Street, he elaborated it.

'Stung in the centre and on both flanks,' he remarked morosely. 'And biffed in the jaw into the bargain.'

'Still, old dear,' murmured Algy brightly—Algy's world was bright again, now that there was no further need to postpone his marriage—'you may meet him again. You'd never really have forgiven yourself if you'd watched him passaging down a glacier. So near and yet so far, and all that sort of thing. I mean, what's the good of a glacier, anyway? You can't use the ice even to make a cocktail with. At least, not if old man Peterson was embalmed in it. It wouldn't be decent.'

'Stung,' reiterated Drummond. 'And not only stung, my dear boy, but very nearly bitten. Are you aware that only by the most uncompromising firmness on my part did I avoid paying his bill at the Palace Hotel? The manager appeared to think that I was responsible for his abrupt departure. A truly hideous affair.'

He relapsed into moody silence, which remained unbroken till the sudden entrance of Professor Goodman. He was holding in his hand an early edition of an evening paper, and his face was agitated.

'What's up, Professor?' asked Drummond.

'Read that,' said the other.

Drummond glanced at the paper.

'Death of well-known English financier in Paris.' Thus ran the headline. He read on:

'This morning Sir Raymond Blantyre, who was stopping at the Savoy Hotel, was found dead in his bed. Beside the deceased man an empty bottle of veronal was discovered. No further details are at present to hand.'

The paragraph concluded with a brief description of the dead man's career, but Drummond read no farther. So Blantyre had failed to face the music. As usual, the lesser man paid, while Peterson got off.

'Suicide, I assume,' said the Professor.

'Undoubtedly,' answered Drummond. 'It saves trouble. And I may say I put the fear of God into him. Well, Denny—what is it?'

'This letter and parcel have just come for you, sir,' said his servant.

Drummond turned them both over in his hand, and a faint smile showed on his face. The postmark was Rome; the writing he knew. It was the letter he opened first:

'I have threatened often: I shall not always fail. You have threatened once: you could hardly hope to succeed. I shall treasure some edelweiss. Au revoir.'

Still smiling, he looked at the parcel. After all, perhaps it was as well. Life without Peterson would indeed be tame. He cut the string; he undid the paper. And then a strange look spread over his face—a look which caused the faithful Denny to step forward in alarm.

'Beer, fool—beer!' cried his master hoarsely.

On the table in front of him lay a book. It was entitled 'Our Tiny Tots' Primer of Geography'.

THE END

Eric Ambler: Epitaph for a Spy
Introduced by H. R. F. Keating

Josef Vadassy, an unassuming language teacher, is on holiday in the South of France when he is arrested on charges of espionage. The only way he can prove his innocence is by tracking down the real spy himself. First published in 1938, Ambler's spy classic brilliantly evokes the paranoia and tension of pre-War Europe.

John Buchan: Castle Gay
Introduced by David Daniell

A splendid story of intrigue and romance set in the 1920s in the heather-clad hills of Scotland, featuring some of the most engaging characters Buchan ever created. The kidnap of a newspaper magnate and the menacing machinations of rival East European factions lead to a tense climax in the library at Castle Gay.

John Buchan: The Courts of the Morning
Introduced by T. J. Binyon

Janet and Archie Roylance are on their honeymoon in South America when they get caught up in a bold revolutionary plot to overthrow a ruthless regime based on greed, corruption and drug-induced slavery.

John Buchan: The House of the Four Winds
Introduced by Simon Rees

Jaikie had been warned to avoid Evallonia on his walking-tour across Europe, but curiosity lures him across the border and into an entangled adventure of political intrigue, kidnap and romance. Set in Central Europe in the 1930s, this is a splendid sequel to *Huntingtower* and *Castle Gay*.

John Buchan: The Power-House
Introduced by Anthony Quinton

The familiar streets of London become fraught with menace for Edward Leithen when he tries to expose the fanatical ring-leader of 'the Power-House', an international conspiracy that threatens the very roots of civilisation.

Leslie Charteris: Enter the Saint
Introduced by Ion Trewin

The first famous 'Saint' novel introducing Simon Templar, a born adventurer with a lazy smile, a dubious past and impeccable taste in ties. When he tangles with the London underworld of the 1930s he may not always stay on the right side of the law, but he is clearly on the side of the angels.

Leslie Charteris: The Saint in New York
Introduced by Jack Adrian

When Simon Templar takes on an unsolved murder case he soon finds himself up against the corrupt mob who run New York City. Charteris is in peak form in this full-length novel set in the 1930s American gangland.

Erskine Childers: The Riddle of the Sands
Introduced by Julian Symons

The world-weary Carruthers and his friend Davies are sailing round the Frisian Islands when they encounter some suspicious-looking Germans and decide to investigate. First published in 1903, this is probably the most famous spy story ever written as well as a classic sailing yarn.

Manning Coles: Drink to Yesterday
Introduced by T. J. Binyon

Young Michael Kingston's life is radically changed when he is singled out by Tommy Hambledon of British Intelligence for undercover work in enemy Germany. This is a gripping World War I spy novel of exceptional literary quality and psychological depth, first published in 1940 and dubbed 'the book that made Manning Coles famous in a day'.

Anthony Hope: The Prisoner of Zenda
Introduced by Geoffrey Household

A masterpiece of adventure set in turn-of-the-century Europe. Rudolph Rassendyll, a well-born Englishman with a reputation for frivolity, proves his true mettle when he saves the throne of Ruritania by impersonating its King.

Geoffrey Household: A Rough Shoot

After his classic *Rogue Male* this is probably Geoffrey Household's most famous thriller. Set deep in the Dorset countryside in the aftermath of the Second World War, the story begins when Roger Taine finds a poacher on his land. Investigating further, he uncovers a neo-fascist plot which he is determined to thwart, but meanwhile he is himself being pursued by the police.

Sax Rohmer: Fu Manchu
Introduced by D. J. Enright

Trailing opium fumes and scents of the exotic East, Fu Manchu has survived from the 1910s as one of the most sinister villains of thriller fiction – an inscrutable Chinaman who detests the English and will stop at nothing to achieve power for himself. Fortunately Nayland Smith is on hand to track him down in his fog-swathed Limehouse lair or in his Eastern haunts and thwart him in the nick of time.

'Sapper': Bulldog Drummond
Introduced by Richard Usborne

Demobbed after World War I and finding peace 'incredibly tedious', Captain Hugh Drummond places an advertisement in the newspaper soliciting adventure. A reply from the young and beautiful Phyllis launches him into a fast-paced adventure of blackmail, torture and unspeakable villainy.

'Sapper': The Black Gang
Introduced by Ion Trewin

The second of the famous 'Four Rounds' of Bulldog Drummond versus the ruthless Carl Peterson, in which Drummond and his pals track down the perpetrators of fiendish Bolshevik plots.

'Sapper': The Third Round
Introduced by Jeremy Lewis

Bulldog Drummond investigates the shady world of diamond-dealing in this cracking thriller of the 1920s, which climaxes in a motorboat chase at Cowes and brings Drummond face to face with an old enemy.

Edgar Wallace: The Mind of Mr J. G. Reeder
Introduced by Julian Symons

What really happened to Sir James's wife? And why should anyone want to steal a load of marble chips? Behind a deceptively harmless exterior, the formidable mind of Mr Reeder unravels these and other knotty problems in an exciting series of investigations into the seamier side of 1920s London.

Dornford Yates: Blind Corner
Introduced by Tom Sharpe

Three gallant Englishmen in their Rolls Royce race 'Rose' Noble and his sinister gang to an Austrian castle, where a great treasure is hidden. First published in 1927, *Blind Corner* is one of the most famous of Dornford Yates's immensely popular novels, whose stylish blend of adventure and nostalgia has kept readers enthralled for more than six decades.

Dornford Yates: Blood Royal
Introduced by A. J. Smithers

While motoring on a rainswept night in Austria, Chandos and Hanbury are ambushed by a noble Duke and become enmeshed in an intrigue of royal rivalry. First published in 1929, *Blood Royal* proves a sparkling addition to the tales of adventure encountered by this formidable pair.

Dornford Yates: Perishable Goods
Introduced by Richard Usborne

When Adèle, beloved wife of Jonah Mansel's cousin, is kidnapped by 'Rose' Noble, Mansel, Chandos and Hanbury dash to her rescue.

Further details about the Classic Thrillers
and about all Dent Paperbacks, including Everyman,
may be obtained from the Sales Department,
J. M. Dent & Sons Ltd, 33 Welbeck Street, London W1M 8LX.

CLASSIC THRILLERS

. . . AMBLER:	Epitaph for a Spy	£2.50
. . . BUCHAN:	Castle Gay	£2.50
. . . BUCHAN:	The Courts of the Morning	£3.50
. . . BUCHAN:	The House of the Four Winds	£2.50
. . . BUCHAN:	The Power-House	£2.50
. . . CHARTERIS:	Enter the Saint	£2.50
. . . CHARTERIS:	The Saint in New York	£2.50
. . . CHILDERS:	The Riddle of the Sands	£2.50
. . . COLES:	Drink to Yesterday	£2.50
. . . HOPE:	The Prisoner of Zenda	£2.50
. . . SAPPER:	The Black Gang	£2.50
. . . SAPPER:	Bulldog Drummond	£2.50
. . . SAPPER:	The Third Round	£2.50
. . . WALLACE:	The Mind of Mr J. G. Reeder	£2.50
. . . YATES:	Blind Corner	£2.50
. . . YATES:	Perishable Goods	£2.50

All these books may be obtained through your local bookshop, or can be ordered direct from the publisher. Please indicate the number of copies required and fill in the form below.

Name ——————————————————————— BLOCK

LETTERS

Address ————————————————————— PLEASE

————————————————————————————————

Please enclose remittance to the value of the cover prices *plus* 40p per copy to a maximum of £2, for postage, and send your order to:

PB Dept, J.M. Dent & Sons Ltd, 33 Welbeck Street, London W1M 8LX

Applicable to UK only and subject to stock availability

All prices are subject to alteration without notice